AMATIMAS—I AM TIME

➤ ◄

Richard Herbert

Order this book online at www.trafford.com
or email orders@trafford.com

Most Trafford titles are also available at major online book retailers.

Printed in the United States of America.

ISBN: 978-1-4269-3863-4 (sc)
ISBN: 978-1-4269-3864-1 (dj)
ISBN: 978-1-4269-3865-8 (e)

Library of Congress Control Number: 2010910537

*Our mission is to efficiently provide the world's finest, most comprehensive book publishing
service, enabling every author to experience success. To find out how to publish your book,
your way, and have it available worldwide, visit us online at www.trafford.com*

Trafford rev. 7/27/2010

www.trafford.com

North America & international
toll-free: 1 888 232 4444 (USA & Canada)
phone: 250 383 6864 ♦ fax: 812 355 4082

PREFACE

There in the viewer, a spark, a light, a ball of burning hydrogen in the measureless vacuum of space. A light is being viewed, A STAR! in the depth of space. There, an object visible and clearly filling the lens of the massive telescope. It was a super giant in the heavens, like a pearl in a huge pool of darkness.

Jan exclaimed, "Why, this is not new; it is the North Star." Albert said, "That's right, the North Star. Can you take a spectrum reading?" "I can but I don't see the reason. What we see is just about what it is, a blue star, about two hundred light years away." Fr. Anthony interrupted, saying, "I have seen the North Star before. It is the star that is always in the sky at the same position in the north. Almost everyone has seen it." "Let's all be reasonable. I would like to keep this as private as possible!" Jan, working on the telescope panel, loaded the image so the spectrum can be measured. "It is not going to be private with a star that everybody can see,"Fr.Anthony remarked. Albert observed, "It is there, and it is something that no one knows about except us right now.""There it is the spectrum from blue to red. The wave length is average; I see no special reason to be alarmed. It shows a blue star of hydrogen, helium."

Albert said,"Now, change the telescope to this setting; might as well be any side. Just one degree to any side of Polaris, the so-called North Star. It is very important to make sure that the star is out of the telescope's lens." After a moment, Jan expressed abruptly: "Wait a minute, this can't be right!"Albert explained, "You have the spectrum on?" "Yes, it is on, and it should have changed." "Jan, it is right. Now just take any side of the star out to three degrees." "Has the spectrum changed?" "No. It's holding steady at the point of the original Polaris reading." "Take the scope to four degrees of the star." Jan looked at the equipment as if it were faulty and then once more did what Albert said. "OK, the readings are back to the normal level of deep space." Fr. Anthony, looking like something was wrong with the equipment, said, "What does this prove?" Albert looked at the priest with great concern. "Fr. Anthony, it is the second sun of our sun. It is coming this way and moving fast." Jan, redoing her setting and looking as if she had seen a ghost, replied, "This is indeed strange. There is something going on here that does not make sense.'"Oh, it is going on and there is nothing we can do about it. It is tired light." "Tired light? That's only a theory, and anyway, how does that matter with these readings?" "It is light that is sure to be visible soon. Tired light is a light's formation of its own nature. It can act in any manner as long as it is traveling in space with all of its properties." "Light is a fixed nature; it travels in waves and changes from the blue spectrum to the red spectrum. Light going towards us is in the blue spectrum and light traveling away from us is in the red side of the spectrum. Tired light would have to be in one of those two spectrums, right?"Jan commented. Albert, sensing Jan's confusion, looked up and said, "The spectrum of blue shift to red shift or red to blue is not relevant to tired light. The North Star is in the blue spectrum, as we can see, and tired light is in the wave of the blue spectrum. So the wave is closer than it appears. And really, it is not the wave that is important, because tired light's irregular acts are the main concern here. We are looking at a compression of matter here. The star is not involved, because it will disappear in about five to six years.' "Ahh, then I can leave. This is five to six years away. I thought it would be tomorrow or this week sometime. Thank God, it is what you said, Jan, two hundred light years away. You know, that is far enough away so that I will be a memory by the time that thing, or whatever is out there, reaches here."

"Fr. Anthony, do you think I would tell you about this if it was in the far future? This will be visible in a matter of months!" "That soon? Then, if that is true, why doesn't the Space Administration know about it? They find everything that's out in space, don't they?" "Not this. Jan knows enough to find almost anything and they do the same. You see, no one is looking at this because they cannot detect it. I might as well tell you, it is a black hole moving and sucking up space in its way. The effects will be known, but it will be too late for a lot of people here." "You can't play God, man! This is something over which no one has control. It's like earthquakes, floods, or bad weather. The church can't be a part of warning people about these perils." "The father is right; all we can do is to face the fact that this is going to happen. And you are certainly right, Albert; these are strange forms of readings. It does look like a compression of matter. I'm sure it will have to be revealed to the Science and Astrophysics departments of the Astronomy Community. It is a powerful discovery." Albert looked up at the sky again, through the open dome doors of the observatory, and said, "That's not what I wanted or had planned to do. Let us remember, this is my discovery and I plan to use it for the good of mankind and the rise of devotion to God." Fr. Anthony replied, "Oh, OK, and you'd also want to meet with the Pope, wouldn't you?" "Yes." "Well you don't have any reason to see the Pope over this, because he is informed about all new discoveries and events that affect people all over the world." "I know this, but this will be something different, in a big way. Both of you sit down over here and let me tell you a story and what I plan to do about it."

Jan and Fr. Anthony moved away from the screen of the telescope and went over to the desk, where a set of chairs were. Albert, standing, stepped in front of them, like a professor in a freshman class. He started to speak, and then stopped and reached into his pocket for his little black book. He turned the pages and then began to look at them and said, "It has been a long time since Jan and I have traveled anywhere." Jan, looking concerned, did not speak. "I was in the old world, the land of the Greeks. It was there that I had a vision, a vision of some people of times past. They were from a time before Christ (B.C.) and were of a holy matter. They had done things to the earth that were of a spiritual nature. The powers they had were supernatural. They organized people to follow the rules of their religion." Turning to the telescope as if to thank God that it had been developed, he continued. "The vision was of this nature: This Earth had, no, we had two suns, the one we have now and the other that was taken far away." Jan wanted to speak, but looked at Albert and then at Fr. Anthony and remained silent. "I know that science has proven other things and those other calculations make this reasoning really hard to accept, yet let me continue. The people and the god that ruled the world in that day had a name, a name that was very close to the name of "Draconis". And their star was named Thuban, a star that is today called Polaris. It is in the records of the Ancient Egyptian tablets from about five to six thousand years ago. This is what the North Star is: Thuban! Not Polaris! Polaris is our second sun coming back in great magnitude and is in the direction of Thuban, or the North Star."

Albert continued: "The gods thought it would help the people of this planet to return to their place of origin. So they sent the second sun on a mission to cleanse the people of this planet. Yet, and this might sound crazy, it was Christ that appeared to correct this, about this time. The Christ, the true God, the Almighty, the God of the people, whatever you conclude, the only God that had the power to change the outcome. If we look out into space by any means known to man, we are being deceiverd. Our galaxy is moving towards what we see as Polaris our second sun. The stars we see are not fixed. Our galaxy is not a fixed object in space, it travels. The Milky Way we look at, that's our galaxy and is composed of the stars that look fixed and measurable. Deep space is not. If you can follow this, Polaris is part of our galaxy and not a part of it. It is the binary star of this solar system and part of the sun which we see. Our sun, the sun that heats this planet, is not what it was back in the day of its beginning. Polaris is now a huge star and follows none of the guidelines of astronomy about its exact size. It will make everything on this planet horrible in its presence." Fr. Anthony interrupted: "All right! All right, man, Ahh, mister philosopher. It is something that is about to happen and it is clear to me that neither you nor anyone else can do anything about it!" Albert looked down and replied, "That is what I would like to tell you. There is something I *can* do about it." Jan stood to her feet and said, "I have seen and listened to enough of this MADNESS! Using God, Christ, The Bible! Albert, the laws of nature are clearly not on your side! Look, it is out there and you are here! Now, does that make any sense?! Does it?"

Albert started walking toward the door to leave when Fr. Anthony said "Wait a minute; we want to know more about this if you will suffer our disbelief. Albert it is your idea, dream, vision, discovery, or whatever! So I am sorry for the words. Tell us the rest of your explanation." Albert continued to walk and said, "I've said enough. Let's go back. There's not much more and I will tell you the rest in the car." "Wait! I want to know about what this has to do with the church and the Pope?" Jan said, listening as she closed down the massive telescope and looked at the sky. The sound of the doors closing filled the room as if a great secret had been uncovered in the quiet, silent night of space. The discovery was there and Jan, still in a state of restrained shock, dragged herself away from the panel. She wanted to know more of the science involved and the reason that the discovery could exist without anybody with a good telescope having seen or reported it. "Jan, don't leave any record of this sighting. It is important that you get the credit for this discovery in the future." Albert then exited the building with Fr. Anthony right behind. "Don't worry about that! MY DEAR"

Albert got in the car and unlocked the door for Fr. Anthony by touching the door switch. Jan, still locking and exiting the door at the front of the building, briefly spoke to the security guard. Glad that he was there, she sped up her walk to the car. "This is something great regardless of what you say about it." "It is something that the science world will be advanced by. Still, speaking for the church clearly has to be kept out of this discovery because of all the brilliant scientists that will have first say about what this thing will do to the Earth." Albert began to drive down the road without saying a word. The road was lit by the headlights as the three of them traveled back to the city. The road that led to the main freeway, where a few cars and trucks traveled with constant motion, was dark. It was here, after traveling about two miles from the observatory, that Albert would lay out his plans—plans that would change the world. It was neither a simple plan nor a reasonable plan, considering how the church was fixed in the middle. The great Holy Catholic Church, nurturing its members daily all over the world. The solid rock of Peter, the only church that has not faded with time, eternally, as its relics and structures still stand. . It is to be said that the Holy Catholic Church, Rome, the Vatican, the nuns and numbers of priests all over the world would have ears to listen. The Pope would be the greatest part of this discovery. Yes, this would be the biggest moment for the Church next after the appearance of Christ. The glory of the Highest and the Heavens shall be witness to the complete devotion to God. The true God, who made all things, God, never-ending and never-beginning, who has watched us all on this grain of sand that we call Earth. Where do we all turn now?

As Albert began to speak the view changed for Fr. Anthony, as he sat looking out the car's side window, and for Jan, who was doing the same. They looked directly at Albert as the cars passed, lighting his face like a lantern going off and on.

"About this is the plan: You may not agree, but it is the only plan that will keep the world in order and protect the world from contagious terror. The first phase of this Black Hole or what I call the Dark Star, is visual. A mass that will shine as brightly as the moon at night and will grow to be a bigger part of the sky, turning the night into a mere shadow. It will light the night sky like the sunset of our sun. So there will be no night as we know it for a long time, a very long time. Yet, with the Dark Star in the sky, we still will have to have lights to see clearly at night. As this matter closes in on this galaxy, the sound will be heard, a sound that will be sure to drive the sane man to complete madness in a very short time. This is the way this star will approach, with terror and emotion. After this, it will be taking in all the matter in its path, just as a black hole does. Compressing matter to the size that even today science cannot calculate. On approaching, it will be so massive that shifts in the dark matter of space will be affected. The waves of the elements, and the matter, will have their effect on the gravitational forces of this planet and other planets in this solar system, so that we will need a miracle to survive." Albert stopped explaining and quickly asked, "Jan, is this the freeway we had to take?" He put on the right blinker light and made a lane change. "What, yeah, yeah this is it, the 5 North." Jan, while in a daze and a state of shock, wanted to ask a question of Albert, but held fast to her silence. Fr. Anthony, leaning on the side of the back seat, was locked into a moody silence and wished he had a place to pray as he pulled a rosary from his pocket. Looking out at the lights of the cars briefly illuminating the back seat, he grabbed the cross. He made a wish to be the chosen one.

Albert continued to share his vision of the events of the future. "It is clear that the world is headed for sudden uncontrolled catastrophes that no one could foresee. However, the population of this planet can be saved from most of the effects of the Dark Star. The Dark Star will get to a point of shifting the way we look at the day and night and the pace of time. The world will surely devolve into man against man. It has been written in books all over the world about the most dreadful word "Armageddon"—or the coming of Christ—or the end of the world. This would be the word on this planet, except for the one thing that I have shown you here. If people can believe that it is not the end of the planet, than we will survive. The worst thing is to fear the unknown and not to remember the word survival." "Fr. Anthony, it is very important that we indeed see the Pope for this reason." Fr. Anthony continued, "I feel the Pope has very little concern for the things that are about to happen. I wish you could clear up why you believe this will help you or your cause." "Well, Fr. Anthony, what if I tell you that I can grow the Christian population by my plan? Would you be surprised?" Jan looked at Albert like he was suffering a schizophrenic moment. "Believe me, it would be a nice idea but totally impossible. You have so many religions that do not support Christianity that it is not an issue." "I can do it with the right support, Fr. Anthony." "Ahh, now I see why you want to see the Pope." Albert stated, "You have the idea but not the reason. It is the answer to world order and the only solution we really have for keeping people sane, at least those that are presently sane." Jan looked at Albert with one eye closed and said nothing. Albert pulled the car off the freeway and onto the surface streets and headed for Fr. Anthony's church, about two miles away. "Fr. Anthony, it is a must that we see the Pope. You can play a role in saving millions of people from sure death. I hate to put it in those terms, but it is true. You have a friend at the Vatican who used to be a priest at your church, Cardinal Manlin. He is close to the Vatican seat of power and should trust you with anything you propose to him." Fr. Anthony replied, "That is correct. Cardinal Manlin is very close to the Pope. I have other close friends at the Vatican that would also do, you know. Still, I can't just say 'I want to see the Pope' to anyone there; they would have to know what it is about." "OK, Fr. Anthony, now we are in the same ballpark. You remember your vows of silence? Just get us to the Vatican. Once we are there it is between Jan, you, and me. We are the only ones that know of this Dark Star. In the Vatican, it will be of a different nature. I will need to have your support to get us there." Fr. Anthony humbly said, "I guess it can be done, if the Pope is there." "Oh, he is there, and we shouldn't waste time in seeing him. I trust you, Fr. Anthony. I am going to book tickets for the three of us two days from now. If it is your intention to take ill or any other sort of excuse that prevents you from being on this plane with us, we will just go alone." "What about my plans?" "You can go; you have vacation time, right, Jan?" Jan looked at Albert and said, "Well, it's about time. The kids will be all right for a week. They can stay with Joel. He likes to have their company at the lake. They do have school. Joel will see that they get back and forth. Besides, they need some strong rules right now. Those grades are getting a little low—Anna, a 'C' in math; I don't know what to say about Peter: a 'C' in science. What kind of children do we have?" As Albert parked the car in front of the rectory, Fr. Anthony explained, "They are growing children in tough times. They are blessed children." He continued, "I will be ready. It is bizarre, but I believe you enough to take a chance on your idea. You know, anything that can help the church can't be that bad. No, not bad at all." Fr. Anthony exited the car and Albert replied, "Vows, father, vows." Fr. Anthony dug into his pocket, and pulled out his hand and showed his rosary to Albert. He walked to the rectory counting the gems."This is our SECRET!! Albert," looked at the priest, and drove off with Jan still looking back at the church.

CHAPTER ONE

Seattle, Washington: three years before Albert ever met Fr. Anthony. Albert was attending the University of Washington to get his master's degree in architecture. It was the perfect school for his theory about what he wanted his building designs to look like. He chose this school because of the vast amount of knowledge in its libraries which would give him access to the research materials he would need in order to study the disciplines that would support his theory on architectural design. Albert came from a middle-class family rooted in Los Angeles, California. His father was a small residential architect, who wanted his son to become one also. But Albert had different plans. He wanted to design more than indistinguishable tract homes. Albert liked the big buildings—the steel, the glass, the perpendicular rails of glistening metal called skyscrapers. For that reason, he wanted to study out of town. He preferred to get away from the wooden mind of his father's teachings about small building design. He could remember when he was a small child, the only child of his parents, being absorbed with the designs of houses. Every toy was of some type of building material or designed to build some type house. Why, even his baby crib was in the shape of an English Tudor house, with a roof and windows. Anyway, it was the books that Albert really liked, because they were the building block of his research.

Albert believed that a structure should be designed to support the angles of the planet. Not to force a design to be nonfunctional by its design, but to be shaped to the area of its locale. He considered this should be done by using the stars to align the angles for aesthetic value. This

1

would make the design more a usable form because it would keep the tone of the structure aligned with the earth. Of course, it would have to function in relationship to the structure, and completely practical thinking must apply. The point of design theory is for a structure to be made for the complete and full use of its designs style. The use of motifs from all parts of architectural history, from Gothic to Postmodern, Romanesque to Ancient, was included in his theory. Albert wanted to study a lot of the history of architecture because he needed many old and past styles to support his new designs.

Albert truly liked to design buildings. He never could be taught to make something original like his father had, some time ago, no matter how small it might have been. Yes, Albert's father always bragged about his design—the attached fascia with the drop-down soffit. Even when Albert was a child, riding in the car, his father would point out one or two houses in the neighborhood on the way to his elementary school with pride. He would say, "Look at that, Albert. See, that's a copy of my design, the drop-down fascia with that rafter outcrop. That design is the future. They are picking up that design from the Sylmar Tract project. Yup!" he would say, "it will make the history books, a design of the future." Albert, looking back to those days, figured out that his father's design was a little spin-off of the Baroque period. Well, Albert had never seen it in postmodern architecture, so it must be original. In the Baroque period, the builders certainly didn't have the material they have now. The drop-down fascia was more than Albert wanted to do as an architect, even if it did pay the bills. Albert wanted to be the top, the number one architect in the world.

Albert thought that his knowledge was good enough, so he took various classes in science—not the science of building buildings, but the science of the universe. It was there that he would change his direction and fate. Albert added a minor in astronomy to his major in architecture. He had taken a couple of classes in the study of the stars earlier, during his baccalaureate studies at University of Southern California. In Seattle, he would meet his wife Jan Stevens, a beauty to his eye as he sat in the classes and studied everything from sun spots to galaxies in formation. Jan, an astronomy major, was very nice to Albert, helping him with his studies of this science. They would become closer and closer friends with each class they had together. Although Jan did not know a thing about architecture, Albert would rattle on about it as if she did. So when the day came that he told her about his theory, Jan began to relate his architecture to her knowledge of astronomy. "Buildings aligned to points of stars for design reason," Albert explained to Jan. That's when it became clear that Albert could be a good friend to her in more ways than one. Even with a full set of classes in architecture and astronomy, Albert made the time to see Jan as often as he could. Jan, who was studying for her PhD, had fallen deeply in love with Albert. Why, it was just about all they really had in common except for both of them being Catholic. Love was what brought them together for life—not the classes, not the theories. Not the stars, and for certain, not a strange happening in space were ever going to break them apart. Between them was some kind of match that transmitted the feeling of being together as husband and wife. And later, they surely did become the couple that Albert Lanker and Jan Stevens wanted to be in wedlock. Although the birth of their first child while they were still in college made this marriage happen a lot sooner, they were happy.

In north Seattle, there was a business that brought Jan to this point in her life. She grew up alongside what her father does, even today: running a family business, a small string of fishing boats. As far back as she could remember, her father was a fisherman sailing the Pacific Ocean. Jan, the youngest child of five and the only girl, was the only one to stay on solid land. Yes, she had been on one of the fleet's ships and had been on fishing runs with her father, but to her it was an adventure. In her early life, Jan was so young and so amazed with the world and the sky that she became confused. But it was there that she found her dream of becoming an astronomer, on her father's boat. She discovered that the stars, the lights in the sky, the shine of a Christmas tree twinkling were positively wonderful sights.

At the age of seven, Jan was tagging along on a fishing run with her father. Fishing all day, it got late and the boats were slowly on their way back to port. The stars came out over the sea and the deep blue sky was a sight to delight her. Her father, with his long beard and deep voice, pointed out some of the beautiful big stars and made a particular point of the North Star. He told Jan how this star stayed at that same place in the sky all the time and never moved. He also told her that if she ever got lost at night, this would be the star to look for. Jan looked at the stars in the sky all the way home. Jan would become an astronomer, even if she didn't know it, at the age of seven. She remembered the experience and it was something that she would never forget. Jan grew up and seriously studied the universe in a professional way, even up to the point of meeting, Albert. She was stubbornly committed to becoming an astronomer. Seeing deep into space seemed to put her dreams into motion of discovering anything and everything that astronomers do to make a name for themselves in history. Jan felt that if you can see it, then it is there, and if it is there, then it is a part of us, because this planet is part of our shared space. Jan wanted to find planets and new stars. Using a radio telescope for deep space, or peering through the latest observatory telescopes, would help her fulfill her dream. It wasn't until she met Albert that her dreams would come true.

Who really discovered the ball of light that came into view? Who really discovered this moving thing out in space around the North Star, the large matter that would be in the sight of everyone's future? Who really discovered this star? Who really discovered this, this, Dark Star?!!! The impact on the world's population as it signaled the coming of the end of all things as we know them. Jan was the one with the discovering mind, in fact and form. But Albert, oh, Albert with his strong will to become something that he was not and someone that he could never be, was the one with the peculiar dream.

Albert's dream was to be a powerful architect. When people looked at the sky, they would be looking at his designs that blocked the space, the air, the view. Now, that would make Albert complete, not his wife, not his bloodlines, only the power of the skyscrapers designed by him. Albert wanted people to slightly turn their heads, make a face, put their nose in the air with greed and hostility for taking their sky away! A designed building about which the history books would say "This is a first; a valuable part of architecture for the world." Still, Albert knew the truth; it takes a company and lots of money to have an even incidental glimmer of putting up buildings of his designs. Albert just had so many dreams. Still, Albert has had one dream that the world could not face because it was so difficult to believe that it could come true!

CHAPTER TWO
The Trip

Time traveled on, and Albert and Jan just got older. The dreams that they initially had together turned to what they really were: dreams. Work became a part of life, like everyone on this planet and in the boundless cosmos. In the silence of the night, there's a sample of what was an everyday occurrence for the people involved. There, on a vertical beam, a construction mark barely visible in yellow pencil. A squiggle and a number, marking a bench-setting for some poor fellow whose mind was not on his job. Yes, some smart person made his thoughts known on a simple I-beam in which a discoverer named Mies did his thinking well. For, if not for this discovery, nobody would have had this clear unblemished surface of structural arrangement in this different type and style. But now it's Mies who loses the purity; it's his mark to understand that blackboards and scratch pads serve no purpose in this area for those who forgot their paying job. Not at all. As it stands, the framework stays as it is: a logo of man's identity, a form of translation, a brought-forth form of communication for visible understanding. Yes, the scene is quiet but it was once loud and full of noise with this squiggle and numbered marking.

"Everyone take a break!" called the foreman as he wiped his nose with his plaid handkerchief, wrinkled and badly faded with smudges and mucus. Albert was a twenty-year veteran on the job and had a nice fat pension due in ten years. "The boss," as the men call him, looked at the unfinished part of the project that his company bid for against a number of full-blown competitors of sharp contractors. The boss was on the job of this multi-million dollar building, for some bank desperate to get its name known in the community in a big way. Yes, a skyscraper made of steel and glass, just like Louis Sullivan, (father of the skyscraper) would have built in his day of glory, with form following function. Yes, the most important thing in architecture beside commissions and opera halls. Oh, if Sullivan had only been a farmer, his worries would have made his dreams different, to say the least. He could have had a more stable form of success with agriculture rising out of the ground instead of tasteless and raw indigestible skyscrapers. He would have liked his products to the fullest and not the dreadful dream of ornamentation. Yes, a nomad to his own form of function was Sullivan.

As the men started to eat their lunch, packs of empty cigarette wrappers gathered in the unfinished cracks, made to hold cement. They started to fill the cracks as the workmen pushed and shoved them down to keep the working space clean. You must understand the boss. He liked to keep the working space spic and span and he is a madman if he has to walk through trash and debris. It was because he makes too much money to have his working space littered with trash. That was the main reason he hired his son Victor, a student working part-time while attending engineering school. He cleaned and swept the premises for his father between each of his breaks, for good measure. The iron-workers had dropped their trash down on his job. A can from one of them hit the boss's newly poured layer of concrete and never to this day was it retrieved. He was very angry about it and actually stalled the crane hauling the I-beams for three hours. Still to this day, his modes of perfection are marked by the single thought of trash and rubbish. You see, he liked his formwork straight and clean, due simply to his training. His technical knowledge of concrete and his high standards of detail are what he likes, rather than his fat pension. With some work being done, the boss sometimes would lose sleep over wet concrete, as silly as it might seem, but that was his job and he was the boss.

Albert made it clear that he wanted to have his work place clean and in the summer of one of the most demanding sessions of construction, "the boss," as the men called him over and over again, went on a three-month vacation. He went to enjoy the magic of the world of Egypt. Its rare structure and beautiful terrain would make him feel like a rare creature himself. But it wasn't until he visited Athens that the boss made a change, a dramatic change, in the way he saw his own identity. Sure, he was happily married and had a set of wonderful kids, but that didn't matter here. Why, his whole dream of being the best construction professional rather than an architect had stopped at a moment's glance. He was possessed with skill and success and the talent and full use of technology. His dream caused a big problem with his family and his company and employees, as he let them know after this trip to the old world. After that trip, he would not work in construction ever again; he quit his laborer's job and began to practice what he went to school for: architecture. In his mind, he thought about the slaves walking hand in hand, creating a megalopolis.

He began to tell his wife about the evil results of the pyramids, but it was the Greeks who really consumed him. They gave Albert the thought that a higher form of people really existed and had made this world—the world of lust, the world of joy, the world of pain and anger. He came to this conclusion within his own mind by his own thinking from his own logical deduction. The boss named Albert was made into some kind of mad dream of the ancient world in his present mind. He once told his wife that the destiny of the world lay in the stars and he didn't know its results. His wife felt that he was very disturbed and remarked that he should not think so hard at work. Yes, He thought in a strange new way, long after he had been sitting on the porch steps of the ruins of Andronicus of Cyrrhus. "The Tower of the Winds," as it is called, with its designed Triton and phases of Horologium, a structure built around twenty seven B.C.

But looking back at the start of this trip, Albert and Jan having boarded a plane, the loving couple waved to their relatives and their three children, Anna, Peter, and Victor, who helped his father on the job part-time. The children, getting older, would be staying with their uncle Joel, a fisherman and Jan's oldest brother. He would take them on a fishing trip up north, since it was summer and they were free from school. All the handshakes and kisses had been made last night at the party. It was a great festivity, with cake, champagne, and balloons. Why, it was the first time the two would be alone since their wedding day. It was a lucky thing that Jan could get the trip; she was given a special discount gift from the company that she was working for, Far-Seeing an astronomy group of scientists studying space. Far-Seeing had contacts all over the world and this location was on the list, and she was also doing such a good job over the years that the company gave her the trip. Albert, as you know, owns his company, a medium-sized construction company with projects all over the country. Albert could take time off whenever he wanted, and he would have done so sooner for this trip, if not for Jan being so much in demand at her job. Both of them had planned this trip for over a year. After they both agreed where to go, Albert was delighted with the savings that Jan's employer gave them via her company's travel agent.

Finally, they were going to see the Middle East and the ancient world. It would be the first time for each of them, as they got on the plane, hugging and blowing kisses to the group of family members. They both whispered sweet nothings to each other and talked about the mystery of the Middle East and the romance of the ancient world. It would truly be like a second honeymoon for Albert and Jan and they planned to enjoy every moment of it. The plane took off and climbed steeply into the sun and off they went on the long holiday to travel the world, the ancient world with all of its mysticism. It was a rough flight over the Atlantic. After a brief layover in London, England, they went on to Paris, France. In Paris, the two had a chance to visit some cafes and experience the wonderful outside dining for which the French as so well-known. The view of Paris with the Eiffel Tower in their range of vision was the most enchanting feeling that Albert and Jan had ever felt. They loved the city; they loved the people; and most of all, they loved the food. Still, the country of the camels and pyramids was all they could really think of; it was to be the honeymoon they had missed. Jan and Albert would be staying in the Egyptian land of sand and old world images for about a month and then they would be traveling to their next destination, Athens, for two months. The center of the Greeks and Greek architecture, as far as the classical design went, was Athens. For that matter, the dreams of the two were very classical by just having a wonderful time. Back on the plane in Cairo, they flew over the Mediterranean and landed at the Athens International Airport, where Albert was immediately amazed by the view of Athens. Jan found that the Greek's homeland had made her speechless after viewing the city from the plane's window, leaning over Albert to take a look from the moment they entered Athenian airspace. It was here that Albert would begin his transformation, unbeknownst to his wife, and known only to him.

CHAPTER THREE
The Dream

After spending a pleasurable day at the summit of some of the ancient ruins of Athens, Albert and Jan ate a quick dinner and went to their hotel room, straight to bed. The architecture had affected the two with astonishment and with a sense of visual fulfillment. They both began to think of massive pillars in more ways than one. After they made love, they finally went to sleep and it was Albert who dreamed of the contents of the ancient world. He slept well and this vision is what overcame his mind and body.

The place of Attica was the first unit of stone at the base of the marble structure. It shall be at a ninety degree angle to the right side of the base. It may cause the celestial pattern to the zodiac signs for the nations.

Therefore giving-Thus-interpretation of the present state-Enough ! Said, the robed god of his statements as he waved his golden staff and walked back to his dwelling. This instruction to the common laborer correlated to the calculations of the unknown numbers. The way of most calculations were done to him was to break each number into two, rather than three to show equal portion. The robed god reappeared and said, What a spectacular display! What a fantastic view for the first god of importance! It will have the main face of the god known to the Greeks as Zeus. It will be the rims of the wharf, for the gleam and glare of all sides of the structure's mega-penetrative walls.

He stood as a feather-light man, made of some fog-like image. He was not a ghost; he was made of wrapped robes and a crown of dried leaves. His name was Panitive Possideous Mandula. His age was unknown but was presented only by the stars, in which the calculations were made by the coming comets and celestial shifts. The speech was clear and as any human, except the interruption of each of his phrases was made with the word, Thus.

Thus-, Make each phase of the cut stone by the measurement of the setting sun's green phase, only seen by the special area of the Mediterranean summit, Thus- In which the speed of light times the distance traveled by that calculation, it will be in the increments of one lunar phase. Thus- The third moon of the planet Jupiter. Thus-By material strength, it shall be measured by the gravitational compression on top of the base of the structure. Thus-The art of each framework expression shall be the zenith of, at all times of. Thus-Entree. Thus-

Then it happened again with the construction process of the fog-like god as he had toiled to find answers and there were no answers to him. It was as new to him as the calculation of the universe. It was as different as the planet Pluto. He was bewildered.

Thus-, The main entree shall be made of the compressed rock of the planet Mercury; it is maintained by the mass of its gravity. Thus-Giving the density of each portal entree a sound compact existence, each wall of the four square corners, shall also contain the substances of the giving stability. Thus-One half the base shall. Thus-Contain. Thus-

As a reference, the only way to obtain the structural substances was by direct contact of the mass. This was done by unknown means to anyone but the fog-like god. His methods were made by his own means and by that he demonstrated his direct placement of the known material.

A small plane flew by and opened its throttle and made a wide turn outside the city limits; it created a distant and unusual sound to the unconscious dreamer. Albert turned in his sleep and began dreaming some more. Almost awakened, he went back to his deep sleep and this time the dream was changing. It was different from the first dream, yet still just as powerful.

The second dream was about a silent looking creature called a Roamart. It stood like a tree, as tall as a skyscraper of fifty stories, and walked like a horse. But it was confusing because the creature was not as it stood. It became a building in which people lived and then the dream quickly changed to the main and most shocking dream that Albert had ever had. He would be the victim of the knowledge, which he would be subjected to, in fact, forever. Because he was part of this dream and not watching it like a dream viewer.

The wall of the last floor was finally put into place. It was as long as the total building, but the year was not in the century of architects Frank L. Wright or Ken Venturi. Wright's cantilever in suspended horizontal fashion would not believe that the style of the modernistic theories were long before the invention of steel and concrete or before the sound of music in human ears. It might as well be said: Venturi started an old idea with his mother's house of angles and half circles. But who cares that the speed of light is only relative to the framework of a fixed object? It only works from one point of view and from the second view it is a crayon drawing for mankind. It is the matter of light and its travel that is faster than its own existence but, it is the element in light that the perdition of the speed will travel faster than the speed predicted. As it stands, the disappointing existence of light, as to where it's predicted target is influenced, is underestimated. By this folly, man must be more than the span of his own existence. Albert came to the calculation, the only reasonable thing by which he could rationalize. It would be said that how is this done? The answer is how! And how can it be? It can only be how it is to be said, the dream continues.

In the said land of Athens, the land of the Greeks, they found their way to find architecture for the natives. By how it stands the natives serve to understand the symbols of the land. Amatimas Draconis, an unknown philosopher, never written about or heard of, expressed his total reasoning of the native people in Greece. It stands as the morning sun and the evening star of the ancient land. The people find no direction from the sun and the sun finds no positives in the people, but the two are the same. They find how the day travels and how they travel by day, but it's no direction. It has no direct persuasion; it finds the causes to the real existences of them. Real is real and fake is not real, but the two prove their existence in time. The two find no direction by the one complete day. But it is the way the two find the day, the complete day. AMATIMAS IS REAL. To see the fact is not a fake, but the unseen fake is not the real. There is not or could not be seen how the fake can be real but to time and that time, not by day. No! No! Not by star, No! No! Only by the product of travel. Amatimas is real; he travels by what mankind has not conceived and he will never find until he views his own existence and that does not work. No! No! It is a fake to say it is real, but AMATIMAS IS REAL!!!

Like the architrave, the pillar stands in place, not by the side and not by the shore because that is only for the reference books. But it is real and AMATIMAS IS REAL, by the travel and Amatimas does travel. What is real? The architrave is proof of Amatimas the philosopher, and the pillar is what? Is the land.

-Thus

Albert woke up from his sleep; he stood up in the bed in a cold sweat, and was totally puzzled by his surroundings. Jan, still asleep, never knew that Albert was in such a state. Taking a look at Jan, Albert lay back down and went back to sleep, or pretended to. He mostly looked out into the room, hugging the covers for support in fear.

CHAPTER FOUR

Albert was at home for months after the vacation in Athens. He still could not stop remembering, and having flash-backs in his sleep of the contents of his feverish dream. Time went by and Albert kept most of the contents of his vision a secret. At times he still had strange ideas about certain things that puzzled everyone around him. Most people that knew him felt that his ideas must have had some kind of strange rational meaning, because he was the owner of the company. His wife would learn to deal with this as an act of nature and believed that Albert had a stress sickness and was trying to fulfill his urge not to be an architect. Whatever it was, it was only a little bit disturbing to Jan until one particular Sunday. Jan and Albert and two of the children went to the local church. After Mass, Albert requested to see the head priest about something that was alarming him. He asked Jan to come with him, but she was afraid because she was really not into church affairs since they weren't really the best of Catholics. In fact, it was a bit difficult to remember the last time they actually attended Mass. Had it not been for the children going to the parish school, they would be just about unknown to this congregation.

"He will see you now," said the attendant to Albert. Holding one of the daily flyers, Albert walked toward the pastor's office, motioning for Jan to hurry. Jan, sitting in the lobby of the rectory, slowly got up with a look of embarrassment as she told Anna and Peter to go to the car parked in the lot. Their other son, Victor, was away at college, still pursuing his dreams of becoming an engineer on the East Coast. A very nice looking rectory and statues, and the woodwork of oak with cherry wood inlays created a feeling of holiness and contentment. But that did no good for Jan's nerves as she sat in front of the large desk, the priest sitting across from her. Albert, looking at a little book in his hand, came out with a shocking question. "How do I get to see the Pope about an important matter?" Jan was about to get up in anger but Albert said, "Please, Jan, it is not what you think. It has to do with you." "With me? We haven't discussed this, and in fact, what is this about!?" In a raised voice, the priest, Father Anthony said, "Come on, settle down. I get requests like this many times. It is not that strange coming from two loving people. Your children were baptized at this church and have attended the parish school. They both are in high school now, if I recall." "That's right." "Well, what is the subject you would like to discuss with the Pope? Is it a personal matter? If you...." Albert interrupted, "It is something that will affect all of us in due time, and time is running out." Jan, staring, but listening to Albert, began to look interested. "Affects all of us? In what way?" Albert looked at Jan as he continued to speak to the priest. "My wife is an astronomer and she has access to an observatory." "Well," said the priest. Albert responded, "It is up to her to let us use it as soon as possible for about an hour." Jan looked at Albert. "Use it? When? Where? Albert, what is this about?" "If this can be done, then you will know all you need to know for now. Believe me, you will not be disappointed. In fact, it will make you famous, along with the church. That is why I would like to get them involved." "And this has to do with the pope? I'm not following you." "No, Father, it is your duty, if I can be so kind to say it, that you be present when we, if we can, use the observatory, and you make up your own mind whether the pope should be informed. I will show you the reasons why and what I plan to do about it." Jan said, "Today is Sunday; it will take about a day to get a fixed time at the Far-Seeing Lab. I hope this is a refractive viewing, because the radio telescopes are reserved for months."Albert responded, "Refractive? That will do just fine, honey. About 10 p.m. is what I need; that should be enough." "OK then," said Jan.Fr.Anthony interrupted: "I am wondering now myself about what this is and what this is about?" "All right, so, I can depend on you this time, Father? I can pick you up about nine o'clock and you can ride with us." "That's fine, I will see you then and remember to keep in mind that prayer is an important thing and may God bless you." "Thank you, Father." They both got up and exited the rectory, shaking Fr. Anthony's hand on the way out. The children, who were still in the car, had no idea what their parents had been up to for forty minutes.

They were at home when Jan asked Albert what that meeting was all about. Home was a three-bedroom house just to the north of Seattle. It was a medium-priced good-looking house with a large backyard and nice trees surrounding the property. Jan waited for a answer from Albert as he looked at his little black book. "I am going to take stock in Earmax and Voices, a manufacturer of hearing devices. This is going to be a good buy for us." Jan, feeling like she was oblivious to Albert, was not going to be ignored without an explanation about what was going on with all this planning. She felt like it was going to be one surprise after another so she began to raise her voice. "Albert! ALBERT! "We have a family to raise and I have a job that does not like me playing with their equipment without knowing what's going o n!" "Honey, calm down, it's not that big a deal right now to tell them anything about what you are using the lab for, except that you want to look at some stars." "Albert! I don't know what stars and why. Why should I be in the dark about this great big discovery, if it really is a discovery? Look at the way you are staring at that little black book." Albert laughed, "You've got this wrong. I use this for notes about different things, that's all, Jan. It helps me keep things in order, that's all! You want to see?" "Yes." Albert gave the book to her and she looked at it and saw a lot of numbers and a couple of names and symbols. "What does this mean, r.a 16 dash +30?," she asked, picking out one of the many lines in the book. "You are the astronomer; you should know!" Jan thought, "Oh, this is astronomy. Let's see; it would be around the Corona Borealis or the Northern Crown. Yes, that's about the position of this reading." "It is confusing, Jan. Let's wait until we get to the lab and we will see if you can point the telescope in the right direction." "Alright! Alright! Still, you know enough to have made me interested now. I will make the appointment and we will have this adventure settled once and for all!" Giving the book back to Albert, Jan walked to the bedroom and said, "It better be good, honey dear." "It will be, and be prepared dear, honey dear."

Monday was a simple day. Both of them went to work, just as they had for years. The children did what high school children or teenage children do, for they were so wrapped up in their friends and outings that Jan and Albert's matters were almost totally ignored, except when they asked for money, like teenagers do. Then it was Tuesday, and the only concern that day was a cloud bank which had moved in and was about to ruin the appointment they had with Fr. Anthony. It got later in the day and the clouds were breaking because the sunset was of a red glow with some sky showing. The darkness rushed in and the stars came out as bright as ever.

Albert wanted to make sure that Fr. Anthony would be ready, so he gave him a call. Hanging up the phone, he was delighted to have learned that Fr. Anthony was waiting and willing to see what this was all about. Albert said to Jan, "Let's go, it's about eight o'clock. "I've got the whole night booked so we won't have any disturbances," Jan answered. They got into the car and went to pick up Fr. Anthony. He was waiting outside by the curb when they pulled up in front of the church. "May the Lord be with you," he said as he climbed into the back seat. He was comfortable with this late-model car with lots of space and the radio playing soft jazz. "How are the children?" Jan replied, "Oh, they are fine, Father. They are getting their studies done." Albert looked at Jan like he was about to laugh. Fr. Anthony replied, "Yes, they are not children anymore, the youth of are generation, teenaged, I might add. It is a blessing to have such wonderful parents that see that they get a good, solid education. Yes! A blessing, indeed." Albert, driving the car, looked in the rear-view mirror at the priest, who was barely visible, and said, "Yes, they do study their lessons; they are good kids."

As he drove up the long expressway, the observatory on the mountain became increasingly visible. It was about 8:50, and it had been a long ride of about forty minutes. They had just pulled into the parking lot and begun to get out of the car when Jan said, "See the far door under the dome? I'll meet you both there." "We'll be there. You gonna be all right? It is dark around the front, Jan." "There is security and I will be all right; just give me about five minutes." They all exited the car and Jan and Fr. Anthony where very interested in what Albert was about to do. They both were looking at the sky on this clear night; the clouds where all gone and the moon had set early. They entered the observatory room after Jan opened the side door and said "lock it" back to Albert. This huge telescope sat in the middle of the room like an eye to the universe. Albert came inside and said, "This will be just fine. I think this is just perfect." Fr. Anthony and Jan were walking toward the control desk and tables, both looking at the telescope's doors as they retracted and the sky began to be exposed. The mechanical sound of grinding gears filled the large room like a rumble of a large boulder rolling down a hill. It was a very complicated device, with the metal framing supporting various points of the telescope that would make the most brilliant engineer think twice. Upward the huge dome went, till it stopped at the point of dwarfing the tallest human trying to relate to vast space. The lights were at different positions in the observatory like they came from hidden walls. The walls were the only thing that could be seen clearly, with the low lights on the control desk. At the desk, Jan's face could be seen lit like a true scientist studying the newest invention of man's technology. For this was the latest and the best view in the area to observe the stars without any chance of getting confused. "Well, Albert, we are here; now you have something to show us." Albert slowly started to walk over to the controls, then stopped and said to Fr. Anthony, "I think you should see what I am doing." "I am here and very interested in what you have to show us."

As he finished his walk to the control panel, Fr. Anthony continued to look up at the telescope, displaying great amazement over the huge device reaching to the open ceiling. Then, as he reached the table, Albert reached in his pocket for his little book and began to flip through pages. It seemed like he had found the right page, but he kept flipping back and forth from page to page. He looked at Jan and said, "OK, here are the numbers for the position." He put the open book in front of Jan and she looked at it. "This is going to take some time. Give me a couple of minutes to turn the telescope and position the lens." "Alright. I am glad you can read the coordinates. We should have no trouble there." "It's readable. I just hope we are going to be able see without having a blurred view. There's a lot of water out there with the clouds clearing out." She flipped a switch and turned on the sidereal drive to match the rotation of the earth and began to plug in the numbers that Albert gave her. After about five minutes of silence, Jan said, "It's ready!"

CHAPTER FIVE

The next day was as if a dream had transported the world to a place that was not real. It was like a place where time had stopped, or as if someone had stopped the Earth from its persistent spinning. It was unreal to believe that something like this could happen in someone's lifetime; it would be enough to send the ordinary man running and yelling down the middle of the street. That was the thought that Fr. Anthony had, and Jan's thought was of running, or at least of being naked and doing a fast jog to mountains. These were not Albert's thoughts; he was so wrapped up in his little black book that it was like he had a second brain. Albert was not afraid of this discovery. He was sort of glad that he had told someone, after years of being silent about it. Now, at last, more than one person would know about his undisclosed dream, his nightmare, his touch of reality which was coming true faster than most people would like. Running from it was not the right thing to do.

Anyway, there was no place to go, because the truth was hard to look at for Jan and Fr. Anthony. Never go anywhere, for it is the planet Earth that is really involved here. Not from the side or from the top or from the bottom shall we go, and that should put the mind in a closed state of false reality. The thoughts of being safe and the center of the universe, like the old church beliefs, was just for sanity, for peace of mind. It was to help all of us believe and fear not. The truth always has the last say; even the astronomer Copernicus could have been wrong. Tycho Brahe, another astronomer, was clearly in a state of making his history so complete that being safe meant to find order by any means possible, even if the scientist

Johannes Kepler was guessing. Let us all think together here about the issues and not go to the safe and peaceful planet Earth. The astronomer Galileo dealt in reality and he had nothing to prove. Like John the Baptist, it was the power that would have the last say. By water, we should be completed for our maker to be proud and delighted. By the blessing of the soul, we are delivered to him, and that is by means that far outdo the human mind. Even if you are right to say so,for such ideas some men have lost. Too strong! Too real! And too much fear! The unused space on the planet left to graveyards and tombs, never to be opened. A vault of fear that Earth is just a rock in a huge pool of the endless ocean, going nowhere. At least we all know that there is no road to be taken, because there is no up or no down or no side when we look out at space.

We look at the sun every day and it fills the planet for us to be around. We have no choice. It is there always and always we spin around it without a second thought. There are stars that come out at night and we have nothing to say about how they act or even if they shine. If we believe in the fear of being alone in this endless, airlessness of space, we can't find a real isolated place in our minds from the Dark Star. A jungle of anything and everything, ready and waiting to jump in our direction to ingest this peaceful planet like a lamb in the teeth of wolves. We need to believe in someone or something that we can relate to. A God, a Supreme Being to save us from being eaten and never to be heard of again.

Who said that we have souls and they should be forever? Well, forever is a long time to have a soul, but now it is time for each person in the whole world to turn to each and every corner of his or her soul. The churches, fixed with the ideal of redemption, always looks forward to the cleansing of soul. It would only be a spiritual affair for them in the soul matter. The love of the Divine shall surely come to light in times of these measures. With any religion, everyone should be given to believe in a Master, a God over this weak flesh of mortal mankind. To have control over them in times of need. To have a place for them in the last of their days. To rescue them from the pain and suffering that is clearly in front of their eyes. The Catholic religion says that the Apostle Peter is head of the church, so then it is to the head that Albert must go. It is the biggest church with the most power and, as Albert plans his solution, the one with the most money. For it is a business now, and religion is just the part that will do the job for people to listen!

Albert is many things from his talents and very informed from his knowledge gained in a dream—a dream that taught him a vision of the

Richard Herbert

world and its people. Call it what you like, Albert is a businessman and his number one client is the Holy Roman Catholic Church.

The three of them, Fr. Anthony, Jan, and Albert had taken the late flight to Italy on the spur of the moment. They were on their way to the Vatican for a reason that would shock not only the Vatican but the whole world. Albert was sure within himself that the main reason was to help the people of the world. There are some acts of a humanitarian nature that the Vatican and the Pope would like to hear, but Albert had never told Jan and Fr. Anthony about the money he would milk out of the church. Complete sinners, have given their hard-earned wages to such a friendly church, would never have been able to imagine that their money would be taken from the poor and needy, now to fund a man and his wild idea.

After thinking about it, as Albert had done, it seemed like it would never be enough. No amount of money can buy life, no amount of money can make you free from sin, and no amount of money can bribe your sorry soul's way into heaven! It is known that heaven is not for sale, not to be bought, and you earn nothing from your hard-earned money by giving a donation to any church; you have to do good also. But make that donation to the one man that can save you from the pain of what is coming your way. A small offering to pay for your sanity and peace of mind is all that is at stake here. Just a part of everyone that will pay for God's sake and not for the sake of God. It's an old church and well-established over the years, decades, and centuries, and with plenty of cash to give if the giving is for the right cause. This church must decide if Albert's cause is worthy of enough merit and status to be granted, and be fulfilled with this holy money—cash.

The plane going to Rome was full, and if not for Fr. Anthony, they all would have had more space and comfort. It was Fr. Anthony, with his peaceful smile and his strong looks, who decided that his vows of poverty could not be broken. It was he who insisted that economy class would be the ideal space for him. It would do just fine for the ride, which had cost him nothing anyway, because Albert had footed the bill for the trip. To Albert, this was business, and if economy class was good enough for one, then it was good enough for all of them.

Albert sat next to Jan in a seat that was one away from the window. This time, sight-seeing and viewing the monuments from the sky was not on his mind. Next to Anthony was an older woman and a youthful man. Fr. Anthony was two rows back, almost at the rear of the plane. Albert had glance back before the flight to see if Fr. Anthony was all right. A vow of poverty was a tough thing in the mist of such giving people as Jan and Albert. They would always insist on the best of any arrangements when it came to traveling. Albert seemed to be happy because of the conversation he was carrying on with the younger woman, who looked clearly Italian, as if she came from the destination they all were headed for. Economy class was just about full of Italians in this part of the plane, because most of the voices were he could hear were speaking Italian. Albert, not in the mood to mingle with any person, closed his eyes and adjusted his seat to relax as if he were about to go to sleep. Italian was not his language and he could not understand a word of it, even if the gestures that he used suggested that he did. Jan, reading a book, looked at Albert as if he had a rough time to go through, with the toughest time now about to begin. She reached out and touched his hand.

Italy! The world was involved in the history of this place and now it was going to be the history-maker once again. To see the Pope here in the Italian air would be a wonderful thing. It would be a stroke of luck to have him here as this party of three arrived. A Pope that loved the people of the world with such a great sense of compassion just might be at home. He is a Christian in belief, the symbol of all Christians if you believe in Catholicism. The number one emblem of the religion for the world to see. Not Christ or St. Peter, if you have read your Bible well, but still the representation of the holiness of faith for the Earth to respect. It is upon this Earth that the church is built, if you can recall the beginning. It is here that the church is built, and much more, for the people of the world to see the representation of God, to worship no one else except the living God that has come down from heaven and saved the world from sin, if you believe in the scriptures, if you believe in the Holy Catholic Church and all who support the meaning. Yes, it is here in the land of Italy that a big church is built, with all the luxuries of time and devotion to God.

Churches for God, a structure, a building, an enclosed space surrounded by statues and fine ornamentation for worship. The church must be the best presentation of God, because there is no one else that has done what God has done and never ever will be, Albert thought. For God seems strange in the mind of most who are waiting to enter the glory of the heavens, the grand reward for being a good Christian in the eyes of many, but not in the eyes of God. God sees all, hears all, and of this human rationality, Albert realized, most of us have blinked once or twice to the divine immortal being. We judge and we should not; we sin and there are other things to do; we believe in being forgiven when we contemplate our wrongdoings.

21

It is for God that we do, not in the eyes of God is there any wrong from our actions, yet in the repentance we are visual facades to tell God our wrongdoings. We know the law of man in the world; it is to keep order and peace. If man's law is broken, then it is paid with human capture and punishment. To know the law, you pay the law and to know you'll get caught in the eyes of mankind, then it is mankind who judges your mortal worth. It is for God to have the last say, the creator of us all to live here on this rock in peace. To have the bowels of rejection loosed us forever if you break the law of God. Yes, heaven is not for those who lie in wait for lambs. We don't take away the belief of being a good and peaceful creature in the land of many. It is upon the eyes of God that we depend, even if we feel the right thing to do is the judgment of others, who play or act God-like. Albert pondered these things.

Hell is forever and that's a long time to be in the arms of anything but God. To be away from the mainstream of life and forever to be in pain and suffering is hell. Looks like a bad thing to have all the praying wasted in a moment of visual gleam from God that nobody on this planet can judge. To condemn you into the pit of fire forever, even if you believe in being forgiven. Repent, as a word, has become a common-day symbol. It just rings the bell that God's eyes are not like ours. He does not blink or take sides or let mankind judge his creation by their means of laws, for He will surely have you counted regardless of who you are. It is the Divine that made it known what He feels should be on His rock of planet stuff, spinning around the sun, whether you like it or not, a ball of fire. Warned every day about his intentions if they hurt, cheat, and don't believe that He is who He is as we wake up every morning to this gas sphere of heat.

It's simple to explain: do good. go to heaven; change and do bad: go to the other place that is not a place that you would like to spend forever. Forever might numb the limbs, the mind, the soul. Why, it's a dog-eat-dog Earth. Survival of the strong and let the weak be weak—it is their sorry loss. Albert thought that it might not be so bad to be rejected and placed in the fire to burn forever. Surely you can get used to it as time drags on. Just like the other place, which might be a truly boring experience, strolling around in heaven. Still, God knows all, and for that thought we run around in our feeble minds and realize that the true God is not worth taking a chance. The creator of all would indeed have forever of good and bad, or good and evil, clearly in mind in making His final conclusions, a well-warned experience that all humanoids in total knowledge could not imagine. We look around and see or hear or feel, on and on, and believe why or how many things are created that do not go without notice. Trillions and trillions of parts of life that the true God has his eyes on and even more, because He is God.

The doctrine of the church is strictly clear that the Pope is not God or even close to being him. He must also be judged and must risk his chance to be on that Virgo scale of justice, to have that good gold of goodness weight down the gravity to keep him up. Get on the weak side of less goodness and it is down on the meter or he must believe in fasting away the weight to become lighter until he does not exist on the low side of the scale. Who is to say who shall worship in what manner of religion that helps the world? There are other religions in the world besides Catholicism. What about the religions that do not believe in the Holy Roman Catholic Church? It is a point of concern with Peter's chair in the closet of the house of God. A part of belief and not a part of the other for future Christians to judge. The Mormons, the Baptists, the total Protestants, the Methodists, the Presbyterians, the Lutherans, and the Shakers, and let's not forget those Quakers and Evangelists. All have some focus of Christ, to judge how he said things or viewed his life. There is Mohammedanism, Buddhism, Hinduism, Confucianism and Taoism, Animism, Shintoism, and Judaism in the view of God, eyewitnesses to the faith of their belief. Who is to say that worship of some form of Higher Being is wrong as long as the aim is to correct the order of mankind. To consider the meanings of God and to believe in the faith of worldly consciousness should be the point. To fight and claw for the right to worship or to not worship because there are some who don't believe at all in God. From complete organizations to cults to passive egoism, it is present in the world of good and evil to load the Virgo scales of religion. Albert leans back and thinks some more.

The world is so old from the human point of view that human beings have no relationship to the past except in history. Old to life-living, and old to religion, and to what is perceived to be God's creation. Strange, for the creation of mankind to be unfolding on this rock called Earth, in this space of a measureless empty vacuum. For God, it is no problem to view every hair on your head, every grain of sand, and the faith of a mustard seed can move mountains. Believing in the road that is the right road could be not such a good idea, even if you do not show it or express it in faith when you are asked in your heart. You believe in God and that's what counts when nothing else matters, because this is what Albert, yes Albert, believes and he is now a true disciple of man's monetary business.

Taking a long look at the sixteenth century St. Peter's basilica, Albert stared at the dome, which reached two hundred and fifty feet above the floor. The dome that Michelangelo made for the glory and power of the Divine. It reached to the sky as if it had come as some holy gift for man to worship the heavens. It was big in stone and nothing was left to say that a segment of stone could not be shaped to express the absence of gravity. Fluted so as to escape the morning dew and the dry heat from the sun, the out lip buttress of this classical orders, right down to the columns. Adorned with the life works of mankind to save the meaning of worship, the chiseled forms of saints and biblical people encircled the building. The piazza of St. Peter's, designed by Bramante, could be nothing but an uplift to the peaking structure of the total building. The Tuscan columns made of travertine coarse golden stone used in old temples enclose the outside area. A natural running frieze in the walls of the open air, the surroundings capture you. A colonnade form and fountains surrounded the obelisk in the center. They show the feeling of being a part of holy ground and holy sky, for it is what people saw, felt, and did that made the stone more than a weight of crag. It promotes the meaning of workmanship to the people who toiled long hours over stone in every way to come together in this Vatican city. Giant pilasters at eighty-feet high drew the designers, Sangallo, Madern, Della Porta. To build from the Roman High Renaissance to the Florentine Renaissance, the blessed, the gifted, the precocity were all a chip of precious stone from the quarry of God-made natural stone.

Fr. Anthony said to Albert and Jan, "Right this way." He was on familiar ground and it was in his hands to make this meeting a reality. The arrangements of transportation and accommodation had all been made by Albert, and now it was Fr. Anthony's turn to get the point to the altar. Jan and Albert welcomed being in a room like an office, after the maze of buildings and security measures. A room of elders sat around a table like an office's conference table. One with the name of Manlin was sure to be in the room, for Fr. Anthony was quietly speaking to that elderly person. As Fr. Anthony talked to him, he also glanced toward the other cardinals in the room. One point was made clear: the only female in the room was Jan and she was in a suitable attire, looking like a lawyer in the midst of clients. Albert, in his regular dark suit, was not in the mood for kneeling and kissing the rings of high-status priests. That's what they were to him; anyone of those cardinals could be the Pope and it was left to Fr. Anthony to get the main pontiff to the table. Still standing and waiting for the Pope to enter, Jan began speaking to Albert: "This is going to be a tough meeting. You must make sure that it is out there and heading this way in a short time." She then asked," What are you planning to do with the Pope's relationship in this matter other than just informing him." Albert looked at Jan while the both of them were still standing and said, "You will know soon, very soon." Just then, with the door still open and with the random peeking in of nuns and clergymen, the Pope walked in. He was with his guards and keepers, three of them in total, which made it look like this was a very important man and his time is not for idle chit-chat. The five other clergy looked and gave their befitting respect to the Pope. Albert walked over and, about to kiss the ring, said, "Good day and how do you feel?" The Pope lifted his hand and Albert kissed the ring and then Jan did the same. Fr. Anthony, giving his respects to the Pope, then gestured for people to take a seat in front of the table. In total there were twelve in the room, almost like the Last Supper except there was one missing. The door was closed tight and all were seated. Albert and Jan sat across from Fr. Anthony and Cardinal Manlin, at the head of the wooden Gothic-type table sat the Pope, and at the other end, his keeper. Next to the Pope were two other clergy in a standing position, as if to translate anything that he would find disturbing and that might need an explanation. Knowing that the Pope understood English, Albert looked at Fr. Anthony and began to break the silence that had the faces of everyone in the room open to receive any information that would ease their thoughts. The introduction of each member was completed, and it was Albert's turn to speak, knowing that everyone in this room was in the dark about what was out in space except Jan and Fr. Anthony, who held their vows of silence. With puzzlement on the faces of the people in the room, only God knows what Fr. Anthony or Cardinal Manlin had told the Vatican staff and Pope to arrange this emergency gathering.

"My name is Mr. Lanker and this is my lovely wife Mrs. Lanker. I have a great concern for the future of the church and it might sound strange what you are about to hear, but please remain open-minded and be very optimistic about what you hear. In this room is where you will be to hear of one of the most biblical events ever to occur in history. I want to explain and make it known to you in particular, Your Excellency, because I want you to be a part of it." In the room, everyone looked at each other in bewilderment as to suggest something strange. The Pope never moved a muscle and just looked at Albert. "In space right now, at this moment, a star is heading to this planet at a rapid pace. It will make its presence known in this galaxy and will forever change history. The star is not known to anyone but Fr. Anthony, my wife, and of course, myself. Now you in this room also know, for I have told to you. I do request that this be kept secret by anyone leaving this room after I have told you the circumstances surrounding this event." Again, the clergy, and even Fr. Anthony, looked confused, but the Pope looked relaxed, listening quietly. "I have had a dream, a revelation, to know the parts of this event that is coming to Earth. It will take its greatest toll on the religions of the world unless there is some countermeasure. As I have said, I know enough about the dream to save many people physically, but I have to admit that the complete end of what will happen over time is very obscure. I do know that I can help in that area when we begin to see the changing pattern of what I call 'the Dark Star.'"

The "Dark Star is a second sun of our own. It is on its way back to its place of origin, not as a sun, but as a black hole, compressing matter in its path. The stars that we see will also be in its path. The Dark Star has become the biggest vacuum in space ever recorded by any device. The reason I tell you this is to inform you of what can be detected and the knowledge of what to detect. My wife has a PhD in astronomy and she agrees with the conclusion of the findings on this subject. I myself am in the building field, and have the knowledge to shape and design any structure possible. Still, the main reason I have asked you here is for money—money that would do the church, this church, the Holy Catholic church, the greatest gift to set history to rest. To set the record straight as far as the Bible is written for everyone and this religion. The money needed for me to do this is one hundred billion dollars." A great gasp arose in the room and a couple of the clergy motioned as if to get up and leave. Jan looked at Albert as if he had really gone mad and she placed her hand over her mouth in embarrassment, with her eyes closed shut. Albert, still sitting at the table, got up, as if it were a good deal. The Holy Father looked at Albert and at his priests and clergy with an uncertain gesture and began to speak, against the wishes of his staff. The Pope said, "We don't have any money for things you have in mind. We get most of our money from our devoted Christians and that consists of donations. You ask for investments in science, but that is really a matter you should take up with your country. The United States is a rich country and has brilliant minds for matters like this and your Dark Star." The Pope signaled to his clergy to get up as he was about to do, as if the conference was over and nothing else could be said. Albert, still standing, said in a loud voice, "Wait!!!" It shocked the room, rather like "who do you think you are talking to?" The Pope motioned again to the clergy to sit back down. His two keepers were in a state of restraining Albert, but not before these words came out of Albert's mouth: "It is you, Pope, you must be the center of this plan of mine! To bring Christians who were not Christians into the church. Ninety percent of the world will become Christians. Doesn't that matter to you?" Fr. Anthony stood up and said, "Yes that does matter." He sat down after speaking and looked around as if he already had chosen sides. Albert continued, lowering his voice and gesturing to the keepers that he would keep the volume of his voice down.. "If you don't agree to this matter, I will fully explain," Albert said, now that everyone was really listening. "You will be robbed of more than half of your flock into other religions, ready to use this Dark Star for their gathering of poor souls."

The Pope looked at Albert in consternation and explained, "But you are after financial gain in this matter. As I stated before, the church is not in this type of business to be investing in science." He stared, as if waiting for a reply and then continued to speak. "You're saying that over half of the devoted Catholics will leave the church is the only thing that has really grabbed my attention. For this, I will be patient for your answers to the problem. I am not a hard man, with ears closed to the voicing of evangelical ideas. I'm waiting for the answer about how you expect me to be involved." Albert went to his chair and sat down with his hands folded, as if he was praying. "OK, now that the madness of what I expected as a reaction is done, I would like you to know that it sounded mad to me too. I am Catholic, too, remember. This is what must be done. The money is really not so important to the conclusion of the plan if we all are going to die. Here is the master plan to save the world from being weakened by unbelievers in view of Christ. Call me a messenger, yet I must have this church, my church, remain strong and holy."

"The Holy Father is the key to have people believe in Christ. He is in the position to do that. It is true that money is needed for various things that I will have rendered. The United States is a big part in this plan, but if they go it alone than it would be a loss for the church. There are many religions in the United States and, for that matter, speaking of religion, the world has its share. Well, in a short time before I make known the exact position of the Dark Star and how to detect it, a plan must be made. This strange star will give a warning of its approaching matter by the calculations I have—something that the world will see in a very short time. If this happens before my plan is put into motion, then the church will be put to one side in the view of science. We have about one month to get this plan up and running. It deals with the buying a seat, which would cost about a billion dollars, more or less, to put the Pope in space. In space, he will present this warning as if you had a divine revelation given by God." The clergy looked at each other as if they wished they could go, after hearing Albert's deal. One keeper began to smile in a manner suggesting that if the room were empty, he would be rolling on the floor, holding his laughter in. The Pope looked down at the table and then got ready to speak, but Albert interrupted him. "The money that I seek is for your good, not mine. The Dark Star will drive the world mad in the coming years with the sound and sight of its approaching. I have my own money invested in two important companies as a safety measure, Earmax and Voices. These two companies make hearing-aid devices. A few small changes to these devices can help control the sure thing about to happen. With this stock, the United States will have to have these devices given to people so that they can function with a bit of sanity. The point is that millions, in fact billions, of them must be made so that every part of the world can have them. There is time to do this and distribute them all over the world. I might add, it would be part of the plan offered by the Pope to the people of the world, at no cost to some and little cost to others. It is up to each country to make this decision. With this distribution of the sounding devices, a cross and the seal of the Vatican would be imbedded in the casing. I am sure that it would not be advertising religion, because it is a "must-have," not an added luxury."

"The United States would be the primary distributor because the companies are located there. There are more and more things, with the help of the one hundred billion dollars that would take people, uhh, to a point safe from real harm with the approaching Dark Star. This star will cause years of events and it can be compelled to be eliminated from changing everyday life for many, yes many, devoted Christians. I will deal directly with you, Holy Father, and your staff of brilliant scholars, about the plans for the countries and people of the world. There is more, but it should be said that the Pope must be in the space shuttle to make this plan work. I feel that you are the answer to this coming star, to keep peace in the world, I mentioned to Fr. Anthony. Silence about this is the most important thing before, or should I say, if, these plans can be set in motion. It will not be long before the star shows itself, and after that, the world will be in a frenzy to find answers, answers that will all move in the wrong direction. The path of science will be ready to explain the situation, not to use it for an religious event, though that is what it is, in reality."

"I will not take your time any longer, Your Excellency, but just to say that everything I have told you up to this point is true. The world is in danger. The aftermath of what will happen, or even whether the world will actually be destroyed, will be in the hands of God. If the latter happens, then it is still a matter that God would look on us as having attempted to bring the word of the true God to the world of many religions. I am not asking that the world become all Catholic in any sense. Spare me! Just that most or some of the non-Christian religions be converted. That is the point for the Pope's message in space and to relate the word of Baptism in terms of entering the faith of Christianity. The message is reinforced by the exact time while in space and the event about to happen. I do agree that it would be time for faiths to come together; still, it will be a powerful message that cannot be denied. People will believe, not by force, but by love, that you the Pope have been sent by God to watch them." Albert got up and acted like he and Jan were ready to leave and then said, "There is a shuttle about three weeks away from being launched into space. It is a tool-testing mission, but this Vatican can buy them out and take over the mission with the right money. I am sure that at a cost, NASA will indeed make arrangements for the Pope to be on board, without the testing required. From this broadcast, the earth would instantly be focused on the Pope all the time. Padre, I am not asking you to lie, fake, or make believe that God has given you a special insight to the future, forgive me. By my telling you this, you are already a part of the future, a bigger part than you think. I have shown my wares, no doubt about it. More members to the church mean more support of the church in more ways than one, in my plan."

The Pope looked at his staff and then at Albert and said, "I will contact you by way of Fr. Anthony when the staff and I come to an agreement on this idea. It is a idea and nothing more! That is a lot of money for me to put into one man's control, and if the agreement is reached, for you! My powers on this must be met by the staff and various financial organizations. We will be in touch and I know you are eager to have a answer on the subject of your plan, because the time is near." Albert went over to the Pope and shook his hand and Jan did the same. Fr. Anthony, who intended to stay behind, motioned to Albert that he would see him later and knew at what hotel to reach him. The clergy, talking to each other about different things, continued to look at the Holy Father for some further response on the subject. The sound of talking, like the buzz after a news conference, was strong and clear to everyone present in the room. The Pope, still seated in his chair, got up and began to speak and then stopped. He turned toward the door and said in a voice that he knew the rest of the clergy could hear, "I must pray and have time in my chapel; silence is golden. I need about three hours." After this, the room went quiet as the Pope left entered the hallway heading to his chambers. Fr. Anthony and Cardinal Manlin would go to their quarters close to the Pope's.

The room was empty now and the chairs were all in place. A gleam of light showed through the stained glass window opposite where the Pope had been sitting. A beam of light from the sun was penetrating through the colored glass of red and blue, as if the room were filled with a spiritual nature. It lit the old carved table in a ghostly manner, making a symbol of a cross in a slant and obtuse figure that warmed the room. The lights had been turned out and no one was in the room except a thing that was left behind: Albert's little black book, placed under the table for safe-keeping during his heated discussion with the Pope. It was left behind for a reason, because if his plans changed, this book would have to be rewritten and already he had many little black books in his collection of notes and calculations. But this one was for the Pope and it sat on the floor in this holy place awaiting an answer that had not been given. The time was near and it would be a long three hours before any prayer could take effect, as the sun slowly deserted the sky. A sky that was not the Pope's or the people of the world's or even the sun's, that shined the light that lit the glass. It was God's own creation and only truly would answer to Him.

CHAPTER SIX
The Waiting Room

In the hotel room, Jan and Albert were talking to each other after finally being alone for the first time since the start of this trip. Jan said, "You really called the shots there against the Pope, didn't you? I'm wondering right now if we will be able to board the plane without straightjackets on. A hundred billion dollars? My God, Albert! That's a lot of money; in fact that's a huge amount of money. It's crazy to ask the Pope for that amount of money. He is the Pope! I know you understood that, didn't you?"

Albert, sitting on the bed, kicked his shoes off and lay down. He put his arm up and behind his head. He looked at the ceiling and wiggled his feet, as if to relax his body. Jan, standing, continued to speak: "This was a bad idea, I know it. My company, or should I say, the company I work for, has a great deal of knowledge to inform the world about this thing in space. Why do, you want the Pope to go into space? Now that is the second craziest thing I have ever heard. Besides, you say you had a dream about what will happen. A dream! Sounds like you should be in a mental institution with electrodes hooked to your brain, so that they can find all of your thoughts and save everybody some money." Albert looked at Jan and said, "They can do that? Read my mind and, let's see, put it on a video tape and play it back and forth for accurate details? Jan! Jan, be patient. It will be alright! Have you seen the star? Now that you have had a little insight into the future, it looks like you want the whole thing. I don't know the whole thing about the future, you know, Jan.?"

Jan asked, "Where did you have this dream?" "On our second honeymoon." Jan replied, "Oh, in the Egypt!" "No, Athens. You were asleep that night. I was standing on the bed in a cold sweat and afraid to tell you or anyone. The knowledge I was given was true, as you see. I'm the same person; you know that. And as far as your being alarmed about how much I know about space, don't be. You know I have taken a lot of astronomy in school with you, honey. With your books and papers and equipment around, I think I can put two and two together about what the Dark Star is. Jan, you are still the scientist; don't forget that. With the right money, I think I will just buy that company that you work for." "Please, Albert, you are really dreaming. I am waiting for the Italian police to knock on the door and arrest both of us for telling the Pope that he must go to space. Now doesn't that sound crazy to you? You really have been dipping into the noodle bag here with a crazy idea like that!" Albert said, "Are you finished now? I know what they are thinking about; it's why didn't they think of an idea like that." Jan asked, "What!"

Albert continued, "The church is willing, whether you like it or not. The Pope is not going to miss this opportunity that would help the church in a spiritual way by going to space. Our main strength here is Fr. Anthony and Cardinal Manlin. They are the ones that will verify the sighting even if it is the last day on the planet, which I doubt it will be. You see, it is not the money to the church; they will make tons more than that with this idea. Maybe five or six trillion dollars if they get just a little increase in members to the church. The real problem is what the Pope will do with the Jews and Buddhists. They will be on the move against the baptism of everyone in the world. It is kind of ironic that if the Pope can do that, not too many people will believe that their religion will be the strongest against the Dark Star." Jan replied, "Are you forgetting that you have no idea what the Pope will do with you? You think it will be easy to give you authority to go on with your plans? Can't you see that I love you, Albert? I hate for you to be hurt for being right. It is true that the Dark Star is out there and coming at us every second. You will be in the spotlight and all the people will want to know who you are and where you live. You know that once the media gets a hold of this, it will be a crazy time. Answers and questions that nobody will be able to respond to, Albert."

Albert looked at Jan and said, "You like television?" "Well, at times." "That's the point I wanted to make, Jan. Your company is big enough to have its own network. You will be the narrator, or anchor person, for a daily broadcast about the Dark Star. If we have the subject, than we have the facts of what this star will do. You will have special guests and all that, but it will be a clear science update, like the news, not like a regular talk show.

Besides, Jan, I have been talking too much anyway. Why didn't you tell the Pope I was going wacky? You know, you were the only woman in the room, Huh?" "Sitting across the room, I was afraid of the Pope, He is a holy man and I just got to thinking about my sins and God." "Oh, got afraid. Well, little girl, say ten Hail Mary's and sin no more. You should be stronger, not with the Pope I mean, but with your knowledge of science—you've got a PhD, woman!" Jan, looking at the ceiling, said "I get the credit for the discovery, right Albert?" "Well, yeah, and then you can send me a pack of smokes and a checkers set to the crazy house while I gaze out the window at the sky." Jan went to the bed and jumped on Albert and kissed him. "I know you are having a hard time. So am I. That's why I didn't say anything about the Dark Star in the conference with the Pope." "Oh, thought you were on the side of the clergy, just about ready to hammer-lock me into the bottom of that building. Those guys are big, aren't they?" "Not as big as your heart is, dear." Albert sat up and said, "What time is it?"

Looking at his watch, Albert noticed that two hours had passed and knew that the Pope would make a decision in about an hour. Albert said to Jan, "I'm going to order some room service. You want something special?" "No, Albert, I will have what you have." Albert picked up the phone on the side table and ordered some steaks and potatoes with a side helping of creamed corn. Jan requested a salad with her order and Italian dressing and a glass of the house wine. The two stood up and hugged as they went and looked out the window to see the breathtaking architecture that surrounds the city. The old buildings looked godly with the shadows of the setting sun on the craftsmanship of their facades. The sky with a clear view of the rising moon gave a tranquil mood to the dusk that was falling on the city. A subdued feeling of looking at the people and cars that were traveling around the city appeared to be in the state of anticipation of any word from the Pope. Or is it just what Albert and Jan believed to be the feeling of waiting for a answer? Albert suddenly noticed that his little black book was missing. He searched his jacket as it lay on the bed and asked Jan, "Have you seen my little book?""No, you had it out at the meeting with the Pope." Albert responded, "Well it might be a good sign if we do get back in the meeting room. Besides, it is a copy and a few notes are in it. Still, it is important to have. If we do get word from the Pope, it would explain some things I forgot to mention."

There was a knock on the door and a voice called out "room service." Albert went to the door and in came a man pushing a cart with a metal covering. The man was dressed in a red and gold lace suit, with a funny looking hat, shaped like a ship. Albert paid the man and said, "Thank you very much." The man replied in some rude Italian after seeing the size of the tip. They both pulled up chairs to the far table by the window to eat. Albert served his wife and they both ate the meal, along with the wine and a cup of coffee. As they were about finished with their meal, Jan said, "It has been over three hours and the Pope said it would take that long for him to come up with an answer." Albert looked out the window as if it was too long for not having heard anything from the Pope. The city was turning into night and you could see the lights of the car's headlights moving through the streets as though nighttime was on its way. The fourth hour passed and then the fifth hour. Albert and Jan, who were on the bed, trying to get some rest, began to look into space with a sense of pessimism. They both were thinking about cutting short the trip, if not for Fr. Anthony who traveled with them.

Albert got up and said to Jan, "Let's go." "Go where?" Albert said, "To the airport. It's a fact that we are wasting our time here. The Pope is not going along with that plan, maybe because of the money or maybe the others on his staff have realized that this can be done without us." "Albert, it's not like that. I am sure he would have told us what he thought if he was not going to do anything about it." "Why don't we just call?" Albert said. "What! We will be on the line for two days with that answering service. They have tours and museum gatherings and various things on that machine. I myself am not in the mood for pushing buttons for an hour." "I'll call." Jan picked up the phone and asked for the Vatican switchboard. The operator replied with the number. Jan, on the phone, looked at Albert as he fell back on the bed and looked up at the ceiling. Jan, still standing and talking on the phone, replied, "Yes, Cardinal Manlin's office, please." There was a silence and then she hung up the phone, saying it was after five o'clock and the answering service was on. Albert said, "I told you that it was. These people are very hard to reach. We have the hope of Fr. Anthony and the best thing to do is to meet him back in the States. At least we know we can reach him there." "But he flew with us." "So? He knows his way home and that's the best thing to do rather than just waiting around. Fr. Anthony is going to give us some kind of word when we see him back in the States."

Albert and Jan were ready to go, and called the desk to ask them to get the bill ready. "This is room five one two," Albert said. "Can I have the bill ready? We will be down in couple of minutes." The desk replied, "Is this Albert Lanker," "Yes." He replied, "Yes sir, I should have told you, but

I did not want to disturb your meal." "Yes?" said Albert. "Sir, a telegram from a Fr. Anthony was left for you. Would you like me to read it? It is brief.""What does it say?" The desk attendant waited a moment and then said, "To Albert and Jan. (stop.) It is taking longer to hammer out the deal. (stop.) Wait there. It looks good (stop.) And I will see you soon. (stop.)." Albert, listening, said "Thank you and we will be staying longer; thank you very much. "We are here to please you." Albert hung up the phone and told Jan of the news. She was wondering about more of the message, but Albert refused to talk any more about it.

CHAPTER SEVEN
The Deal

"WHAT! "WHAT! I am the one that should be going into space! I am not as old as the Pope. He might fall asleep when we contact him up there!" Cardinal Manlin replied, "I am the Pope you know!" Cardinal Boush said, "You know, we all can travel there too! Your Excellency it should be someone that has a stronger will, physically!" "Wait a minute!" Fr. Anthony said, "The Pope needs a space suit. Who is going to take care of that?" Manlin said, "NASA I guess? It is their spacecraft and it should be their job to make the arrangements for what the Pope would need to fly into space."

There they were, in the chambers of the church, with the walls filled with masterpieces and with priceless statues in the coves of stone, images of saints that looked so real that they could come alive. The ceiling extended at least twenty stories high. Gold trim was placed in places that accented the room with the sense of wealth. This secretive chamber was a sight to behold, if you were among the gifted to be granted entrance. But this place was for the most important staff of the Vatican, and there they would make the arrangements for what would come to pass. Some of the members were standing about their throne-like chairs and others were seated as they talked. Yet, there were only ten of them in the room discussing a solution.

"No! No! No! I am the Pope and the people will believe me. I am the man to do the job here, so let's get this show on the road! Now, what about the money that this Mr. Lanker wants, Fr. Anthony?" "Well, I have looked at the figures with Manlin, and he says that the Swiss banks could handle that amount of money." "No! No! Anthony, not who can handle the money! I asked you who will control the money! Don't think for one minute this guy is going to have a free hand with a hundred billion of the Vatican's money in his neighborhood bank!" "He knows that; he has a company and he knows business," Fr. Anthony said. "He realizes that there are channels for moving around money of such a huge sum." "Alright! Then the next thing we must do is to come up with an answer about this baptism idea." Manlin replied, "Now that is brilliant! I have to say now that's the best thing I have heard come out of this Dark Star idea. You see, the church is in the position not to lose anything, only to gain everything." The Pope replied, "What! What! Manlin! Do you think the Jews are going to fall for that? Just toss their lifelong religion and go get baptized and become Christian in one day? No! No way! Is that going to happen? I don't think so. And what about China? Now that is a world in itself. They don't change easily. The way it sounds, the Asian world is not going to start detaching from their religion. No! We need some angle beside the baptism one. You know, blessed Christ! I get shivery when thinking of a massive baptism. That's in the Bible. You get enough mad people in the world doing that and Yep! There it is: the old Pope's head is on a plate as the target. Or should I say his head is on the plate with a space helmet on." Fr. Anthony replied, "That would be history repeating itself. That does not happen." "Let's go with the baptism; it's the beginning of our religion." Yes, it is the right thing to do because, you're right, we are in a crisis here. We'd better get to the task. Well, this Albert looks to have a good head on his shoulders. He's got enough ideas that it should work. Look at us. We are fighting over a done deal that's really clear. The church will make money even if we get only another ten percent increase in membership."

"Get Manlin and Fr. Anthony to take care of the money distribution, and Fr. Boush and the others to take care of the world membership drive," the Pope said. "OK," everyone in the room replied and they all got up and left the secret room in the Vatican. This was not a place for the members of this great organization except for those that have rank, and not for the members of any Christian faith in the world do they enter this place, for it is not the Catholic's main concern in this place, a place of worship and forgiveness that this deal is made. It is just the fact that the Catholics have the sustained truth when times are tough. Feeble-minded doctrines among all Christians all over the world that seek for the real truth. The real materials that endured in history which were made of strong virtues and strong facts. So facts and reasons that the main history of Christ in full glory existed in material forms were saved somewhere for truth. The glory of history that changed the world for them that believed in nothing! No facts; none at all, of what really happened in the time of Christ if not something was saved. You might ask yourself, in the time of your own worship, do reason and logic really exist?

It is the Catholics that have the facts in the matter of history in the forms of relics. The leftover goods of the truth of something that happened in those days of religious strife that the good God had won. It is not for the religion to say if fact and logic is one central thing, because the Catholics do have the facts. In St. Peter's church, there are many traces of articles that point to the truth that cannot be denied. The truth of being a Christian is to believe in God, the God that was on the cross and died. The God that rose to pay the price for our sins and give us the truth. For it is a fact that we all are sinners and with sinners of any faith, the facts are always what counts. It is what humans do; faith is unseen and it never tells its reactions about what it does. To believe in the unseen or unpredictable is faith in our eyes. For God sees all, hears all, and knows all. He is God and God answers to no one. The symbols of His messages are part of his infinite power to believe in mankind and mankind to believe in him, because male or female, we all are human and God knows the limits of human belief.

To say it was a reason for one powerful church of God to have a stronghold on religion is not the reason. The Catholics are old, and with an old religion, people will do what people have always done: preserve the faith over the passing of time in a manner that God will approve of. A style that will make the simple life of a person a mission in time to the Almighty. To keep the spoken word fresh in the mind and the facts made not to be forgotten. The Holy Spirit is in faith and fact, yet we would never know of the two. We believe in facts, and facts are things that happen for us to witness to. Yes. Hear it! See it! Feel it! Say it lasts a while and then fades in the sun. Faith never leaves us or never changes the meaning of God for the use of facts. As the relics grow older, they are the facts that never will be changed in the present For relics of the past are what they are, and every Christian's faith should bow down to the Catholics for having the facts. But, that's NOT Christian-like because, believe it or not, they are on the same side when the true God is Jesus Christ. How shall they worship Him is a debate of any religion, and how does any community really believe anything could be? Is it by fact or by faith? Cardinal Boush pondered these things in his mind.

It was up to Fr. Anthony to call the Lankers in the morning, for the debate among the clergy had gone on well past midnight. The call came in the morning while Jan was in the shower and Albert was eating a small breakfast of hot cakes. He was about to take another sip of coffee when the phone rang. The message was to meet Fr. Anthony at the same place they were last time, in the conference room at the church.

This time, Albert did not have his little black book. He had forgotten it under the table and he was glad to see that he was going to go to the same place where the book still was. Jan, out of the shower and getting dressed, asked Albert who was on the phone. "Fr. Anthony would like to meet us this afternoon about one o'clock in the conference room." "We will see if the idea is church-worthy. Are you sure they will accept your idea? Well, if they called, it is a good sign, honey." "I think they bought the idea. It is the only solution they have for this matter. Yes it can be done differently, but it is better to have a plan that is really already in motion." "It is ten o'clock right now; let's see some of the Vatican while we can." "Do you have the Sistine Chapel in mind, Jan ?" "Yes, the fresco on the ceiling by Michelangelo, and the Dispute of the Sacrament by Raphael, and Christ's Charge to St. Peter by Pietro Perugino." Albert replied, "Let's go. If you mention any more, we will be here until we grow old." Albert got ready, putting on his watch. He looked at the time and said, "We've got about two hours, so let's see and run. The appointment with the clergy is at one o'clock, so there!" They went to the elevator and out of the hotel to sightsee the Vatican.

They both entered the meeting room a little exhausted from seeing an eyeful of art and architecture in the Vatican. In the room were Fr. Anthony and Cardinal Manlin, standing up, waiting for the Pope to arrive. Fr. Anthony gave Albert the thumbs-up sign and continued to talk. Jan, standing next to Albert, said, "Be strong about your ideas, Albert, this is the final plan until we go home," and then she grabbed his arm. Albert knew that he would need to have everything in order about what the series of events would be. On the table, in front of the same chair that Albert had been sitting in the day before, was his little black book. He walked over to the table and picked it up and placed it in his upper pocket. Then in came some of the clergy and then the Pope entered the room. One of the Pope's keepers said, "Your Excellency," and everyone paid respect. The room had the same people as it did when the Pope was there the first time for this meeting. Twelve people in total, including Jan and Albert, except this time there were two nuns, raising the total to fourteen. Albert looked at the two nuns as if he wanted to tell the Pope of their presence. But the Pope beat him to the question, saying, "I'd like to introduce to you Sister Irish, my financial advisor, and Sister David my speech writer." Albert looked at Jan as he pulled the chair to sit down. The sisters nodded their heads in acknowledgment to everyone. Jan looked at Albert, as if to say, "You gotta be good to have them here." The sisters took the two empty chairs along the far wall, opposite Jan and Albert and behind Fr. Anthony and Cardinal Manlin.

The Pope said, "Mr. Lanker what will you get out of this?" Albert looked at Fr. Anthony and then glanced at the members around the table and said, "A hundred billion or more." The Pope said, "What!" Albert replied, "A hundred billion or more; you see, I need that much for the things I want to do. The church should be repaid as an investment, if you want to look at it that way. A trillion dollars or more in about two to three years. After that it's anybody's guess because of the new membership into the church as a result of the Dark Star." The Pope looked at Manlin and said, "Is this possible? I mean, can Mr. Lanker handle that much money?" Albert interrupted and said, "I will assure you that the money involved here will be enough to have everything planned go smoothly and soundly. There are communications and satellite feeds that will have to be done to reach all the major religions on the planet. The point is to have most, if not all, of the civilized world see you. The third world and isolated people will have to be reached. They will need technology to help them see you before seeing the Dark Star."

"The United States and some other countries around the world will help with reaching and delivering some of the devices to help the people deal with the events that the Dark Star will cause. As to my concern of being in the spotlight with this idea, I think not! In fact, I plan to build and be in a distant place away from the cities and clear of fame. As you know, my wife is an astronomer and is highly educated in astrophysics. Her company has access to many companies and organizations all over the world. So, it would be an advantage to have Mrs. Lanker in the spotlight in my stead. I feel that a science channel would help everyone with the information about the progress of the Dark Star. Of course, there will be nothing but the best scientific minds on a interim presentation of this channel to assess the Dark Star."

The Pope answered, "We are pleased with your plans and feel that it will be a positive thing for the church. So, I have brought along Sister David and Sister Irish to help with the planning of the two things that

I feel need the most attention." The Pope, looking at both of the nuns, motioned to them to take a seat at the table. They moved their seats next to the Pope, with the help of the keepers, and then one of them opened a suitcase and from there the keeper handed some formal papers to Albert. "As you can see, these forms are made out in your name as a contract to our financial coffers," the Pope said. "It is to insure that the money you are given is well-recorded for your sake and ours." The Pope then lifted his hand and said, "Sister Irish, please." She was a large nun with a heavy body shape. Her wardrobe, the typical nun's attire, was the only thing that made her look different from a banker. She had a veil over her head, as though there was a large amount of hair was underneath her habit. She was serious in voice and stance as she began to explain the paper placed in front of Albert.

"This is a document to state the meaning of the arrangements of the Vatican. If you'd like to go briefly over them, you will find all the documents in order. It is our agreement that you will, in a explicit manner, perform certain duties to the Catholic church for the purpose of presenting an aggregation of people's thoughts. It furthermore explains that the direct motivation of your intentions is in an uncontestable function to the Holy Roman Catholic Church. Also, imbedded in the statement pack is a clearly written clause that Christianity is steadfast to any and all religious motives in your goals. In any case, it is not to isolate any certain Christian religion or bring about the discord of any Christian organization as mentioned." Sister Irish queried, "Is this clear to you, Mr. Lanker?" Albert looked at Jan and said, "Ahh, it looks to be in order." Sister Irish, standing next to the Pope, retrieved the document that the Pope had signed, and motioned to Albert to do the same. Bringing the same pen to him that the Pope had used, Albert signed the document. Sister Irish asked, "Did you have any questions?" Albert smiled. "Ahh," as he looked at the twenty papers underneath the first one to be signed, "Naa, I mean, No."

Sister Irish, placing the papers in her case, pulled out another set of papers. Going around the table and handing a set of papers to each of the clergy who were seated there, and to the two keepers who were standing, she stated, "Everyone in this room except me and Sister David has a document with his name on it. This is a commerce deed to the church, the Holy Roman Catholic Church, for the instruction of capital to be distributed to Mr. Lanker in the form of real money, United States dollars. This will be done in conformity with Fr. Anthony, i.e. code 1182 and Cardinal Manlin, i.e. 4739-b. In this declaration it states that the

Swiss Bank and Chase Bank of Chase shall have the sum of one hundred billion dollars deposited in the names of code 1182 and code 4739-b and of Mr. Albert V. Lanker. So, Mr. Lanker, it is not that the church doesn't trust you with the monetary sum, it is the fact that the pecuniary sum must be made in this manner for the assessment and other capital gains taxes. This is a real solid agreement that will give you total usage of the cash, excuse my expression. It is, of course, fitting that the other two parties in the covenant, Fr. Anthony and Cardinal Manlin, be informed of any transaction of funds. I am sure this will be more than sufficient." Fr. Anthony and Manlin both signed the documents with their own pens; Albert looked at them like he had just done the impossible and then signed the document with his pen. After that, everyone in the room signed the document in front of them and then passed the paper towards the Pope. Standing next to the Pope, Sister Irish was collecting the documents and placing Albert's and those of code 1182 and code 4739-b on top of the stack of signed papers. The Pope looked at Albert's document and glanced at the endorsement and smiled. He said in a low voice, "That was quick." And then the Pope looked around the room to see if anyone had a comment.

Sister Irish said to the Pope, "These documents will be notarized and placed in the vault. I would like to mention that all documents from this room are not to be discussed with anyone that is not in this room." 'As far as you all are concerned, they don't exist." She walked over to Fr. Anthony and then to Cardinal Manlin and placed a brochure in front of them. She then walked around to Albert and gave him a brochure identical to Fr. Anthony's and Cardinal Manlin's. "These are the codes and accounts you will need for any transaction to be done. I would like to mention that all three of the trustees in those accounts are present. Knowing that this is intended for Mr. Lanker, it is his code that will transfer any funds to any company or business or organization. It is Mr. Lanker's responsibility to act as the sole agent for disbursement. He has this power to use as he sees fit—to purchase, rent, lease, or whatever, to allocate his plan of funding the Dark Star project. Finally, all transactions will be transmitted from my office in the Vatican. Any questions from anyone here?" No word was said by anyone, just facial expressions of concern for Albert.

Sister Irish, her briefcase in front of her, ready to leave, said, "You are now going to have a new location, Mr. Lanker. You will be a resident of California in the center of the state." Albert said, "But that is farm land." "Yes, it is an empty monastery with a huge amount of land there. This land and the building need to be built into a productive area. Since this venture covers a number of years, it is the Vatican's request that you take our offer. It is easy to say that you will be a farmer, but we know you will be much more than that because of your building knowledge. You will be provided with everything you need for development besides the use of the Dark Star coffers. I ask you, are you willing to take this offer, Mr. Lanker?" Jan looked at Albert and said, "My job is in Washington." Albert replied, "I think we can arrange this transfer; it couldn't be better." Jan, looking at Albert, said nothing. "OK, Mr. Lanker, this deal is set." Sister Irish opened the door and walked out to her office down the hall. The Pope, looking at Albert and Jan, said, "This is a gift with no strings; you have made a wise choice."

The Pope then looked at Sister David, who was about the most beautiful nun you have ever seen. Her eyes were of a confidential nature, with a look that showed the goodness of her heart. She was neither tall nor very short, yet her shape was almost beyond perfection. She talked like an English teacher, with every word pronounced clearly. You had the perception that she was fluent in many languages, and you would be right. The Pope said to Sister David, "You have some words to say to me about what should be said about this Dark Star?" "Yes! Holy Father." Sister David said, "The main reason for the church to be vocal in this presentation is to bring about baptism. To do this effectively, baptism will be the subject of the speech the Holy Father will give. Mr. Lanker, do you feel the world will have a sight of this Dark Star in the day or in the night?" Mr. Lanker looked at Fr. Anthony and said to Sister David, "It won't matter for the first week after the Dark Star shows; it will be visible. After that, it could be seen during the day if you look for it, yet at night it will be as bright as the full moon, about at four to five apparent magnitude. Yes! It will be pretty bright day or night."

"OK. The speech the Pope will give will consist of a presentation at the moment before the Dark Star appears and will conclude with direct instructions to the world in all languages spoken by mankind. It is the goal of this speech to stress the importance of baptism before and after the appearance of the Dark Star. Mr. Lanker, can the exact time of appearance of this Dark Star be calculated?" Albert, looking at Sister David, scratched his head and said, "I think I can get it down to the thirty second range. It should be around there in the seconds of time." Sister David said, "That's good. Now, my office will handle the arrangements for the Pope's travel with NASA. I understand that certain channels must be opened, Mr. Lanker. The President of the United States should be in a position to fulfill the request for the Holy Father, I understand." Albert replied, "Yes he is; still, NASA must meet the guidelines of space safety. It is clear that the European program has some strong leverage with NASA as well." "Yes!" Sister David said, "They will have the equipment needed for the Pope's venture into space." "Well," Albert said, "The mission is about three weeks away and we have about two or three days before NASA starts rolling out the spacecraft." "Yes," Sister David replied, "it is mandatory that NASA be told as quickly as possible about this mission."

Albert pulled back his chair and stood up. He said, "Now, we need this mission to space to have a silent code. It is clear that the media will be all over this, if they get a whiff of what is going on. I personally implore you all to let the word of this venture be made known the day before it happens, not before! Let's name the reason for this mission as a concealed science project. That way it will be in the news, yet it would not be announced until the day before; we will be need to hide the Pope for this to work well." Sister David said, "This can be arranged."

"OK!" Said Albert, and then he looked at Jan as he stood by the side of her chair; she began leaning back to view Albert. "My wife, Mrs. Lanker, works for a astronomy group. It is important to give her first crack at the measurements of the Dark Star. I would like her to be given the credit for discovering this because of her background in astronomy, and the company should be a done deal with me owning it. Now that puts the Dark Star under the control of what we have planned. All the scientists in the world will be fighting to have information on the Dark Star to tell the world. This position will give us the advantage of transmitting data to the world from this company named Far-Seeing. Of course, this will be the science side of the Dark Star. As soon as it is known to the world, all the telescopes on this planet will be directed at the Dark Star. I will set up radio and visual telescopes with the Far-Seeing company; by using a radio interferometer, they will make an array to receive data from the Dark Star." Jan looked at Albert and said, "Thank you," and smiled. Just then, the room was filled with applause. The Holy Father even clapped a little and smiled at Jan. She said "thank you," to everyone present.

The meeting was over and everyone walked out, congratulating Albert and Jan .Fr. Anthony was the last to give his regards to the two. Fr. Anthony said, "I'll see you back in the United States. There are some details to be taken care about my church up north. Looks like you will be in California from now on. I think that's really nice." Albert replied, "Yes, looks like I'll be a so-called farmer and I've got a church for you. Anyway, take the offer if you can be around the area. You have done a wonderful job for me. I don't know what I would have done if you did not keep the faith." "Look! It's no problem; you had an idea that was really hard to believe, so remember THAT! I have seen with my own eyes, remember!" Albert shook Fr. Anthony's hand, "I'll see you in the States." Leaving the Vatican and checking out of their hotel, Jan and Albert were on the plane to America.

CHAPTER EIGHT
The Mission

Jan and Albert got back to the States and to their home in Seattle. Their three children were informed about the move to Merced, California, and Victor, still in college on the East Coast, would be staying there to complete his studies. With time at hand, Albert and Jan began to move mostly everything to the deserted farm, which had a medium-sized house and lots of land. Albert envisioned what he wanted the farm to look like and it would mean some years of construction. Upgrading this farm, with even a monastery on it, would require a lot of demolishing. Albert had family in California; his parents were glad to learn that he would be living in the state, even if they were further south, in the Los Angeles Basin area. During the transition, Albert was on the phone often with Fr. Anthony and Cardinal Manlin about the money transfer arrangements for the Pope's trip. The money was under Albert's control and he would make sure that the plans stayed on schedule. And the time was imminent, with an an almost-empty house to take care of the Pope after his arrival in the States. The public was in the dark about what the Pope was doing because the public thought he was still at the Vatican. You can blame that on Sister Irish and Sister David, not to mention Cardinal Manlin and Fr. Anthony, who had carried off the biggest cover-up that the Vatican had ever known.

In a small jet that the Vatican leased to hide the fact that the Pope was leaving the Vatican, he flew into America. It was feasible to leave the Pope's specially prepared jet back in Europe to avoid detection, so it was left in the hanger in Italy. Now the Pope was in Washington and was quickly met by the ambassadors from the United States and Italy under a seamless shroud of cover. Cardinal Manlin had made this meeting possible by communication from the Vatican earlier. The Pope was then taken to the Capitol building where the White House staff and the President were waiting for his arrival. With dark tinted windows, the three vans passed through the streets and lanes of the city without anyone knowing who was coming to see the President. As well, it was nighttime and most of the earlier events around the White House with the media and people were gone.

The building, covered with lights, stood like the pearl of the free world. A home to the people of this country, not physical, but spiritual in nature. It was a good symbolic building where declarations of both war and peace had been made. The tall columns of classical order created the feeling of complete order. The mandate to place this country under God and freedom to all who enter the borders of this country is inscribed on the walls. The White House, a place for the people of this country who believe in freedom for all. But it was night, and who is to say who will be stopping in the home of the President.

"Right this way" as the group of Vatican people and some of the President's staff walked to the oval office. The Pope, among the group and without his regular attire, looked the oldest; this gave him the privilege of walking in front of Fr. Anthony and Manlin. It was shocking to the President as the Pope walked in, dressed like a business man wearing a suit and tie. All the rest of the Pope's party had on priestly suits, and overcoats concealing their clerical collars. They all entered the room and closed the doors as the Pope sat down in front of the President's desk. The President, looking at the group, sat in the large chair of his office and said, "Yes, what can I do for you, Your Excellency?" Cardinal Manlin, who was seated next to the Pope, glanced at the Pope and pulled out some papers. Cardinal Manlin got up and placed the organized papers in front of the President on his oval desk. The other people in the President's party were in the room and looked at the group of Vatican clergy with great concern. As the President read the papers, the Pope broke the silence with the words of, "You can do this, Mr. President, can't you?" The President looked at the Pope, "It is a matter of importance to you and the church, isn't it? I have certain powers that determine what I can do and cannot do. This request to NASA is certainly going to take some time. Executive orders go only so far in the arena of science exploration that NASA falls under. Also, the Congress must be informed with the judgment of this request for review." The President, looking at the final paper, lifted his eyes and said, "You are willing to pay the United States a billion dollars, is that right?" Fr. Anthony, who was standing, said "Yes, the Vatican will pay the sum of one billion dollars to have the Pope, at his own risk, on this mission that is about two weeks away, with no liability to your government or NASA. The Vatican will take all the risk of this mission. If you can get the Pope on this flight and this flight only, NASA and the United States government will be compensated with the complete sum of one billion U.S. dollars at this moment."

The President looked at his staff and said, "If it is that important, let me wake up some people at the main base." He grabbed the phone on his desk and asked for the Pentagon. The conversation went on for about a minute and then the President hung up the phone. "Let's make this happen, Your Excellency; the flight on this mission is a low level tool mission and is not an important science or military one. Of course, all the missions that NASA sends into orbit are vital to the space program, except some have more importance than others. NASA does take in civil schedules for flights of satellites and experiments at times that they are funded by various groups. I feel this will be one of those groups, pardon the expression. I think you got a deal." The President looked around at his staff and said, "About the money issue; one billion dollars is a lot of money to spend. Some spacecrafts cost around that much. I'm sure we can make some arrangement for lowering that cost." The Pope replied, "No, this is the price I am willing to pay. Because of the short notice, it is only right to have your government compensated for that sum. I am not interested in how you divide up the payment, because it must be recorded in the files of your government as more than a mission to NASA. There will be questions. I think it would be better to mention it to the American people when this becomes public," he said, with his eyes turning toward Cardinal Manlin. "The Vatican is not unknown to the world and this payment will discourage all other attempts by people or governments to try this feat."

The President looked at the papers on the desk. "I am still in the dark about why and at this time you would want to go into space. It is so sudden and it looks like there is really no point, given the trips you have undertaken, to South America and so forth." The Pope, looking at the President, said, "It is very important to use this platform for the message I have to deliver to the world. You, Mr. President, will be informed of the outcome and will play a big part, beneficial to this country." The President, without further conversation, looked again at the papers and signed them, and handing them to his secretary, said, "Keep this under the code of secret seal." Then he stood up and signaled to everyone in the room that this was a secret. "This is a private matter and should not be made known until the Holy Father wants it known, understand?!" Everyone in the room replied, in a low mumble, "Yes, ahh, yes."

They were all ready to go. The President was talking briefly with the Pope when a staff member intervened, telling the President that the chopper was ready. The President motioned to the staffer, all right! It was one of the President's helicopters and it was on the landing pad outside the White House. The Pope and his clergy, Fr. Anthony, Cardinal Manlin, and the two keepers were to board the aircraft and be ready to be delivered to the airport. From the airport, they would be flown from the Pope's private jet to the space center in Florida. All the plans for the Pope to go into space had been made by the Pentagon brass, so things were to follow those orders. It is about money; the money the Vatican paid by the transfer from the Swiss account that made things go well. Albert, in California, had made that possible. He had already put the bank transfer into motion, with the last codes of Fr. Anthony and Manlin to finish their passwords and had designated to what account the money was to go. It was Albert that knew this would be a good idea because NASA was eager to have their mission in the news as much as possible.

It was to be one of the strangest two weeks for the Pope, especially his getting a crash course on being an astronaut. He figured that if a monkey could go to space, then it should be a piece of cake for him do so too. His health was good for a man of his age, and it was the safest spacecraft known to man, so NASA felt they could do the job. A job that would make the world's concerns take a backseat to what was going on with this mission to space. With the help of the military, it would never be leaked to the public or media, until the Vatican wanted it to. It was not difficult for the Vatican to cloak the disappearance of the Pope by saying he was in deep seclusion and would not take any appointments. And those appointments that he did have would be rescheduled for a later date.

As the Pope and his clergy spent time at NASA, Albert was being contacted by them regarding anything they might find strange or out of the ordinary. Albert, still busy with the final stages of his relocation of things from up north, was ready to start planning the design of the land he had in the middle of California. He looked for an architectural firm named Peterson and Associates. He would buy this firm after looking at the urban planning experience it had in Los Angeles and New York. It was a small firm and had not done any really big projects for a long time. Albert would remain in the background of his projects, with the development of his corporation name "Ultra." Now with the money, Albert could go on his long-time mission of building. Albert would buy out Jan's company and almost all the hearing aid manufacturers that made devices he felt would be useful to him.

It was the final week of planning for the Pope's visit to space. So Albert began to make plans for Jan to make known the discovery of the Dark Star. He had Jan fly back to the north to her job site at the observatory and set up a remote communication base with the media and science world. Albert and the children would see it on television at the farm as soon as the coverage was on-line. With the spare time that Albert now had, he could make some preliminary sketches of this flat farmland and try to see what he could do with it. He had thought of plans that would make the farm look like a multiple-building project with all the needs of farming crops and more. That is what would be needed in this part of the country. Wheat, corn, and beans would do well if he could get the help he needed for planting and reaping those crops. He would need a good crew, and Albert would erect a living quarters to the south for a crew of well-determined people that loved to farm. Anyway those plans would be in the future. Right now, it was time to get the world well-educated about the heavens. This was the week for the Pope to reach the world and give his message to them from the space shuttle.

The Pope was shown all the things he had to do to be a good passenger aboard the spacecraft. He was shown the basic needs he must attend to, like bodily functions and how to use these devices for that. He was given a ride in the artificial gravity machine to simulate the launch of the spacecraft. He went through a number of other endurance tests that would have him ready to go on the mission to space. Fr. Albert and Cardinal Manlin were at NASA to give support and also to hold on to the Pope's holy garments. His space suit, provided by the European Space Program, was a perfect fit, with the Vatican symbol and the Italian flag on each shoulder. It was the keepers' idea to have symbols on the Pope's space suit, because it would be clear that the Pope is a man of God and should have his identity made known every second to anyone who looked upon him.

It was about time to tell the public about the Pope being in the United States. Albert contacted Fr. Anthony to tell him that everything was ready for the people to know of the Pope's presence in the country. Two days before the Pope's space mission, Fr. Anthony instructed the media that his message must be aired by all major networks simultaneously. It would be late at night the day before blast-off of the shuttle when the public was told of the Pope. Fr. Anthony gave the instruction to the rest of the clergy at the base that he would tell the media of the Pope's voyage into space. The task of informing the media would begin with a tip-off to the President via a phone call from the Pope. NASA was very happy that the mission was going smoothly and all parts of the previous mission planned had been reassigned, including the astronauts. This crew would have a five-member team, with the Holy Father included. Two flight commanding officers were men, and one mission technical officer, also aboard was a woman. The other astronaut was a science officer, whom the clergy requested from the scrapped mission that the Pope took over. The Pope was part of a science team on paper that hid the mission from the public until now. It would be the most watched NASA mission because of the Pope being in his senior years. The mission also included a fix-up job for a small satellite. It was ironic that it was one of the Europeans' weather satellites.

It was eleven o'clock Eastern time Sunday night. Albert was planning on the news to travel fast once it had been released. Albert knew that on Wednesday about seven o'clock Pacific time, the Dark Star would be visible. The news media were already in a melee trying to get to the spacecraft's base in Florida. The news of the flight was announced publicly at eleven o'clock on the east coast, and it hit the west coast about eight o'clock. Just enough time to not make the World News broadcast and just in time to have the late news catch the shocking story. Radio stations were broadcasting the news and wondering what was going on and how the Pope got into the country without anyone informing the public. At the White House, the news media fought for seats after being notified that the press would be allowed in for a meeting with Pentagon officials. That would leave about six hours to blast off the Copernicus-Emissary mission. At NASA, the mission had been named for the astronomer Copernicus, who was wrong with the sun being the center of the universe. Although Copernicus was right about some things,, that was not the point. Copernicus was just the vehicle for having dealings with the Catholic church.

The media was given the word and it began live coverage from the NASA site; even background coverage of certain people involved was released to the media. The church where Fr. Anthony was the pastor in Seattle, Washington, swarmed with reporters. Fr. Anthony had spoken first to the media about the presence of the Pope and his mission to go into space. The coverage was complete in all ways, with stories of the Pope's history and his position among the world's society. Also, the background of Fr. Anthony was connected in some media circles with Cardinal Manlin. The Vatican gave only one public statement. They expressed great concern for the safety of the Pope and that it is the will of God that the Pope express himself to the people of the world in many ways that people would cherish. The churches around the world were glued to every possible nuance of this great event. A rush of planes and ground transportation flooded the lift-off site of the spacecraft. All regular broadcasts on the television were overruled to make room for round-the-clock coverage of the Pope going into space. Nuns, priests, and children rushed to Florida, made possible by Cardinal Manlin, to feel the support of the church at the site. He had given free round-trip tickets on any airline with complete transportation to see the Pope go into space. Of course, this undertaking was governed by the established Catholic church in the United States. Cardinal Manlin felt it should be considered as part of the budget of the Dark Star project, and Albert and Fr. Anthony agreed. The College of Cardinals were in an emergency meeting about this adventure of the Pope and why it had not been made known to them beforehand. This almost created a rupture in the church because, Cardinal Manlin and the keepers had not sent word of the news regarding the Pope. The only thing that made them all in agreement was the authority of Cardinal Manlin, who was a big part of the college. The same thing happened at Fr. Anthony's church, with the dismay of reporters parked outside the church and asking questions about the priest. All of them there were puzzled, because his contacts with the Pope were news to them. Most in the area were shocked and still could not believe that Fr. Anthony was involved with this event.

Albert was the only one to be at ease. He had moved to California weeks ago, at the same time the farm was being sprayed because of the bug problems in the soil. It was a peaceful place, with the two teenagers happy to be there. They had lost their friends in the move, yet with their own telephones, it would be no big loss; just bigger phone bills. Besides, they had more space, a lot more space to do what they wanted with their newfound rooms. The schools would be a travel, but the oldest kid drove and they both would have to share their time. Albert knew that in the long run, this would be too much for them, and in the future he would have to agree for both Peter and Anna to live with his mother and father in Los Angeles to continue their schooling there. As Albert sat in front of the television, the news of the Pope was on every channel. He began to fall asleep, looking at this with ease because neither his name nor Jan's was mentioned in any of the reports. Albert leaned back on the couch and slowly fell asleep, dreaming slightly about Amatimas.

Soon enough, the television blared out: "This is the National News Report, The Copernicus-Emissary Mission, and this is your anchor person Tom Bevel. Our latest report is that the mission of the space shuttle is on schedule. This is a seven-day mission with a most unusual passenger, the Pope. What a surprise to us and the world with the announcement of this mission. We would like to mention that NASA has had about every new first in space, yet this one is likely to be the biggest one of the decade," Tom Bevel remarked. "Sending the Pope into space will mark the first time that any high order man of God has gone into orbit. People are wondering what the Pope will be doing in space, besides just going along for the ride. It is our suspicion that the Pope will be addressing the people of the world with a holy message. The Vatican, quiet concerning this trip, has referred all inquiries to Cardinal Manlin," Tom Bevel stated. "Manlin is at NASA right now and we have a feed from our remote transmitter there. Cardinal Manlin, this is Tom Bevel with the World News, I have a question for you." "Hello, yes this is Cardinal Manlin." "Yes, Cardinal Manlin, do you have any information about the message that Pope will give on his journey into space?" "Ah," Manlin replied, "it is his own message to the people of the world. He has written it and it's a message that I really have not read." "Manlin, does it have to do with his latest trip to South America or the upcoming trip to Greece?" "No, I don't think so. It is, ah, ah, from my view it has to do with the world of Christians. I really feel that he means to express a devotion to the church in some way and to bring about support for the Christian faith. Of course, I myself have no idea of what the message is and would only be taking an educated guess, knowing the Pope personally." "Cardinal Manlin, it is known that there were some strings that had to be pulled to arrange this trip. I have one question? How was this kept out of the public eye and the news so long without anybody knowing about it?" Manlin replied, "Ah, that was Fr. Anthony's planning. He is the one you would want to talk to about those arrangements. Thank you very much, Tom, I must be close to the Pope right now. Thank you very much and may God bless you."

Back at the base, with about two hours until take-off, people were still arriving at the base. It was so jam-packed at this short notice that the National Guard was called to direct traffic. All cameras went to live broadcast when the Pope, dressed in a space suit, was ready to board the shuttle. The Pope gave his greeting to Fr. Anthony and Manlin as he boarded the van. His keepers were already on the van as a security measure. The Pope, seeing the cameras, gave a little wave of his hand and a small smile showed through the space helmet he was wearing. He was ready to fly into space for the good of the world, because it was not to be a fun trip or a trip to make of the Dark Star to the planet. With the news of his going into space, it would be the greater news that all the clergy looked for and not what he was about to reveal. He would be the main person to deliver that message because Albert had a plan that he wanted to work according to the book.

With minutes left until countdown, the Pope was ready, the spacecraft was ready, and the crew was set to fly this holy man into the great immense frontier of space. They would orbit the Earth many times, but it was like being in deep space. Even though it is close to the seashore, it is still a part of the total sea. Its waters are all concurrently one piece of the total mass; that's what was intended in Albert's plan. To be at the point of space to give the message that this planet is part of the total mass. He felt that the world would and should relate to the meanings of being all together on this planet we call Earth. Albert had sat on the couch all night with the remote in his hand. He was not asleep now, thanks to the phone ringing. Albert finally answered it and Jan was on the line. "Albert, is this you?" He replied, "Yes!" Jan continued, "The news is full of this! The Pope looks like an astronaut, did you see that?" Albert replied, "That's what you need to go into space; you have to have the right equipment." "Well, anyway, this announcement of the Dark Star, well, will the media be here at this site?" "You'd better believe it; these guys get around. Be sure not to disclose much about me, only that I am your husband and that I have nothing to do with astrophysics or astronomy. Jan! You understand?" "Yes, I understand, but I feel that you should be known to the public." "Jan, that would create a problem. Make your discovery a random one. you know." "Like what?" "Like by chance?" "Yes, like some strange mistake in setting of your equipment; that would do." "Well, I'll think of something; I'll make it look good." "Thanks, honey, and honey, remember, it is Wednesday at about seven o'clock." "Yes, I know that! I will be all on it; remember, this is my discovery, Albert, OK?" Albert then gave his regards to Jan and hung up the phone.

CHAPTER NINE
The Universe

At the base, it was time to see history put on a new face for the world to behold. The press conference with the White House had just begun to answer questions about the space launch. The military officials had shown up to talk about the mission with the Pope, now ready to go into space. They explained that the reason for the national security surrounding this mission was to stop any left-wing action aimed at the space mission. They further clarified that the mission was Top Secret to the public and that they had this planned at the request of the Vatican. They did not go into detail as to why the Pope would be going on this mission, only to state that the Pope asked for the use of the shuttle to express his message. The Pentagon officials were not clear what the message would be, but had a clear understanding that they were to take direct orders from the President. The cost of the mission was mentioned to them and they just said that it was funded by the Vatican. Without further explanation, the officials adjourned the press meeting and went into their chambers.

The time was at hand, with the countdown coming near on the Copernicus-Emissary mission. With the message of a lifetime, it was not going to be easy to talk to the people of faith who were not Christians about their beliefs. No, something they would not want to hear, when all their natural-born lives had been spent in another faith. What can be said about a message that could have been delivered from some other source besides the Pope making his speech in outerspace. It is easy to have the leader or head figure of any faith tell his people what's right and what's wrong. Why should this be this church? The Pope is just a man of the cloth, and from where things stand, he is going to support his beliefs and his church. Why, if someone wanted to be of that faith, then it should be no problem for them to join anytime they wanted to. Still, that is not the point here! It is to let the world know about what this faith believes in Now! That's the mission at hand. Because as it stands, this is God's creation and it is God who created all of us in this belief. Yes! May it be in. Godspeed!

"This is mission control, with a standard two minute hold at T minus fifty minutes and counting. We'd like to mention this is a planned hold at this time," said John Tittle, the launch coordinator. "Countdown resumes, and the closed loop test and mid-line activation is performed. T-minus forty minutes and counting, start of the pre-sequence has commenced and final cabin leak checks are completed, with the cabin vent being performed. Pressurization of the orbital maneuvering system and guidance navigation control are done. The main engine controller preflight bite check is done and cabin vent valves are closed. The countdown clock will hold at T-minus twenty minutes, another planned hold," Tittle remarked. Then the final ground crew cleared away from the pad. Tittle continued, "The console programs are verified and check of the launch window and collision avoidance are done. Status of landing sites is done and all test team personnel switch to channel four-four-seven. This is John Tittle, and we are holding at T-minus twenty, and all preflight alignments are complete. We are ready for the transition of the oxygen purge system right now. The countdown clock will continue in thirty seconds to the next stage of launch unless the recommendation to hold the launch is performed."

The crowd outside the base was huge; people from all parts of the country had arrived at a moment's notice. On television, on cable, on radio and even in some late newspapers were seen to have news of the Pope's trip into space. In small towns and big cities, it was news, big news! From coast to coast and from pole to pole, the news was traveling fast that the Pope was going to space. All the countries that had any piece of electrical knowledge had a way to hear or see the news at-hand with exhilaration. Cardinal Manlin had arranged to reach all parts of the world with the communication of this event. He leased large screens; he bought air time on radio, and nearly bought a satellite in orbit to make sure that China and other non-Christian countries got a good part of the news that the Pope was going to give. All languages and all symbols were translated to make sure a clear delivery of the Pope's speech would take place. All of the Catholic churches in the United States were notified of the Pope's travel to space. Also the news was given to all the Christian churches that could be reached to inform them that this man of the cloth was about to address the world. It took a lot of people to do this, with the College of Cardinals and bishops all over the world selectively communicating via phone calls to people and churches around them.

"The next hold will be at T-minus nine minutes," said John Tittle. "The countdown is resumed with the purge of the fuel cell. The oxygen purge system transition is completed and now the uplink loading preflight system for backup is completed," Tittle explained. "T-minus sixteen minutes and counting with the water spray boiler quantity being verified. Performing the reconfiguration of helium cross-feed valves has been done with the adjustment of the fuel cell. High flow rate for left and right solid rocket boosters has been performed. General purpose computer dump is completed." John Tittle continued, "This is a planned hold at T minus nine minutes. This is a planned hold and the readiness of the launch team is verifying the weather and forecasts to meet the launch criteria." Now the countdown is resumed and the auto sequence has been started and the orbital access arm is pulled back. The auxiliary propulsion unit pre-start with the auto arm device has been armed at T-minus four minutes and counting. "Verifying solid rocket motor ignition and initiating space shuttle main engine purge sequence with the body flaps in launch position," Tittle stated. "The closing of the topping valve and liquid hydrogen chloride vent valve have been set at full. T-minus one minute and the heaters are turned off. Now verifying critical commands and ground power removal. Stand By!"

The spacecraft sits on the launch pad with the eyes of the world glued to every movement. All broadcasts are turned on with radio and television with the silence of dead air, the only sound being from John Tittle. "Attention! Operations review board, the vent door of the shuttle's engines has begun." Tittle continued, "Start! solid rocket boosters and auxiliary power unit, START! solid rocket booster gimbal test, begin suppression water fifteen seconds. Perform high point bleed valve and close and stop helium fill, TEN SECONDS! Clearing hydrogen burn off, START! system ignition and go with main engine start. Inhibitors are removed from safety range and main engine three is started. Main engine two is on, then main engine one is started. T-minus zero with ignition and hold-down release command. LIFT OFF!"

A loud sound of the rocket was heard; like a bomb of nitroglycerin, it filled the air around the pad. It was a sight to see in person, because the media never could give the full effect of the open sky and this craft's power.

It elevated slowly and began to speed up as if gravity were the only force of nature, and yet gravity was brought to its knees. Up the rocket went after it cleared the base and laid out a huge amount of smoke. The sound was shattering with power from the engines; it left no doubt that it would reach top-speed shortly. The crowd watched, with their heads following upward, as the spacecraft went up to the heavens. Up it went and after the two side engines had been freed, John Tittle broke the silence, a silence that all the broadcasters were afraid to break. Even the radio transmissions had not spoken a word. The sound of the shuttle was the only noise on the airways. "This is John Title and we have had a successful launch with all systems working well. The shuttle will be entering orbit momentarily, at an altitude of one hundred and ten miles above earth. The crew has reported everything is going well with the special passenger, the Pope. This is John Tittle. I thank you for watching the launch of the Copernicus-Emissary mission. From now on, communication will be done via Mission Control."

It flowed into orbit at a speed of thousands of miles an hour. The Pope was in a state of amazement because of all the power of the spacecraft's engines underneath him. He was experiencing the feel of gravity pressing him into his cockpit seat as if he were being crushed. After thanking God for a moment, he was standing brave to the effects of the launch. It was when he began to get weightless that he knew that he was in space. The crew looked around at the Pope, wondering if he was all right, knowing that Mission Control was monitoring every heart-beat and pulse-rate from all of them. One of the commanders said to the base that "the Pope was along for the ride with flying colors." With the shuttle in orbit, it would be hard work for the crew; as the gravity got less and less, the straps and tags began to float. In orbit above the planet was something to observe as the windows began to light up from the earth below. You could see the sun, as bright as any star, and out there, light glistening off the moon and planets with a great array. They would be in a polar orbit rounding the planet, with a speed around seventeen thousand miles per hour. To the crew in the spacecraft, it would seem like a walk around the park, not feeling the speed at all.

With all the systems of the shuttle completed, the crew began to get down to the business of the duties of the mission. The Pope had nothing to do except to wait for the first broadcast from Mission Control. Most of the talk from Mission Control had been directed to the commanders, for system checks and orbit calculations. The Pope did have one thing to do, with the help of the systems specialist, and that was to get out of his space suit and into some lighter apparel. He floated in the cabin like he was a bird with a little more grace than an older man would have. He got the feel of space really quickly because he was not taking any chances with his movement. Holding on to something with each movement made him look almost like a cane would have done him good. Although he did not experience space sickness, the Pope would not want to eat anything when the food was ready for the crew. He stood in the window, looking at the earth and the stars like a small child. Yet it was in everyone's minds that the Pope was full of glory with the power of God's creation. He could see the oceans, the land, and the clouds, all in arm's reach of the shuttle. Still, with religious symbols and pins, it looked like a prayer was being made by the Pope for the people of the world as he looked out the window. The most powerful realization that set in on him was that this planet was truly out in space. The word space was not a thing, but a limitless place, with no up, no down, no side, and nowhere to go. It was strange to think about it with so much darkness and vast distances unfilled. The Pope was hit with a new and powerful realization of the meaning of the claim that God is love. This life-filled planet called Earth was all that existed to the Pontiff. Seeing it was like a living rock in the midst of this huge universe. The cameras were about to turn away from the ground crew in order to broadcast pictures of the inside of the shuttle to the world. It would be the first telecast and the world wanted to know how the Pope looked in space.

In the dark of night at a place in the heart of Africa, it was serene. The people of this land were out for the night in their own way, something natural to them. Out in the darkness, these people, with the sky lit like it always had been, saw a transformation. The stars are far and show like little lights in the sky. To them it was nothing new to see Sirius in the sky or Vega or Deneb. It was a common thing to them to view the universe in all its beauty at night. Not even the red giant Betelgeuse, in the Orion constellation, ever meant that much to them .It was the moving stars that made these people think. Sure, there would be a flying star sometimes, like a meteor falling from the sky and lighting up the night that might make them take notice. This would get the attention, at times, even from nomadic tribes and wild animals. Satellites had flown over this distant land for years. In the sky, with a slow orbital motion, the satellites would move silently. But no, these lights were manmade in the huge sky that have the darkness a sense of newness. The moving star drew their eyes upwards in the cool of the night. A moving star was flying in the very sky that they owned by tradition. They noticed it on its way to the north, brighter than the other moving stars, yet not as fast tonight.

It was the shuttle in space with a special man in its cabin flying by. To them, it was just another moving star, except for the brightness of it. A little more brilliant than the larger stars in the sky, which made them look and follow. It moved to the north around the sky, where it passed low on the horizon until it went by Polaris, the North Star. A gleam in their eyes, a flick of energy, a pulse of charged particles caught the night. It was strange to them for a second or two, and then it was gone. Words in a language that years of history still had a hard time translating would be said to each other. Something that the domesticated world would never know of the observation, had taken place because they were first to see it. To see history and not know what was going on with the rest of the world. These people were nomads from the years and years of traditions and beliefs. They traveled at night and hunted and sheltered themselves as best as they could. Primitive in nature and civilized in thought, they were the first to see this shine of light in the sky. Not the moving stars in the sky that they knew fly by the night; something else, making its path, unaware that it was some spacecraft or satellite. Of course, they knew of the modern man, but never understood that his technology could create light in the night. The moving stars could never be of man's works to them. Sure there are planes that fly and the boats that sail, yet no ray of light in the heavens would be attributed to modern man. Not to this tribe of hunters, in a land where every minute is full of danger from the wild beasts of nature. Large game is no new thing to them, because they must survive in this danger. This is their land, and their prey wait for them just as they wait for their prize food.

It was the strangest thing that happened that cool night in the nomad's land of darkness. As the tribe saw the moving star, the leader of the group went to the water bag, a bag of animal skin of a prized catch which was skinned and cleaned for reasons of making a water storage unit. He grabbed each person in the tribe and poured the rare water from their travels over them and washed their heads. Each of them was christened with the water and then dusted with the dirt of the land around them. It might have been the way to cloak their mortal body or it was a ritual done to the sky. Why it happened, nobody knows, yet it did have something to do with the sign they got from the heavens—something that was not told to anyone, because there is no way of communicating with civilized man in his terms. These people had learned this from the tradition of their past, handed down through successive generations by way of interpretations and rituals. How old was this tribe? Old enough to know that the sky is changing, and changing in a way that would be apparent to them very soon. It was here that the first sight of the Dark Star was seen. Well, it might have been their discovery if Albert could have told them that the rest of the world could be talked to. In the primitive world, it was not news to them; it was something they knew innately, and conceived to be trouble. That's why they performed their rare and once-in-a-lifetime baptism. That is what the civilized man called it and maybe they knew of a Man that is God to them and who had instructed this single tribe to perform an act to join His glory. Christians, maybe, or just call them nomads, living in a primitive world. You see, these people don't care about money and luxurious living. Those are things they never had, and, as they will to live luxurious it is just the price of the game. The skill of the wood, the shape of the rock, the color of the paint will do just as good as money. It is to them that will be the ones to suffer if not for a airlift to drop something that could save their traditions. Not to say that some people are not enlightened about the rest of the world. Not to say that the Pope is in space and the whole world knows it in some form or another. Not to say that the Dark Star is not years away, only that the whole world will be affected and the entire population of the world will feel the effects of this event very soon. Albert thought of the nomads in deep dark Africa—too !

CHAPTER TEN
Erroneus Deception

The spacecraft remained in high orbit, in a perfect position, circling the earth from pole to pole. The crew was ready to plan the release of the satellite into its location from the shuttle bay. They have been downplaying the special passenger on board in order to give him a chance to rest during these hours of anticipation. There were some live pictures of the Holy Man in space that kept the public informed of the Pope's well-being. Most of the information about the shuttle was brief and to the point for now. The news media, still filled with this event, had never stopped for breaks of the live coverage. It was a history-making event for the spacecraft's families and friends, all about the number one Man in the cabin of the shuttle. Even some of the news dealt with the best positions to see the space shuttle as it flew by. The best views of the spacecraft were in North America and some parts of Europe, with some cloud cover blocking the view of those who looked to the sky. In the southern hemisphere, it could be seen also, with the news reaching the total civilized world.

North, in the Seattle area, Jan was patiently getting down to business, making the appropriate arrangements for recording her discovery of the Dark Star. She needed to have all of the science associated as possible to have a part in and credit for finding this strange and critical star she would reveal. Jan would contact the Central Bureau of Astronomy for the purpose of putting her name on the position of this star. It would go almost completely unrecorded, because of the news of the shuttle at hand. The recording was well in advance of the event, which Albert told Jan to do because of the flux in her readings. This would put all scientists and astronomers, not to mention the astrophysics gang of technical brain surgeons, all running to the observatory for facts. It was going to be a strong and demanding Wednesday for Jan. The time was hours away and the Pope was still preparing his speech to the world. At this moment in time, it would be the facts according to Albert's calculations and now it was coming true; visual indisputable evidence would become known.

The hour had arrived for the phone call from Albert to Jan. It would give her permission to go with the recorded data of the Dark Star. Jan, in her observatory office early Wednesday morning, had made herself a cup of coffee and read through the newspaper. Reading the news of the Pope's travels and seeing Fr. Anthony in the photo came as no surprise. Cardinal Manlin from the College of Cardinals was mentioned, along with the affiliation he had and that his main idea was seeing the Pope in space. She smiled, and read on when the phone rang. "Hello Jan," Albert said. "How do you do, my wonderful husband? Are you lonely in California?" "Yes, I miss you." "Yes, I know; same here." "Well, are you ready to become the most famous astronomer in history?" "I guess that's the title I will get and I want it! It does sound good with my name when it says, 'Jan makes the greatest discovery in mankind.'" Albert replied, "It's your baby but don't get too informative; just give the facts. Jan, have you got a name for the discovery?" "Well, it looks to be a what science calls an object from the Ursa Minor Quad. It could go in any manner like that, except I made it clear to not name it the Jan Star. No, I'll leave the name up to the science debating staff. Besides, they will call it something—the data is here." "That's fine. I like the sound of that. I am really intrigued to know what they will name this." Jan replied, "Yes, I am too." "Let's run the discovery now, Jan. Let the cat out of the bag, honey. I'm going to be watching you on television, so look good!" "OK, I will go with the recording and I will keep you out of most of the questions if they ask." "Love you." Jan hung up and went to her computer and began running the data. It was Wednesday morning and the Pope was about to give his speech at noon, only a few hours away.

Albert took a seat in front of the television at the farm and the news changed to a live picture of the Pope in the space shuttle. He was dressed in a beautiful tapestry and lace vesture with a Chi Rho symbol on the front. An overlapping stole of the same material, made of fine woven fabric, showed the chasuble. It was hard to recognize what it was, with the weightlessness of space lifting the garments softly up and down. Some Celtic crosses were on some of the ends of the stole and vesture with inlaid golden silk. He was sitting in front of the camera as the Pope looked directly at the lens. One thing was clear: with all the nice wardrobe the Pope had on, the miter he had on his head stood out the most. It had a large Chi Rho on the front and looked completely out of place on a spaceship over this planet. The thought was shocking and you had to pay attention to every word this man would say, simply because of the miter. Albert knew what he had done in this planning of this trip. The effect of the mission was to use the Pope for his good and for the world's good; also, he knew this was the only way to do it. It made the head of the Catholic church look worthy and strong in ways that could not be done by any other means. The Vatican was now off the Earth with faith and into space where all the planets were, and in theory, the teachings of this establishment could spread the message on to new worlds. Because it happened here and here is where it began, that a God in the flesh rose on the third day to save the sins of the this Planet we call Earth in the Christian belief. As the camera remained on and the picture of the Pope was present, he began to speak, a laced paper book in front of him.

"Hello, people of the planet where we all come from. I send you welcome from aboard the spacecraft called the space shuttle. I embrace you for an important message I must bring forth to you. The peace of mankind is a substantial part of the well-being of the world. It is the fabric of civilization; it tolerates no suppression of the facts. We must all strive to maintain it, for the well-being of ourselves and our children and children's children. As Christ has taught us to do, we must love one another. We should all run from strife when the times of our own lives are in troubled waters. Peace should be preserved at all costs when your fellow man is in danger of confrontation. The peace of the world is at hand, from small to large countries of this beautiful planet. I look down on the oceans and the mountains from this ship of peace and say to myself, what an astounding God of creation He must be to give us such a living planet. I am not leaving out the poor and unproductive areas of the Earth, yet the blameless land should benefit by the copiousness of the rest of the land on this great planet. Help the poor in all ways, as Christ has done for us, for we are indeed poor in the view of the universe around us. We are the needle in the haystack, the grain of sand of the many shorelines. We are the fish in the ocean of multifariousness. We are the leaf on the vine that reaches out to eternity. I beseech you to remember the Word of God for my sake and yours. Love thy brother as thyself and be slow to anger, for the time is near. This is what I tell you to remember always when the time is constricted and pain and suffering is near."

The Pope changed his booklet, which he had in front of him and began to read from another one that was handed to him by one of the astronauts. On the ground, people were glued to their television screens and radio transmissions for the words from the Pope. All channels carried the message, because now the people began to fear what the Pope was about to say. The Pope continued, "I use the Holy Bible, the Gospel according to Luke 1:11, 'AND THERE APPEARED UNTO HIM AN ANGEL OF THE LORD STANDING ON THE RIGHT SIDE OF THE ALTAR OF INCENSE.' I believe that this should guide of the directive I want to share with you all. I mention this act to you not only because I am in an order of the Holy Catholic Church, for the good of this institution, but to all Christians and non-Christians of this great planet. To all religions, the Jews and diverse religious orders of the whole world, I appeal to you that baptism is the key to my mission here in space. Not to force you to choose this way of God for my sake, but for you to walk the way of our Lord and Savior Jesus Christ. To become a Christian is the greatest gift to mankind. It travels the way of the living God. I do not despise other religions, for their faith has proven dedication in history. Yet, the time is near and time is running out for us all. Choose baptism at any Christian organization that leads to the way of Christ," the Pope explained. "If the Catholic religion is best for you, then so be it. Still, whatever the Christian faith you choose, get baptized if you have never been."

"In conclusion, I have been given insight to know, through prayer to the almighty Father, that an event is about to happen that will change the world as we know it. Shortly, there will be a sign from the Heavens to show all of us the power of God. It is a natural event and threatens our lives forever. It is as a warning that I tell you this. It is not the end of this planet, yet a moment for us to begin to love one another. The best way of doing and showing love is through Jesus Christ, who taught us all how to love each other and to sin no more. For it is sin that leads us to death, and in that sinful state, we are of no use to each other. So, believe in life and living in harmony with each other. I cite a quotation about love from Hannah More, an author in the eighteen century. She states, 'Absence in love is like water upon fire; a little quickens, but much extinguishes it.'" The Pope put down his paper and again finished his directive by saying, "I as a symbol of the Holy Roman Catholic Church, after the manner of St. Peter, relay the message from Christ, that upon this rock I build my church for all to worship Him that is called the Christ." The Pope then wiped his face with his stole and kissed it, as if he were in great fear, and said, "We will see the fury of the Heavens within the hour."

The Pope signaled to the cameras to be turned off and reached for the device. On the ground, the media were all searching for answers that something was about to happen. People in their houses went outside to look at the sky. All over the world, there was a rush to look at the sky, day or night. Leaders of other religions expressed outrage, blasting what the Pope had said about what was happening. The nerve of this man to force his faith on the world, the religious world complained. And then there was about ten minutes of nothing in the sky and people began to believe as they always had. It was a hoax that the Catholics had perpetuated for some strange reason, people thought. The most common assumption in people's minds was that it was for money; everyone knew that the Catholics were trying to rule the world. Then it happened, as they stood in their shoes or sandals or boots, or even just barefoot. The airwaves fell silent, with all broadcast and radio transmissions suddenly going off the air. It was a full streak of a neutrino burst that smashed into the Earth. It lit the shadows, indoors and out, with a light that blinded the eye. It lasted about ten seconds and then it was over—the first phase of the Dark Star's arrival. The transmissions were still out and even the phones went dead from the burst. These particles went straight through the ground and everything in its way. Shock was everywhere, because in front of those who were standing outside, even in the daytime, there it was! Over the pole to the north, a huge object, like an eye spinning around. The Dark Star had appeared like Albert said it would. From the southern parts of the earth, where the North Star was not visible, the Dark Star's outer edges could be seen. It was spinning and taking in planets or stars, but it was so far away that you could not tell. With small tiny objects in the circle, it appeared to be headed this way, yet it was so deep and far out in space, and its size was so big, that it frightened the onlooker. Whoever looked at it was bewildered that it was part of the sky above them, larger-around than the sun and the moon. People stared as though they were in a hypnotic state, even while driving. Communication was interrupted for some time. All telephones and electronic communications were still off-line. Everyone was afraid.

Albert was at the farm outside taking a look at the sky around him. He figured that the neutrino blast was very strong for something so far away and he had not planned on it being that powerful. He could not call anybody for awhile so he began his plans for the projects he wanted to do with the farm. About an hour later, he could hear the phone ringing. It was Jan, and she was excited about what just happened. Albert had turned the television off because of the blank screen, but he turned it back on. "Albert, did you see me?" "What!" Jan explain, "I announced the discovery of the Black Hole neutrino burst. Did you see the broadcast?" "The transmissions from here were out for a long time." "Yes, I know. Still, they went back on and I was on the air about twenty minutes ago. We got a full computation status of the energy and distance of the Dark Star. It is at a distance of about twelve million light years away and traveling at double the speed of light." "Jan! Jan, don't get too technical with the distance and speed of travel. Stay with the energy." "Well this was the data from the science feed. Besides, I got the credit for the discovery and I thank you, my husband." "I told you it is your baby. By the way, have you talked to the kids lately?" "Yes, all of them called after they saw me on television." "I'm the only one that missed it. Guess I'll see you on some news reports anyway. Did you experience any blank vision?" "Sure did; it was the wave of a particle stream that passes through the matter of everything. It affects the optical nerves in the eyes. So the feeling of blindness is the result." Albert replied, "Must be the neutrinos carried with a deuteron shift or something. That would explain the positron effects of the transmissions." "Could be that. You know, all of it is completely harmless from that distance. Well I mean, it is not that strange; we have this stream every day. In a blast or eruption of these particles, it would only have an effect that is not lasting, if any." "Well, let's see if I can get the Pope home; his job is done." "That was a wonderful thing you did. I watched every bit of the Pope's sermon. I'll be here, if there's anything, I mean anything you want, call me." "I know you are busy now. Love you, honey." Jan replied, "Love you more," and hung up the phone.

CHAPTER ELEVEN
The Sky

The land of the Middle East, the genesis of the ancient religion, would never be the same. They all looked at the sky and wondered what could this possibly mean. Taking the Pope's word with a grain of salt, as they always did, only because they were Jews. They don't have trouble with becoming anything else but more Jews. Now they all wonder what was in this sign from the sky that made them all think about their faith. Was it the way the Pope said what was going to happen? Or is this the man sent from God to guide them to the promised land? They wondered about his message of being baptized and changing faith with great concern. Most of the Jews did believe the Pope and were prepared to do be baptized at some point in the future—a future that was going to deliver another heavenly sign for the Jewish people to believe. They were slow to take the facts of this sight in the sky as a warning to them to change and believe in Christ and baptism. Besides, there is no reassurance to most of them that this thing out in space would last any more than a week or two. Their leaders called it a fraud of false religion and not a work of God, and most of the Middle East with their other religions followed that thought also. They felt it was a devious plan to abolish their old religion by the powerful United States as a trick. The astronomical warning was in the minds of most of people in China, where there had been no belief in the pontiff's speech as it was heard loud and clear, until the sky uncovered itself. It even showed through the clouds, which were pretty thick there in China, where minds began to change about this object. Most people watched it like a light show that had to do with the shuttle. The only good thing that happened with that country was that it was around morning and most of the people were already tending to their everyday business. It was about as bright as twice the magnitude of the moon in the day-lit sky. Through fear alone, they would learn to believe in the expanding matter in the coming weeks. With the view becoming a wonder to behold, it was something the Pope said that translated to many scholars would make enough meditation to their religious values. The same would be done with the belief of this sign in the sky as being a hoax. Albert knew the views would be all over the place, with doubt and speculation of a staged act that the Vatican did with the help of the United States, a plan to dupe the world with science tricks.

It was at night that the reflection of what most thought to be a black hole in space, based on the shape made it the look of fear alone. It spun in slow motion, the center being the brightest area. The color what most scientists were particularly confused by. A deep blue, green, and yellow lined the outer edge of the huge object. Closer to the center, the colors changed from a light red, like a Christmas tree bulb, to a bright bluish white with streaks of dark green in a pattern that changed in a moment's glance, almost like a mirage that skipped through the space around it. That caused the measurements that scientists used a false reading of the center of Dark Star because it was light not seen in history books of this formation. It would be Jan's discovery, and Albert had given her the key to unlock the mystery of this object. The star was being interpreted as being exhausted, fatigued, haggard, drained, wearied, just plain old tired light. She had the answers and she was the only scientist on this planet that had advanced the measurements to come up with some accurate readings.

Soon, the science community started putting together a pack of the world's top scientists. Far-Seeing was on the list of the group of scientists to study the long-term effects of what they called the Ursa Star. For now it was just a light in the sky, as strange as it was, because the effects of it did not change the weather or change the heat from the sun or even the moon's golden glow. To the public, the panicking crowds never existed; they were more concerned with the Pope going into space and his landing. After only two days in space for the Pope, NASA decided to cut the mission short because it was twenty hours after the concerning appearances of Ursa Star.

"This is Tom Bevel of the network and we have experienced a blackout of our transmission and broadcast. Well, we are now contacting Houston for word about the Pope's mission. Let's wrap up the events that have happened. The Pontiff had finished his message to the world and then the lights went out here at the station. Just a minute!" Tom Bevel listened to his ear piece and wrote down something while on the air. "Yes!" he exclaimed. "Ah, ladies and gentlemen, we are going to a live feed in New York." There, people were looking up at the sky at the Ursa Star. "Hello, this is Charles Headly of Station WGNN. Yes! I am here in Times Square with a crowd of people. The people are seeing what they call a supernatural occurrence of some sort. A miracle in the sky, they're calling it. The traffic is stopped and throngs of people are looking from their windows, from their roof tops; everyone is looking at what is in the sky." "Charles, this is Tom. Did this happen after the Pope's sermon?" "Yes! Yes! This happened about a couple of minutes after the Pope's speech. There was some kind of wave of blindness that everyone experienced; I know I felt it!" "Charles, Charles, Yes! Here at the station, we felt the same." "Well, looks like everyone is all right now. There is a light in the sky that has remained; I don't know what it will do." The city is on alert because of the huge crowd here. I am sure most of the cities in the country have some type of gathering." "Charles, this is Tom. Can you get a shot of the sky there in New York?" "Yes, let's turn from the crowd, give us a moment." The camera turns from the large crowd, almost like a New Year's gathering, but much bigger. "Yes! There it is!" The camera zooms in on the Ursa Star. "Yes, we see it!"

Now that it was on television, the people that had not seen the Ursa Star could now see it and hurried to gaze up at the sky from their location. Even Tom Bevel, after looking at the monitor, left his desk to go outside and look at the object. Still holding a microphone, he walked down the halls of the studio as the picture of the Ursa Star filled the television screen. With a camera man accompanying him, he broadcast from Los Angeles and brought the object into view from that location. The sun was just going down and the sky had a small amount of stars with some clouds dotting the horizon. And there it was. Tom Bevel, being handed a handheld microphone, unlike his neckpiece microphone, said, "My God! It is a big object out there. Excuse me, ladies and gentlemen. I just had to see this object that has people running to the streets to see. Yes! It is certainly in deep space and of a large nature. To you the viewers, I would like to ask you to be calm and remember that this is being seen by, in fact, the whole world, so we are all together here. This is indeed amazing; it is out there just as the Pope said it would be."

It went on and on with most of the news stations, along with scientists from universities and organizations, trying to explain the object. The same thing happened to the President at night when he was watching the

Pope's newscast. Sitting in the Oval Office with the First Lady, they were surprised by the message the Pope was giving out. It sounded impossible to convert the members of the religions in the countries that had been of different faiths, the President thought. He knew that it would take some act of God to have them believe the Pope. But then, both the First Lady and the President experienced the neutrino blast of protons that took them by surprise. With the loss of vision for awhile, the President sprang to his feet and said, "What is this? Did somebody nuke something? What in the hell is going on?" His wife, looking at him, said, "The TV is dead! Try the phones!" The President went to the phones and they were also dead. At that time, an aide named Bill came in the room and said, "Mr. President and First Lady, we have lost transmissions from the rest of the world." "What did you say?" "We are experiencing some strange outage of all electrical transmissions." The President: "What! Transmissions are electrical; I don't want to hear that! Get me the Pentagon, even if you've got to hook a string to two cans! Get them now! There must be some explanation of this!" The aide quickly ran out the room to tell some staff members to get to the Pentagon.

After about thirty minutes Bill came into the room, where the President and the First Lady were talking about what the Pontiff had said and how he planned the trip to space. "Mr. President, it is there;" with the look of fear in his eyes like he had seen a ghost. "What is there?" "The...The sky thing; I don't know what it is!" The President, looking at the First Lady and then at Bill, who was pointing at the ceiling, asked, "Is it outside?" Bending down to look out the glass doors very slowly, the President told his wife to stay right there. Trying to see the sky from a low position, while he walked closer and closer to the doors, "I don't see anything!" Just then, a Secret Service agent came to the glass door and said, "Mr. President, look at this!" It was about eleven o'clock on the East coast, with the sky clear and stars shining, and there the Dark Star stood. The President went outside and looked to the north and said, "Holy Moses, what is that?" He looked at it for about ten seconds and called for the First Lady to take a look. She looked at it. "Is that an explosion out there? It looks like a star." They both looked at it for a while and the crowd of staff members and even the Pentagon officers had arrived, all looking out of the Oval Office at the sky. The last thing the President said before he went indoors was, "How did that man know that?!" referring to the Pope.

Inside the Oval Office, the President sat at his desk in that big leather stuffed chair and wanted answers and wanted them now. There were about twenty people in the office: staff members, Pentagon officers, and others. The Pentagon member General Casey Thorn said, "Mr. President this is a natural occurrence. It is deep in space, in fact, it is light years away." "You tell me this when I just went blind today? Is my mind light years away too?! Tell me I'm losing my mind!" "No, Mr. President. That was some form of wave of atoms in space reaching us and then passing through the planet." "Tell me, does anything work as far as communications?" "Well, this happens from time to time, like sun flares we have. I assure you that everything will be online shortly. There is no damage to our satellites and our computers. Don't forget that if we get the disturbance, everybody gets the same effect." "What kind of scientists do we have? Looks to me like the Pope is the only one who knew about this event. Now I call that crazy! I sent that man into space and he is up there now! Do you know what the people will think of this?" One of the staff members answered, as the crowd looked around, as they heard this for the first time. "Mr. President," Casey said, "The Vatican has been studying space for a long, long time. They have all the earlier astronomers, Tycho, Kepler, Galileo. Why, they even go back to Aristotle's writings in their vaults. There is no shame there about tracking and observing astronomical objects. If anything would happen like this, it is good that it is in their hands. You do know they are looking after people too." The President answered, "So this is not a strange event? Why am I the last to know about it? My God, man, we've got NASA!"

As the discussion went on, including nothing new about who to point the finger at, the television came back on after being blank. "This is Tom Bevel of the network and we have experienced a blackout of our transmission and broadcast. Well, we are now contacting Houston for word about the Pope's mission. In wrapping up before these strange events just happened, the Pontiff had finished his message to the world and then the lights went out here at the station. Just a minute," Tom Bevel went to listen to his ear piece and wrote down something while on the air. "Yes!" he explained. "Ah, ladies and gentleman, we are going live to New York."

The President, after looking at the television, said, "All right, someone turn that off and you people get out of my office. Go to national alert, now that we have some phones working! I can't believe that this is happening. We are going to have every nut case in the country trying to explain this thing in space to support some cause or another. All right! Move! And put the National Guard on call for the major cities that have the public in the streets looking at this thing." Casey came forward to the President and said in a soft voice, "We got this covered. In my opinion, rely on the Pope. He has the clean deck of cards when stirring the masses about whom to believe. The world will look at the peace to bestow. We've got the protection from the world and from both sides of the coin this looks to be a natural act of God." Relax; he is on our shuttle." The President looked at Casey. "You think you can deal me a good hand and get the Pope home safe and sound?" Casey looked at the ceiling and said, "You are holding all the aces

They were up there for a long time without communication from Houston or the launch base at Cape Kennedy. The Pope and the crew members were in a daze over what they were seeing out the window of the shuttle. It was the Dark Star, without the atmosphere interruption to change the view. They didn't even have the horizon to get a fix on the dramatic picture of this star. It sat out there like a large eye, with no face for a context on which to focus. It was just hanging in space over the distant stars. It looked to be no match for the helpless planet Earth in its path. Even the sun looked powerless to match the size of the Dark Star. With various colors of blue, it clearly looked like the most powerful thing in space. Engulfing space and chewing up the matter of the universe at will, to make it into who knows what. It was big, and getting bigger, with a slow spin of a drain in the ocean of the cosmos. They gazed at it for some time until they were so concerned about the sight that their communications became second priority to their minds. A few comments were heard around the cabin, like "We are going to die!" The technical officer was the one with the most fear, because the neutrino blast had made everyone blind for a short time. To her, this was a big thing to fear, until her vision was restored and she could see the Dark Star out the shuttle window. In fact, she had been the first one to see it, while everyone else was focusing on their position in the shuttle's cabin. The Pope was at the time going over his presentation to the people, in anticipation of the debate he would have when he arrived back at the Vatican after they landed. This would be a private meeting with the College of Cardinals for the sake of instructing them. It would contextualize the aim of their mission to the church. A little less than an hour had passed when the sound came over the cabin's speakers and into the ear plugs in the crew's headsets.

"This is mission control. Over! Mission control! Contact mission control. Over!" "This is Houston. Over! Respond shuttle crew, this is Houston. Over! Acknowledge!" After the sound coming from almost all the communication channels to contact the shuttle had been cleared, the commander answered. "Houston, we are here!" Finding that Houston had contacted the shuttle, mission control responded, "Glad to see you're still up there, transferring to Houston." "Thanks, Tittle." Houston responded. "This is Houston and our monitors are online. We have readings and are now rebooting some of our computers. Vitals are good, with cabin pressure and technical setting in the stable range. We have you at an altitude of one hundred and twenty-two miles on the apogee side. Elliptical slide to the perigee of one hundred and three miles. Do you confirm, commander?." The commander looked at the lowest computer monitor and said, "That's affirmative!" Houston continued, "We have you at a speed of sixteen hundred and eighty-seven nautical miles an hour at a latitude of minus thirty degrees and forty five seconds past the equator. At an longitude of eighty-one degrees and twenty-two seconds west. Do you confirm, commander?" "That's a roger! Looks to be a confirmed reading."

"OK," Jason Pert of the Houston control center said, "We have had a bunch of problems down here. With the vital data here, we see you all are fit and in good shape. How is the Pope's attitude and visual condition? Are cameras still down because of the interference from the burst of energy in space?" The commander replied, "Looks good. Say a word, Your Excellency?" "I am feeling well. Looks like we are in the hands of God up here." "All right, commander, go to channel three seven; we are going to have to cut this mission short at the request of the President." Everyone in the shuttle looked around like it was the right thing to do, considering the big thing out in space giving out strange readings of energy. The commander replied; "One question on this star we see out there. Any word of what it is?" "Well, we've got a pretty good station up there and the Hubble telescope working on it for data. Your mission is complete with the deployment of the satellite and it's good news there, with an orbit right on the money. Now we feel that this mission has been a success with the Pontiff and the deployment. We just don't have the devices on board to measure any of the strange star burst. Standby." The commander then went to the channel that Houston requested. The rest of the crew started preparing to put their space suits on. "Commander? This is Houston." He replied, "Yes, Houston." "OK," Jason replied, "We are downloading a program for re-entry in one hour. We have clear weather at Kennedy, so we have a go for landing at zero two hundred hours. It will be a night landing, so we will want you to stay online with the computer plot and no-go manual, confirmed." "Roger." "Confirmation of data on main computer." The commander answered, "Confirmed data locked and loaded." The second commander on the shuttle flipped two switches and looked at the first commander and said, "Suit up. I've got it from here." The Pope, in his suit and strapped in his seat, was ready to go home, a trip that he would never forget. Now when he looked at the sky, his view would be much longer and deeper in space, because he had been to the mountain.

After being in space almost three days, the shuttle was ready to come home to the planet. News had been travelling fast with this mission, so the media was there at the base, ready and looking at two strange things for the public to see: the Dark Star spinning out and heading this way, and the Pope on the shuttle coming from the opposite direction to land. Anyway, the whole world heard the message, being played over and over again in most countries, so that the word would get out. Cardinal Manlin saw to that with Sister David, and the power of the Vatican. Fr. Anthony was in circulation, too, making sure that Albert's orders were fulfilled with Sister Irish. Yes, the Holy Father was on his way home after a long journey, the longest in history for the Vatican and for any man of the cloth.

CHAPTER TWELVE
To Analyze

In anticipation of the Pope coming back to earth and landing at Cape Kennedy, the President had a lot on his mind. The late hour at the White House did not stop calls from all over the world from coming in. Most were to the sighting of the Dark Star but others were from leaders of major countries wanting to talk to the President. He mentioned to his staff that he would not take any calls on any matters at hand and would be in contact later. He and his chief advisors were in the Oval Office, holding a conference to impose civil order on the country; the surprise of this new star in the sky had made things troublesome. They thought that most of the people would look at the Pope as a threat to national security, with his being in the country. The President did not feel it was an intimidation to the people and country any further, after debating the Pope's presence. The President wanted to meet the Pope when he returned from space, yet there was not enough time to get there from the Capitol. So he personally sent some of his top advisors and governmental leaders to take his place, under the authority of the full Presidential seal. The Pope would stop by the Capitol on his way home to the Vatican, so the President would see him there.

In the night sky in some parts of the country, a streak of light split the darkness like a shooting star. It was the shuttle coming home with its heat tiles being polished by the elements in the atmosphere. A booming sound hit the sky like a drum or like the falling of a gavel on the top of the famous St. Peter's Basilica's dome itself. An ending to the mission was at hand, with a crew of astronauts the world had never seen. At fifty nautical miles to the base, with an altitude of forty thousand feet, the crew, still dazed from having been unconscious, was awake and ready for the touchdown. The shuttle, completely on computer control, was doing well managing the cross-turbulence over the base. On line after a correctional turn that took place in the plunge to Earth, the shuttle began to become visible to the people on the ground. Lights flashing on each wing and one on the top of its tail, it looked like a bird as gas fell from the tips of the large engines in the rear. With the condensation of air along the bottom of the orbiter, a long stream of vapor was being left behind the path of the craft.

"Attention, this is John Tittle of mission control. The shuttle is online and will be landing in two minutes. Look to the southern sky at twenty degrees and you can find a visual. I would like to thank all of you for your support of NASA'S Copernicus-Emissary mission." This was heard over the loud-speaker at the base, where the crowd was only half as big because of the time of night. But still it was packed with people, because thousands of flash bulbs went off as soon as the shuttle was within range. In the cabin of the shuttle, a few commands to the commander about the readings on the computers could be heard, to which he replied, "Roger."

Looking at the shuttle landing, it was kind of a strange picture with the sky lit up like a second moon. The Ursa element was in the sky and here is the man that put it there, most people thought, but then, some did not. The Pope had talked to God and we are all going to die! Why was this done? The small sleepy children in the crowd asked. Why? Did he make us sin? Why? Do we have to be baptized! Why? Why? Why? Now? The questions would never stop and the Pope knew it. So, when the shuttle landed, the presidential helicopter was waiting for the Pope, who still had his space suit still on, to take him to the Capitol, as you might guess, with Fr. Anthony and Cardinal Manlin and, yes, the keepers were on board the flight. As the Pope got off the shuttle, he reached his hand toward the sky in sight of the people. The cheers from the large crowd rumbled through the darkness. It was like the final winning score in a ballgame. The noise was loud and got louder once he had left the stairs and kissed the ground. The Pope kissed the earth not only out of tradition, but also because he was a little frightened about the new light in the sky that had so puzzled everyone. As quick as could be, the Pope was airborne again in a presidential helicopter to the White House.

Actually, on the way to the White House, he was examined by a member of NASA medical staff. The quarantine for the Pope had been lifted because of his age and his position. It was clear that it was a chancey mission, and that goes for the effects of space as well. The Pope was experiencing some effects due to the gravity, but he was getting better with each second because of the short time he was in space. As a special flight, the presidential helicopters would fly all the way to the White House because of the timing. The long-range helicopter would be in Washington DC in about two hours, enough time for the President to get a handle on things with the Pentagon, and with the nation now on alert. It was a wise choice to leave the Vatican's leased jet at the base and fly it in route later to the White House, because there was a problem with reporters and crowds flocking the plane at the airport in Florida. On board, the staff and clergy were watching the news on the monitors, and all communications from the nation about the Pope. It would be early morning when they would arrive to see the President. The four astronauts that went into space with the Holy Father were already on the television. They were commenting about what he did and how they reacted to the presence of the Pontiff.

In California, Albert contacted Jan with some measurements on the Dark Star, or what the science groups were calling Ursa. It looked like that would be the name of the star, considering that they never knew that Albert was really the one who found the star. He did call Jan to tell her that another burst of neutrinos would come in about four days or less because of the way the light was forming. Jan had reached an understanding with that concept of the Ursa Star because she had looked at pulsation of the star's center. It was back to work for Albert, starting his building spree, because now he had the money and that made the difference when you are now the wealthiest man in the country. And now the main concern of the President was the Pope, after tracking the money flow from the Vatican. He would have some really interesting questions for the Pope once the President got the Pontiff in his office. He was going to demand answers to some of the questions because it was just not the leaders of other countries that wanted them, but the American people wanted them too! Even with the Dark Star coming to Earth, business is business in the running of the most powerful country on this rock. It was the pace and quantity of support for the Vatican that made everyone in the Capitol look firmly at what the scheme meant, with this solicitation of baptism to all the people of the world. It could be seen as an insurrection against the country's values, being that the United States is a free country. In one way, it could be interpreted as a form of trying to take over the country, with the masses of people in support of the Catholic church. Yes, the President flew the Pope directly to the White House with his keepers and staff. As head of the church, the Pope was now really on the hot seat. Sometimes you may wonder if the repetitions in history are in fact really true when it comes to religion.

The media was in force around the White House with crews of personnel around the grounds where the helicopters were about to land. "This is Tom Bevel of the network and we have word that the helicopter containing the Pope is due in minutes. After a very successful trip into outer space, the Pontiff will be transferred here to the White House after a shortened mission. It was a night landing flanked by two military fighter jets and then the Pope was quickly whisked away to the waiting helicopter sent by the President. There, there along the horizon we can see the two helicopters coming in," Tom Bevel continued. The cameras viewed the helicopters flying in, with the morning sky in the background, in level formation and then descending towards the White House. They landed and immediately out came the staff and some of the clergy.

The first helicopter just sat on the landing area and no one came out of it. The small crowd of people that came out of the second helicopter stood at the door, as if waiting for the Pontiff. And then the Pope came out, dressed in a vestment of holy attire and his small skullcap, He walked toward the entry to the White House. He seemed not to notice the hungry crowds of reporters looking for a glimpse of the Pope. "Tom Bevel here. And we have just seen the arrival of the Holy Father at the White House. We have been informed that a press conference will be held sometime shortly about the events surrounding the Pontiff's visit to space and information about the Ursa event in space. This is Tom Bevel at the network, now back to your local station and the regular broadcast in your area. Thank you."

The clergy and staff members walked into the Oval Office, with the pontiff behind them. Talking with the Pope were Fr. Anthony and Cardinal Manlin, in a discussion about the next plan for the Vatican. It included making it possible for people to have easy access to the rite of baptism. They walked into the Oval Office where the President was on the phone, looking tired from a lack of sleep. Everyone was seated and chairs were set up so that the Pope would be in the best position to talk to the President. The President hung up the phone and began to thumb through the papers that were on his desk. He looked at the Pope and said, "Glad to see you made a safe trip into space, Your Excellency." The Pope replied, "Yes, it was a wonderful experience." "I am sitting here wondering about a couple of things in the presentation you gave while on this country's spacecraft." The staff looked at the Pontiff with concern and the clergy looked at the staff with the same idea. "It is the position of this country to have freedom of religion in all ways. We do not make issues of church and state a commonplace, and we do not support the rights of one religion is greater than the other. It is the right of the people of the United States to have this choice for the good of the country. Furthermore, it is the position of this office that we find that this undertaking of religion in the situation of presenting a strange or a abnormal event is like using the barter system to approve of one certain type of worship. I am not saying that the Catholic Church is behind the appearance of this Ursa Star, but your promotion and salesmanship is a matter that must have had some other intent besides the idea of warning the world of this event ahead of time." The Pope looked at Cardinal Manlin, leaned over and whispered into his ear, and then motioned to the Cardinal to speak for him. The Pope was tired and he did not want any mistakes in clearing up the subject matter that the President had presented him with. Cardinal Manlin knew what the Pope wanted to say because he had helped the Pope out previously when he was having trouble with his voice. Cardinal Manlin said, "Mister President, the Vatican does promote the bringing of new and unknown human beings into the Catholic church. The church's position on the sale of its religion to the world is a twenty-four-hour campaign. We have done nothing wrong from the point of view of the laws of the church or of your country. The Pope is a known figure; by basic fact that his position is stated to be of one faith and religion, in which he carries both the power and the obligation to relay the message of Catholicism. The division of church and state does not apply to this subject because of the large Catholic population in your country."

The President looked at his staff members and asked one of them to bring him a folder. The President set the folder on the desk and opened it. "In this folder, prepared by the CIA and FBI, is a joint file about national security and the whereabouts of certain individuals that have interest in the Vatican's affairs." The Pope looked at Cardinal Manlin and Fr. Anthony. "Your Excellency, we have information that a Mr. and Mrs. Lanker have been in the area of the Vatican in the past weeks. I ask, you do you know these people who, I might add, are United States citizens?" The Pope began to speak and then whispered to Cardinal Manlin again. Cardinal Manlin said, "Yes, we know those people; they are devout Catholics. Yes, we do have the respect to keep the dealings and arrangements, if any, with the two a private matter with the church. Any questions about them should be asked of them. We do understand that they have not broken any laws, so I really feel the matter should be taken up with them. Also, they are dear friends of Fr. Anthony and the members of the clergy, not to mention the Holy Father." The President, immediately aware that this conversation was not what he wanted, realized that he was getting into the affairs of the church that would put him in a position of suspicion in international affairs. That would make him look like he was against the church's affairs when he was the one that had approved the Pope's journey into space using the space shuttle. His position was to uncover any covert action that the Vatican might have with the Ursa Star out there to take over the United States. The President was sure that the views of the Catholic Church were in line with the belief in the United States' Constitution and for world peace.

The President stood up from behind his desk and went to the Pope and said, "I am glad you are safe and so I won't trouble you any longer." He then kissed the ring of the Pope and signaled to his staff members to help the Pope get to the Vatican safely. The President offered to have the military fly all the way to Italy to escort the Pope's jet home. But before leaving, the Pope did finally speak to the President. "I will pray for you, Mr. President, and let the strength and peace continue with the gift of two wonderful people that this country has produced to see that the faith of God is alive and always present in the world. They are good people and private people. Don't ever forget that the Vatican is not without examination in dealings that concern the Roman Catholic Church. Our files are more than twice the size of these people, Mr. President." The Pope looked at the ceiling in puzzlement and said, "I thank you and God bless you; these are indeed trying times." The Pope left as the President, with a smile on his face, looked out the window of the oval office and said when everyone had left his office, "God speed, Your Excellency."

Well, as it happened, the country was in good hands with the sitting President, because on the following day at the press conference with the President, the Lankers were not mentioned. He had instructed the governmental offices all the way to the Pentagon to protect the security of the Lankers, without them even knowing it. There was one thing that could not be kept secret and that was that Jan was the main scientist for the YDS channel. It had worked its way into daily reports on the Ursa Star. And, yes! The Pope was met by throngs of people at the Vatican after his return. He continued to hold strong ideas about his message and he instructed the clergy to welcome people of all other religions to the sacrament of baptism.

CHAPTER THIRTEEN
Farmland

The beginning of the day was like the soft wind of summer, a cold chill to the finished creep of stagnation which had made the feel of winter in the air. It was not cold, yet it was not warm either, and the sky made a statement about that. Low clouds draped themselves over the mountains like a mist of smoke from a huge fire. The sun was coming up early and it began to brighten the sky. Still, it was not enough to hide the stars, and the moon was not there at all, not in the sky of darkened blue and black water.

Albert said silently to himself, "I've wondered now and then about UFOs but I never believed in them. That's just too far for my mind to grasp onto. I thought if there was going to be a UFO sighting, it would be on this morning, because it was now the time of winter. The storm that left the small amount of clouds in the sky was just about right for anyone to catch a glimpse of a strange light. Anyway, I did not sleep well last night and thought I would get up and watch this strange universal happening while I can. Well, you know it could have been any morning, any morning for the past year, because there are only nine more years to go."

"I looked east toward the sky and the sun was rising, as it has always done for year after year, day after day. It was not new to the sky and surely not new to me, that ball of fire and its golden glow, heating up the climate to bring in a new day. The night was rough and not only for me but for everyone on the planet. Rough enough to break your sleep, to give you a cold sweat, to forget about how much rest you can get. Still, it was not enough to let your mind over-think itself, night after night."

"Sometimes the rain is good for sleeping. It gives you time to think about the things that need to grow, to spread their roots into and over the ground. Yes, the rain eases the mind somewhat; it takes you away from things, far away at times into a different time, when the nerves were not so tight or we humans were not so worried about the unknown. Yep! Looks like a UFO to me that changes every night, or should I say, every morning. Well, every early morning when one is chilled to the bone and no matter what you do to get warm, it still does not cure that harrowing feeling."

"In the distance, you can hear the rumble, the sounds of air pushing and pulling the darkness apart. It sounds like sandy rocks falling down a mountain and becoming a river of dust. The sound of silence has been gone for decades, with the traffic, the planes, and everything else that man has made that speaks. Still, the Dark Star dominates the morning with a sound of perturbation. It is the morning and the day is yet ahead."Albert!" Jan called, "You out there? Put the coffee on and get ready for work! It's five-thirty in the morning!" Albert replied, "I know that. I was just checking. It has rained all this week!" "You should know that you can catch a cold outside, with the dampness still on the ground. Make some coffee. I don't want to be late this morning."

It was a big place, a flat and dry stretch of land with the fields ready to be planted. Lines of grooves followed the curves of the earth, as if they went on forever. The fields were clean of the latest crop of wheat. The ground should give up good crop this year and be full of healthy plants for a good harvest. It was good farm, well-maintained everyday by the crew that Albert has had for years. It was a well-paid crew of true farmers and that's what good pay does, a group of people who take pride in their work and are not afraid to get really cold to the bone. Still, there is a row of trees, large trees, in the north field. Alpine trees sit out there like a forest and this forest of trees somehow humanizes the land. They give the sense of place, creating a sense of presence to what is left of what has been built on this land. If you look long and straight to the northeast, you can see the hills, so far away that only at sunrise or sunset do you notice them. They look huge up close, but at this distance they look like small hills that would be easy to climb. As you can see, it is a distant farm away from everything that exists in the modern world, but not away from the road or the sky, for jets fly and cars pass by at a distance sometimes, and you can hear them clearly. Forty miles to the closest city where the lights dance in the night sky, like a party, like a show, like the stadium lights that break away into the night sky and glow a football game. Out in the flatlands is where the action is gone, no traffic, no blaring horns that draw your mind to look at the neon signs. Not at this place; at this farm, the feeling of nature the sense of mankind is present.

Near the house and barn and the silos is the dish, the communication disk with all the technology beamed down from space. A full range of everything that is in the news and will be in the news from any city asks for with the right channel code. Being abandoned is not a possibility for this farm. That's because the bigger cities buy natural foods and why there is so much land, yes, flat land to feed the city.

At first, the sound of the silence seemed to be broken by what is going on with the creation of those dishes. That is the sound of the sky, the population thought, and some big satellite is doing that as part of beaming its signals to the planet. It was analyzed and calculated, oh so carefully, on the basis of what scientists believe brings atoms together, until it appeared and it was no longer a puzzle to figure out. It revealed its existence and the race was on, like a rush of mystery. One felt that this planet was not alone in the dark sky and not a piece of what has always been. It was this planet's turn to be a part of something special, as has always been planned.

As Albert walked, he noticed that the workers were heading to the barn. Today was a work day and the fields needed to be maintained. The south field was ready to be looked after, as part of the rotation schedule that has made this farm such a productive one."Here comes the crew!" Albert called out, as he climbed four stairs to the back porch and then opened the door of the house and went in. Jan, the coffee is ready." She had been upstairs, still in her nightgown and robe, as she walked down the stairs and entered the kitchen. The kitchen was a huge one, with a center range and large table connected to it. The cabinets of oak, stained in a light maple, were absolutely breathtaking with the halogen lights highlighting each positive point. The appliances were all a matching set of the latest built-in models. The floor, a specially designed light color with mixed squares, blended into the bare walls, some bare, some wallpapered. It brought out the rare paintings and the metal sculptures that were conversation pieces. The window drapes were fine, giving the view of being see-through, admitting light to the few small plants that were sitting on the sill. Outside of the interior curtains, heavier drapes fell for shutting off the view, as if no window was even there. When the drapes were shut, this simple design gave a completely closed-in effect, almost like blinds or shutters. Next to the coffee machine on the counter that ran around the whole kitchen, Albert poured two cups of coffee .Jan, sitting at the counter which is connected to the range and is used as a breakfast table, looked at Albert. "A little cream and sugar like yours will be fine." Albert looked out the window and then proceeded to bring the two cups on saucers to the table. "Do you remember your first couple of broadcasts at YDS?" Jan replied, "Yes, that seems like decades ago." "Well," Albert responded, "it seems like the science was wrong on the estimates." Jan replied, "The estimates were such a rough guess then that it was just as good as an educated guess." Albert looked at Jan, "Yea, I know that, but it did solve the problems and did warn the people. Even now I think about that broadcast. It was good, because it showed that you, Jan, could do the job, even after all I'd put you and your family through, not to mention us and the children." "You know, they are not children anymore. Besides, Albert, you were the one that captured my heart. I never would have believed that you knew so much about people. The way you handle yourself with all those big and powerful people is something I'm am really proud of. You really deserve everything you got because you just are so kind." Albert took another drink of coffee. "No, not me. You are the one I'm really proud of, sticking with me through thick and thin." "You have everything and much more. I'm the lucky one. Yeah, I am really lucky that I don't have a doctor or lawyer or some factory worker for a husband." Albert looked at Jan as he took the last big swig of coffee from his cup with a smile on his face, trying to hide it in the cup. It is because he saw what was coming and without breaking into a laugh, he just held the cup up to his face. Jan spoke: "I'm married to the richest man in the world," and she laughed and then grabbed Albert by the shoulders and hugged him and kissed him on the head. Albert lowered the cup and just laughed like he couldn't hold it back. Jan kissed him some more."Look at me, am I silly? I got to go to work! See what you made me do." Albert, still full of light laughed." I am a fan of yours, too!" As Jan walked out the kitchen, past the maid's room, and to the large staircase to the upper rooms, she could hear Albert's quiet laughter in the background as she viewed the living room with a smile on her face.

The living room a large room was with studiously designed woodwork. The furniture consisted of ancient sofas and antique chairs and modern couches in a material of high quality. On the walls were many different paintings; both originals by artists from decades past and new works were hung on the walls. The large picture window which stretched up two stories, with various panels of stained glass in different corners, provided much of the lighting. The view of the farm and some of the barn area could be easily seen out the window. The drapes in a matching fabric complemented the woodwork. There were various statues and metalwork sculptures in corners of the room, not to mention the huge and well-designed table in front of the seating area. The look of the living room was that of a well-furnished and comfortable museum. The soft carpet and mixed wooden areas made the room look so relaxing, even at a glance. There was no distraction, nothing out of place, in any part of the room. Even the well-designed chandelier fit well in the context of the walls and paintings. The collection of beautiful materials was just mind-blowing because of the rarity and quality of each masterpiece.

Given the fabulous living room and kitchen, you can imagine that it was just a tip of the iceberg. The farm was not an ordinary place. It had all the right equipment for farming and for taking care of crops. With the equipment and tractors and silos, the main house was still the centerpiece of the property. The whole property had almost the look of a small college campus, with an observatory, a lab, and a medium-sized gym, complete with swimming pool. Yes, it was well within the plan to have this farm as a safe-zone for the Lankers and their friends. Even an underground wine cellar, with the finest stock of spirits from all over the world, had been added. This was the place to be if you wished to view the Earth's future as shaped by your own decision—from your calculations, from your answers, and if you had the guts to give a helping hand to the world. Sometimes money matters, and sometimes it does not Anyway, it was too late now to really care about how you got to this point or to wonder if you really did the right thing. The plan has made Albert wealthy and very happy to have the chance to save not only himself but also many others. Where did it start, and why? Who knows that the moment is here and that everybody will be affected? It is the destiny of the world; in fact, everyone depends on him and nobody really knows who he is. He's just a farmer in the suburbs on the flat, distant plain where the stars are so bright that loneliness never enters the mind, only fear. The fear of the future, the future that has became something that has come earlier than expected, and faster than what was planned, and quicker than mankind can imagine.

Jan came down from one of the upstairs bedrooms, walked into the kitchen, and said, "You still here? What's on your mind, honey?" Albert replied, "Not much. I think I'll help the guys outside to plow some of the fields today. I'm just waiting for them to set up the tractor and get the fertilizer loaded into the spreaders." Jan grabbed a Danish from the breadbox and poured herself another cup of coffee. "Lizzy is here. You want her to make you some breakfast?" "No, she is sleeping. She did such a good job with the kitchen last night after that dinner party for us. It's all right to let her sleep in. You going to drive today?" "I think so; I'll call Thomas to bring my car around." Thomas is the butler, who lives above the garage to the right rear of the mansion. The garage is filled with a number of cars and limos, clean and polished. Also to the rear of the garage, there is a heliport where Thomas can roll out the helicopter from the garage. "Be sure to get some lunch. I'll tell Lizzy to have that ready for you. I'll be home about two o'clock. That's about all the broadcasting I'll have to do today." Albert replied, "They keep putting on those special guests. Amazing, the theories they come up with, Jan." "Yeah! But it is my selection, so don't get upset. They have some interesting ideas on gravitational shifts." "Really." Jan takes the last bite of her Danish and hears the horn blow from the front of the house, and sees a blue late-model sedan waiting for her. "Yeah, honey, it is general information, so don't worry; it doesn't conflict with your theory." Jan kisses Albert and heads for the front door and out to the circular driveway, where Thomas opens the door for her and gives his smile and a good morning greeting. Albert goes to the maid's room and talks through the door, saying, "Lizzy, make a light lunch. Not too much. I'm in the fields." "Ok, Mr. Lanker, it will be ready about noon." Albert walks out the back door and heads to the barn where the tractors are located. He notices that Jan is driving south down the long road to the main freeway about three miles away. He says hello to the workers and begins to climb in one big green tractor with large tires. Albert looks over the steering wheel and checks the outside with a quick glance and hops into the seat and pulls the key from under the gas pedal.

In the cabin of the large plow tractor, Albert gunned the engine and began to lift the hydraulic booms to drive the tractor down to the south field. The rain had made the ground a little muddy, just enough to be like packed clay. The fields had drained well when they got wet, yet you could see the tracks of the large tires eating up the ground as the machine went by. A number of acres needed to be dug up to turn the soil, a process that would keep this farm healthy. In the fields, Albert could see the main house and the barn, sitting out in the middle of the farm, and he checked his radio in the cabin, which had all the devices like a car. He checked that the light was on so that he could be reached, being so far away from the large complex of barn and house. He intended to drag a fresh row for about a mile, which should take about ten minutes. He planned to he do about mile square of field today. Albert turned and looked farther south, toward the church and monastery, another huge complex in the distance, beyond the large ditch in the fields that was used for drainage. He turned the tractor to the north and plowed another row as he gun the engine. The spreaders, three of them, with a dump truck were heading to the west of the same field he is tilling. While he was running row after row in completely straight lines, he began to feel fatigued. After about an hour and a half of driving, he checked the gas tank and noticed that he had enough gas left, and decided to go in for awhile. Albert looked again at the church off in the south. As he turned the large machine and headed that way, he noticed a sunbeam shining down on the church from the clouds that were clearing the sky. Albert saw this beauty and began to think about how he designed that church and how radiant and heavenly it looked. You did an excellent job, he said to himself. It was a completely picturesque view of the holy structure, barely visible from the top floor of the main house. He was just amazed at the beautiful view, and he pondered.

CHAPTER FOURTEEN
Broadcasting

"From Earth, it is about as big as it is with a circle going around the planet. You see it is about as big as you believed it would be. Any bigger, it would not be what it is now; any smaller, it would not be what it is going to be. If you look at it from that view, then to those who feel that it is too small have just became a small group of a lot of planet to forget about. And that's what it is all about if you can picture the Earth and where we all are," the narrator said.

"This is Channel YDS, a community network and your host tonight is Jan Lanker." With a graphic of the solar system spinning and all the planets going around the sun, the camera zoomed in on the planet Earth, and then standing on the planet was Jan Lanker, looking up and reaching her left hand out and then her right. After that the camera started to zoom back and she put both hands together as if she were pleading in prayer to the heavens. The introduction stopped and a huge screen was draped on stage and out came Jan Lanker, dressed in an office-type women's suit, a fitting look for a female scientist. She walked to the middle of the stage, and as the screen in back of her began to change, she leaned on a small podium in front of her, but then sat in an office-type chair on the stage.

Jan said, "It is about ninety three million miles, somewhere around that. It is our closest sun and it's about four light years from the next closest sun. Not far at all when you think of how big the numbers are compared to the rest of the space out there or anywhere else in the sky. So let's look at this space and how this space we travel in is structured. Light years means the distance that light travels in a whole year, with light moving at about one hundred and eighty six miles per second. If you can picture that, it is fast enough to travel distances in the solar system in very little time, so we are very small compared to this speed. Putting that speed in relationship to this planet, you can imagine the speed I am talking about. Now without looking at the math and the calculations, let's make this a bit simpler and less technical. The farthest, or at least the most distant, object that all science can agree on is about twelve billion light years away. Maybe, or maybe not. Regardless, it is a long way out there. You can figure that if this is the point of distance that is so far away that it is more than three times the existence of this planet, the star or numbers of stars or whatever exists and is transmitting light for that distance must be of a huge magnitude, at billions of light years. Without going into the science of distances, such as parsec or astronomical distance, let's say it is a long way to travel." Jan turned to her right.

The screen behind her changed from a picture of the Earth to a picture of the sun. "This star is a medium star compared to the stars in the space that we see around us here on planet Earth. It is medium-sized ball of fire, or more specifically, hydrogen gas. It is a burning-hot ball of fire, at about five thousand degrees or around that. What I am saying is very simple: compared to the sun, the Earth is about the size of a pea sitting next to a big beach ball. This is what I want you to remember because it is the topic of this show today. Most of the suns or stars we see or have been detected in the vastness of space have this most important aspect. Most stars include two stars together, one small and one bigger or, as we scientists say, a binary system. Two stars in orbit, two stars together, vast distances apart, yet still both of them in or around the same space. Again, without going into the details of drawls or super-giants in star terms, let's say that the orbits of this type of system are the most important thing." The screen changed again to a picture of two suns and an outline of their orbits. Jan explained, with her laser pointed to the screen. "You may not understand this like a scientist, so I'll make it simple. Here is our sun or star and the solar system, and here is what we believe to be a second sun. Whether it has ever been seen by astronomers is insignificant, because it has never been detected in full until now. Oh, but it has been seen and studied as something else, maybe like a galaxy, because of the spiral effect of it. Yet, they all were wrong: no galaxy at all. It was not that long ago that an astronomer discovered this by chance. The reason for this discovery has a lot to do with tired light. Yes, tired light—light that travels so far that it becomes a different type of detectable wave and never makes it into the calculations of any science detection. I guess what you cannot see, you cannot really be sure of, to a point. It is there by means of detecting the stars and points of light in the vastness of space." The screen changed to a new picture of what looked like a spiral galaxy. "Yes, this is it and it is heading right for this planet. It has grown in size and is getting bigger and stronger in its orbit. The last readings of this object have given us a speed that is about a thousand times the speed of light. It is increasing its speed every day. Yet, the only thing we know about this speed is that this object is acting like a black hole, where the gravity is being compressed to point of total weight that is mind-boggling. Now that we know most of the general terms, it is very, very important to state where and why this event is happening. It is the first law of nature to find the point of origin of this event and we have found this point of origin to be our solar system. Not only that: this galaxy, or should I say this vast galaxy, is about seventeen million light years wide, yet this mass is ten times that. It is the biggest size of anything ever detected as moving toward us in the vastness of space that we know about to this date. The science of this subject is very unclear about how one single star can develop into this mass of such a huge existence without collapsing in an early stage of development. It could be like a super nova or a white dwarf in the last stages of a star's development."

The screen changed to two objects, one small and about the size of a golf ball and the other as big as the screen itself, with small lines of white, red, and blue coming from this object. Jan turned to the screen, away from the podium. "This is about the size compared to this galaxy and we know that in this galaxy we have over a billion stars. The size of how many stars have been engulfed by this matter is un-measureable. To this day, it is clearly unfeasible to measure what the size of this object is. Our latest data has come up with a new size, of a thousand times the size of our own galaxy. This detectable source of energy is about seven billion light years away and traveling at a speed we have so far failed to measure. We do know that it is moving faster than what can be measured by light years. The most recent data shows that it has traveled a billion light years in a very short time, and at this speed it will be in contact with this galaxy in about nine to ten years. It will be even more visible in about five years. Also, since this void in space of compressed matter is so large, the effects on this solar system are as yet unknown, with the gravitation pulling and pushing space in its path. Even from this distance, it is still a rough estimate that about seventy years is a good calculation because of its acceleration of speed and size. Without going into theory or the calculations of blue and red shifts of light, it is a fact that the calculations of tired light must be taken into account. We have made this calculation based on twelve billion light years of quasars. We have to do away with the old calculations we used based on the luminosity and relationship period of light, like that in Cepheid variables measurements. We still believe the quasar calculation is the best we can do because this energy form comes from a far greater distance than this measurement. Using light shifts of pulsars is the only detectable manner we have to really calculate the speed of it. As we know, it is changing matter in its path and that this changing matter and its surrounding matter have given the science world a new definition of terms defining light and how matter reacts. This reaction does not exclude sound and radiation and other acts of nature. We will persevere in detecting this material event to the fullest, and we must remember that we are all together here on this planet Earth."

The screen went up and Jan Lanker slowly walked off stage, then she was seen on the top of the planet Earth. One hand up and then the other. The camera slowly rolled back and she brought both hands together over her head in an act of prayer. With both hands together, her head bowed downward and instrumental music began as the scene faded away. "This is the science of the world channel coming to you once every week, Channel YDS, a community network. Now back to your regular network."

CHAPTER FIFTEEN
The Architects

It was just about noon in a long day and the city was in shadow, like a huge cloud of new-found moisture that wrapped around the buildings. The top floor of this brand new building was a good site to see through the haze—the flat land and the mountains, and the small people appeared like ants on the ground looking for food. It was there that the work was to begin on a new building, designed of steel and glass that would shine like water in the sunlight. The combination of straight lines and blue mirrored-glass square windows was a wonderful idea to make this building. A new idea, a totally new way of making buildings called skyscrapers.

Arthur called to the top designer, Andrew in the architectural firm on the top floor of this skyscraper: "Come here and look at

this front entrance to the coffee shop. If we would put in some more doors, the space would be a lot bigger and we could use this empty space under the stairs for seating. I still think the three-floor run of stairs for the lobby should be scrapped because of the elevators on the south side of the building. It has no function here. If this was a state building, it would look nice, but in an office building it takes up too much useable space." Arthur continues, "You know, you are right with that observation. Still, my hands are tied with that design change. The client wants that in and in that exact place, He feels it will be the move of the future for some strange reason. I talk about it all the time to the consultants. The engineers are not happy with it and I really don't blame them. It is wasted space that could be used for something else. It seems useless to have elevators and stairs on the same floor for presentation, where foot traffic will be going floor to floor.

I don't know what to say about it or how to retain this client and his bad idea." "The design is workable from the outside. If this building were not so close to the sidewalk, we could move the whole thing closer to the front doors and take a floor rise out. This would take the gradual rise of stairs to two floors, instead of three. Still, that is not workable because of the space in the front of the building." "Well!" Andrew replied. Arthur explained, "OK,k let's do this, come up with a design with the stairs out of the lobby and give a full range of view of those elevators from the front desk. The manufacture of these new designs is just the wave of the future and I'm sure that elevators will be in the works of all buildings in the future; there's no doubt about that. Look how the concept made this building we are in more useable? Why this client wants to hold on to the grand staircase is beyond me. The space is what sells this building and how easy it is to get to. It is almost like this person wants to hold onto the past designs of older buildings that are not as tall as the ones we have now." "I don't know! I just don't know what this is all about! You know the office needs this contract and it is a hard one to keep. The firm's reputation is at stake here and this building just might make this firm look like a backward design group of gothic architects. Well, I'm going to get a bite Andrew. Work on that new design and let's make a go at doing something to meet this client's taste besides this horrible idea of stairs going up the middle of a lobby that can't be used." Andrew responded, "I will try it. You know it is a design change from the start. I still can't understand why he wants this space. It is such a waste in the lobby where a lot of activities go on. I'm off to lunch too, got my wife waiting at the cafe downstairs. We're going to do a little shopping today. It will be a couple of hours before I get back, Andrew. Once we start looking, it will be some time before we stop or run out of money, whichever comes first." Andrew laughed, "Besides, it will give me time to think of some solution for this building. I might run across some new idea buying dishes or plates. I know I'm not buying these stairs." Arthur laughed, and both of them walked down the hallway and out of the office.

The man stood like a good statue of corporate weight. He was the client and the head of Ultra, a power-house corporation. He was to stop by the office Tuesday but decided to stop by the office today, Monday. It was good news this man was to bring to the architects, really good news, for the project had been giving the architects a bad time. He entered the office's lobby and the receptionist was on the phone talking to the suppliers of various products for steel-fastening devices. Julie, the receptionist, was explaining to them that "the orders of Mr. Peterson were to go with the first designs on sheet one hundred and seventeen of the shop drawings and that would do the job for the first of the fasteners to be mounted in that part of the building." She listened, and then replied, "I'm sure that's all he said to tell you if you called, and it would be all right to go with one hundred and seventeen at this time." She hung up and noticed the tall man standing in front of her desk with the dark blue suit and a green tie, looking around at the walls. The walls were filled with photos of buildings, big and small and short and long, about twenty of them in frames, each lit by a spotlight. He glanced and spun and then he looked at the receptionist and said, "What a collection of buildings. All have the same type of style and quality. Looks like mine will be a break from the norm for these guys." "Pardon me?" Julie said. "Oh, I'm Mr. Lanker, the client for the Star project. Is Andrew around? I have some things to go over with him. I didn't call or make an appointment because I just didn't have time to get to my secretary. I just thought he would be in about this time, working on that project." "Well," Julie explained in a friendly voice, "He is out on a lunch break and is due back any moment. Can I get you a cup of coffee and a Danish? It should not be too long." "Just coffee with a little sugar and cream, thanks. I have a tough day today and have to get this out of the way before I get back to my office." Julie got up and went to the end of the lobby where a small opening was and got the best-looking metal-rimmed cups on the shelf above the coffee maker and poured some coffee into the cup. She asked, "That's with cream and sugar, Mr.Lanker?" "Yes, about two cubes would be all right." As she prepared the coffee, the phone rang. Putting the cup on a saucer, she walked over to Mr. Lanker who had taken a seat next to the far wall of the lobby, where a small table stood next to a number of chairs. Dashing back to her desk where the switchboard was, she sat down and answered the phone. "Andrew Peterson and Associates," she said. "He's not in at the moment. Can I take a message?" She grabbed a pen from the cup of many pens and pencils on her desk and began to write down a few names. Then she explained, "I will see that he gets the message. Thank you." Hanging up the phone, she looked at Mr. Lanker as he searched through a little book he had pulled out of his coat pocket. He was checking for a pen and he looked through his suit pockets again and again. It looked like a common thing to do, with one hand holding the page open and the other on the feel for some writing device to make a note in this little book. He pulled out a gold pen and began to write on a page about in the middle of the book after turning a page or two. Looking at the notation, he placed the pen and book back in his coat's upper pocket and began to drink the coffee.

Noticing the photos of the buildings again, he got up to takes a closer look at one ten-story building of stone and glass, staring in particular at the lower part of the picture. The picture was about eye-height on the wall. He stepped a little closer to the painting. As he pondered the picture, the door opened and in walked Andrew. Mr. Lanker turned in the direction of the door. Andrew, looking the other direction while entering, spoke to Julie, asking, "Any calls?" "Mr. Lanker is here." He replied, "Mr. Lanker? Here in the office?" Andrew did not notice the tall Mr. Lanker because the lobby was made with corners and plants, a well-designed lobby with very interesting things to look at. Mr. Lanker, hearing this, said "Right here, Andrew." Andrew turned in the direction of Mr. Lanker: "Oh my! Mr. Lanker, I didn't know you would be here today. I am so sorry to have made you wait. Let's go to my office." They both shook hands and began to walk out of the lobby down a small hallway that was opposite the front door.

"Have a seat." The office was classy, with leather chairs and old statues in certain places on pedestals like Doric columns in marble. The paintings on the wall were of fine art and framed in classic wood and gold-leaf. There was a relaxed feel to the whole office with a view of the city behind Andrew's desk. It was not the drafting room or the meeting room. This was where the deals were made. To the right of the office, there was a bar, and in front of that, a long table capable of holding sheets of drawings, with a number of leather chairs surrounding it. The office was the place where the two of them would argue through what each of them wanted to do. The look on Mr. Lanker's face suggested that he was not in the mood to study how relaxing this office of Andrew could be. He was out for answers and not to listen to objections from Andrew.

"Mr. Lanker! This building of yours is going on schedule and it is under budget so far. I am a little surprised that you stopped by to see me. Is there a problem with anything, or something you are not satisfied with?" Andrew had his hands folded on the desk, on top of a small folder. Mr. Lanker went to his coat pocket and pulled out a little black book and turned very slowly with his legs crossed, and leaning back in the chair, said. "Well, that's good to know. The reason I stopped by is that this design that I clearly stated to you some time back is my concern." "Hmmm." Andrew explained, "Yes, yes, this is going on well, I got the chief designer to clearly reproduce the things you wanted in the building. I do have to state that there are some problems with some of your requests." "Oh?" Mr. Lanker asked? "Yes. There is a problem with the stairs on the first floor. The space allowed in that area is not the ideal design for that this building's type of structure. It is a problem to design around. I am concerned about the square footage and the placement of certain shops or offices on that floor. The stairs create a big problem with the foot traffic and entrance ways of the lobby. It is just too big to make that floor functional." Mr. Lanker glanced down at his little book and then looked Andrew in the eye with a cold stare. Andrew, a little shocked, said, "It's a problem that can be solved, though." Mr. Lanker put the book back in his pocket and said, "A problem? Do you have the designs for that lobby? Not your designs, the designs that I gave you some time ago?" "Yes, that is the source of the problem. It has a large stairway with so much space in the front of it that the function of the elevators is in violation of the code." Mr. Lanker explained, in an unhurried voice, "Get the plans. This is a multi-million dollar building and with that kind of money—my money, I might add!—it can be done the way I want it done. I will not settle for anything less." "Let me get the chief designer's latest drawings for that stairway. Excuse me a minute!" Mr. Lanker gave Andrew a look that said "make it quick."

Andrew got up from behind his desk and walked to the door, heading down the hall to the production room. There were about four or five draftsmen in the room. Two of them were working on a remodeling project, a small job that did not pay well. There was a design room, over to the side, where Arthur's desk was covered with a set of Mr. Lanker's drawings for "The Star Project." Arthur was not there and Andrew looked for some sketches of the lobby area. He grabbed a group of drawings and headed back to his office, looking at them and turning them from side to side. He entered his office. Mr. Lanker was still sitting in his chair, but he turned in the direction of Andrew and got up. Andrew placed the drawings on the large table and Mr. Lanker walked over for a look. He pulled a chair out and sat to the left of them while Andrew began to thumb through them. Eventually, the last drawing was given to Mr. Lanker and Andrew explained,; "That's about it for now." Mr. Lanker said, "This is not good enough. These drawings should not be to form. These are just design concepts, right?" "Well, some of the drawings should not be done to form." "These are just schematics design concepts right, Andrew." "Well, well, some of these are going into production, like the shops on the first floor. That's the best we can do, with those shops being on that floor. The others are designs of the stairs in the lobby." Mr. Lanker flipped through a couple of drawings and stopped at one in particular. "Is this all you have of the stairs? You see, this design here is what I want in the lobby. If you have to cut out something else in the lobby, then cut it. The stairs are the main and the only important thing on this floor. If you have to make a smaller space for the shops, I don't care. I don't even care about the shops at all. You are filling space for no reason there. Make it anything. A landscape architect might be able to do something with it; give it to them to design that space and bring the elevators to each side of the stair case. I won't accept any other design." "Yes, Mr. Lanker, I will do that." "Another thing: when will I see some progress on this? I want some progress with this building at the site that I've just came from. I don't mean to put you on the spot, because we do have a contract. But when you tell me things are on schedule, I have to wonder." "Mr. Lanker, the building is not having a problem. The site is going well. The city has put its normal holds on certain things while waiting for an inspection. We have to delay construction until we get the go-ahead from the city. That's a big hole in the ground, as you see, and we will be filling it shortly. The foundation footings are set and ready to have the steel structure put in them. It should not be that long before you see some framing rising out of the ground. Mr. Lanker, it is going well. The engineers are ready, too. I expected this will all get moving in about a week or two." "I would like to know about the designs of the stairs and any changes you intend to make to any other parts of my building. I would like to be informed, Andrew. I was just now in the area and thought I should stop by after I saw that big hole in the ground with nothing in it." "Mr. Lanker, we are progressing quite well with the consultants and associates; we anticipate no problems with construction." "I hope not, with this idea. The stairs in the lobby are a very important symbol for this building and I'm really not in the mood to tolerate any exceptions to that design I have given you. Do you understand?" "Yes, Mr. Lanker. No changes will be made to the design you want." "Another thing, Andrew. My accountants have reported that you have been paid the third installment on this project. That's a third of the actual cost." "That was to speed up the consultants' work on the interior and the plans for the upper parts of the building.". "The floors, the upper floors, are to be constructed using certain products, and it would save you money if these products were bought right away, not delaying until after the construction has begun. I requested that things be done this way after a debate with your office. Mr. Knoll, I believe, was the person that I talked to, and to whom I sent a letter of confirmation." "OK." "Andrew, if he said that's the way it should be done, than it should be all right. Just remember, Mr. Knoll works for me and so do you, Andrew!"

Mr. Lanker, his temper rising, continue, "This, is my personal project and I could not help noticing that your lobby is filled with my pictures of my buildings, you know." Andrew stood up and said, "I believe you are wrong, Mr. Lanker. Those photos show all different sorts of clients in different parts of the country. How can you say that?" "Take another look, Andrew," Mr. Lanker explained, as he reached into his coat pocket and pulled out his little black book and slowly rose out of his chair with an undaunted look. "The Madison Park project, a condo development with a clear skylight for each unit is mine. The Boller building, a glass barrel vault in the lobby with steel inlays, is mine and I believe Mr. Toolie made it clear that there should be an additional vault on the second floor. The Anderson County hospital? Let's see, it was the slanted beam construction, made of poured concrete with steel beam connections that spaced the glass of a double covered roof in the lobby area and all the outer rooms. That one too is mine. Let's see, there was the Anderson Medical group, and Mrs. Paul Haskel. And you know The Home and Savings Bank of Middle Town? Should I continue, Andrew?" "No, Mr. Lanker, you have made your point. I will make sure that things are in accordance with your request." "I hope you do see the point. I know what is feasible and what is hot air here, Andrew. You get those trucks rolling with that steel and start filling that hole in the ground! I've got some shopping to do. You continue to deal with Mr. Knoll and I want you to send him a full design of the stairs in about three days. Have it in his office by then, understand? I would get Arthur on the job immediately if I were you! I would make sure he gets it done. Ahh, remember Mr. Richards? How is that lawsuit going? You know, you didn't put those double glass windows in the last part of that Heritage building, the twenty to twenty-ninth floors. I really hate to see you lose the commission on that job. Such a nice looking building. You know, Andrew, it does not sway enough to require single glass or another product to augment that assessment. I see you got the message about lay-away products." Andrew, who's will was broken, explained, "Ahh, Mr. Lanker, about that, could you speak to Mr. Richards about that? My lawyers are costing me a lot of money there - project there - glass windows, building there--AHH AH." Mr. Lanker, with a stare and a gleam in his eye, looked at Andrew and turned to the door as he walked out, saying, "Three days on those stairs and there will be no exception." Andrew turned around, walked over to the chair, and sat down with a sigh of exhaustion, as if he had seen a ghost. "Unbelievable," he said to himself in a soft shallow voice. "I thought I was the architect."

CHAPTER SIXTEEN
Big Business

Albert's had his work was cut out for him. With so many design concepts that he would like to build, time seem limited. He was glad that he had an architectural firm that he could control to do his work in a short time. He would not always contact them personally, because he did not want to draw attention to himself or the others around him. He had had enough of the Lanker name, in the news with Jan and the YDS channel on the air every week. Things had gotten to the point that most of the major channels all over the world would tune in for the latest update about the Ursa Star. It seemed a little too simple that some of the connections with NASA and the government scientists would seek out Jan's company, Far-Seeing, for information on the Ursa Star. Albert thought that Jan's presentation on television must have been one of the key factors; a woman with a nice could do wonders for a television audience. But, then again, people in the science world were almost always interested in facts and "figures." The other side of the presentation was basic, and left to Jan's interpretation. Besides, she was strictly business-like and would check with Albert every day for a critique of her latest show. Still, with the sole access to the space telescope and some of the missions into space, Far-Seeing had become the number-one science network and information center.

Albert did something that pleased Jan. He brought down Joel, her oldest brother, a corporation head of Far-Seeing. It was a chore to persuade him of the opportunity at hand, yet with Jan's new-found fame, he finally liked the offer. Albert thought that the money connected to the position did the job, but Jan said it was not that; it was only that he loved his little sister so much. Albert would have liked to believe that, because he did not tell Jan that he had bought her family's fishing company and put the title in her name. Jan found that out later, but not a word was spoken about the matter. She lived in a world of love and power, and to her, it was love. Albert would still think of Joel as a man out of his depths, because his passion was fishing and he always had a love of the sea. So, while Jan's love was strong, without some really good incentives, a fisherman would never agree to an office job, no matter how much money was at stake. Albert knew it was probably the strong family ties; Joel indeed did love Jan. He was the best man at their wedding and that might had convinced him to take the position.

Albert needed more people that he could trust to run things in his plans. The Ultra Corporation was becoming stronger and stronger in the U.S. economy, and he needed more help. Being an only son, his family was small; his parents were retired and busy with the children going to college down in Southern California. Jan, who did have other brothers, warned Albert about rest of her family up north, not to transfer any more of her members. Albert agreed that it would be too much of a demand on the rest of Jan's family. Her father was still going out to sea and fishing with his new fleet of boats that Albert helped arrange. Anyway, money was never a problem with Jan's family because they owned a fishing company. Although with Joel helping out Jan, he made sure that the top-of-the-line equipment was included in the package. Albert did not mind that because the Stevens family was a fisherman's family and it was kind of ironic that feeding the people was their life, and now Albert had begun to realize how he loved the world of farming along with his buildings. It was just a human nature thing, just inspiration. Albert felt at ease as Ultra began to dominate people's lifestyle.

Albert contacted Fr. Anthony, who was now the most famous priest in the Seattle area. He was still at his church and was busily into his duties, with an increased number of baptisms scheduled on the church's calendars. Albert phoned and left a message for Fr. Anthony to contact him in California. It had been about a year since they had spoken together. There had been a lot of correspondence between the two, and also with Cardinal Manlin. As head of Ultra, Albert would need more people to run the hearing aid project that was about to be launched into action. This project would build even more buildings under the name of Ultra. He had help from his father with business contacts who were certified to be a strong squad of professionals. His father had had dealings with them before and was happy to make the introductions to Albert, his only son. Albert's mother was so proud of him, even with his children living with them, that she would tell them about their father's childhood all the time. Albert would hear about that from them, and would still wonder how, with all the sky being eaten up by the Dark Star, he really was blessed now to have calmed the world down from going into hysteria. It was truly in the hands of the top scientists and what the Pope would say about things to come. Yes, any message from the Pope was now being seen first by the President as a security matter. In fact, they had all become really good friends; for any need the Vatican had, the President was quick to offer assistance.

Fr. Anthony got back to Albert around the end of the day. Albert, still pulling together some things at the farm and making plans for some new buildings, had gotten a little busy while waiting on the call. "Hello," Albert said. "Yes, Lanker? What can I do for you?" "Fr. Anthony, long time no see. I hate to bother you now! Well how are you doing anyway?" "Fine. Albert, is there anything I can help you with?" "Ah, Ah, yeah, I got a company in New York ready for production and expansion, and I need a top personnel officer to run the distribution from there. I know what you are thinking, Fr. Anthony, you have your duties to perform and I am not recommending you for the position. I am wondering if you have any idea of who I could use. I have utilized all the people around me, so I've run out of people that I can trust with the operations of the company." "Albert! You own that company, don't you?" "Ah, yes." Fr. Anthony continued, "It is under your control, so you should have no problem with the staff as long as you have control of the operations. You have Ultra, and all those other companies must answer to that company. You have all the power of the company, or should I say, the control, with the Ultra monopoly in the market. Albert, I see the news." "Well, too the company Voices and Ah, I might as well add the company Earmax; they are in another part of the country not close to me. You know the production must be supervised very careful because of the small symbol going on these devices. They have the emblem of the church on them, as a reminder to all who receive them that the church is the sponsor, and to those who can't afford it, ah, it just seems better to have them in the church's prayers. Another thing: With the governments that plan to acquire their devices, it is clear that it be made without any design disputes. I feel that even the United States will be required to buy so many that it would force all other companies to be taken over by the government." "Well! You do have a point there! It is a concern to have the right people in the right place. I do see the problem that could develop in relation to this project."

There was dead silence over the phone for about ten seconds and then Fr. Anthony said, "Let's see, I am thinking of a way this could be solved. In fact, I think this will be the best thing to do in this case. I'll have Cardinal Manlin contact Sister Irish. She has some really tough business people that could take a position in those companies you are mentioning, Albert. That would take the control of the production in the right direction and with the purpose you want. About the governmental takeover, I wouldn't worry about that too much, because they will just tax you enough to take their share of product. Oh, yeah, I think this would probably be the inevitable answer for almost all your holdings and companies. These companies will be tax-free from any charges that the United States would try to impose on them." "Maybe international trade and the military, etc., all fall under a whole lot of United States interests. It is possible." Fr. Anthony replied, "You see, church and state is something the Vatican does not have to worry about. You did the right thing with the control of the funds. You do know you are the richest man in this country, so the United State is your friend, just like it is a friend to the Vatican. I'm sure the US government will make some kind of deal with you when the disbursement is ready to be shipped. Albert, I'd like to mention that you have done a great job with the church; everything is up and going, so you take care of yourself and your family. Things will find a way of working themselves out." "Yes, they do. I'll send you a letter about the position I need to fill, if you can help. It is the only thing that I am concern with." "OK, I'll get in contact with my people here and send it through the suitable channels." Albert replied, "Thanks, Fr. Anthony." He replied, "No problem. You wonder why the vow of poverty is a good thing for us? We have a job to do. Hey, I hear you have a helicopter at the farm. Hmm, seems like a nice deal." "There is space for you here. Construction on the monastery is going on and the church plans are going well. This is an offer. Ah yes, make me a promise, Fr. Anthony: you come christen the church when it is ready!" "Now that's a deal! I'd be glad to! Albert, give your family and that famous wife of yours my regards." Albert replied, "Will do. Take care." He hung up the phone and went to work on what he was doing with a surplus of delight. Albert briefly looked out the window and noticed that the sky was clear though the sun was beginning to set. It had been a tough day for Albert, but he did get a lot done on the farm and his building plans. Most of all, he had set his mind at ease somewhat with the planning of the Dark Star. For Albert had made himself a rich man even though the end of the world was at his doorstep.

CHAPTER SEVENTEEN
Computation

"From Earth, it is about as big as it is with a circle going around the planet. You see it is about as big as you believed it would be. Any bigger, it would not be what it is now; any smaller, it would not be what it is going to be. If you look at it from that view, then to those who feel that it is too small have just became a small group of a lot of planet to forget about. And that's what it is all about if you can picture the Earth and where we all are," the narrator said.

"This is Channel YDS, a community network and your host tonight is Jan Lanker." With a graphic of the solar system spinning and all the planets revolving around the sun, the camera zoomed in on the planet Earth, and then standing on the planet was Jan Lanker, looking up and reaching her left hand out and then her right. After that the camera started to zoom back and she put both hands together as if she were praying to the heavens. The introduction stopped and a huge screen was draped on stage and out came Jan Lanker. This time the stage was set up with chairs and a large table to face the cameras. Jan's chair was over to the side because she was the interviewer, almost like a late night talk show. It was a well-designed set with the floor embedded with small lights that moved in a slow time flow. In the corner of the stage were models of various space satellites and telescopes. One large model was of the Hubble telescope that is stationed in Earth's orbit. This was going to be a panel debate that would feature the most important minds in the world. They had brought with them the data from their own research that they had been hammering out to explain the Ursa Star. This debate was to be held on all channels because of the recent burst of neutrinos on the planet, which the panel would also have to explain to the public. The emission had caused some bad situations for people all over the world, including plane crashes, car wrecks, people falling from some of the most dangerous places. The neutrino bursts had been on the increase since the appearance of the increasingly close Ursa Star.

"Our guests today will include Brad Thomas, astrophysics pioneer and editor of magazine, *The Scientific World Around Us*; John Captain, PhD, the director and instructor of NASA's deep space unit department; Jeffery Philips, PhD and chair of MIT's astrology department and noted for his work on the Big Bang theory and the blue and red shifts of astronomical objects of the present day; and Fili Guter of the World of Stars organization and Yomme Tuts, both having done work on galaxies and black hole theories with gravitational shifts. Yomme Tuts is the number-one astronomer in the world, with the notable discovery of the comet Pertily and asteroid cluster Harblum he is also number one in the field of radio telescope technology with the company Apparent Magnitude. We have a strong panel of scientists from all parts of the world today," Jan said. "This group of individuals will give us all some precious knowledge about the Ursa Star out in space, heading toward Earth." Jan sat down in her seat and asked if anyone of the panel would like to start the debate. Fili Guter, motioned that he would like to start with the presentation of data from his lab.

Fili Guter said, "Good day. I would like to open, hmmm, with the probability, hmmm, of position of, ahhh yes the Ursa Star. Looking at the data, hmmm, it is very closer than it was, ahhh lets say, hmmm, the last seventy-two hours. Hmm, Yes! A powerful enlargement and hmm, a, I mean an, most extraordinary increase in speed. Yes, hmm, data shows this finding with the reading at, hmmm, zero two five hours to, ahh yes, ten minutes and eight seconds, of the Greenbank station." Jan asked, "Is this from your latest data feed in the loop, because we have been someone sharing the information with the interloop on the online science computer network." Fili replied, "Hmm, this is not shared data; hmmm, it is independent research, with the calculations of gravitational proton shift. Hmm, it will be fed to the loop." Looking at his fellow scientists, Yomme said, "Ahh, twenty four hours, yeah, soon, shortly, hmm, I am reviewing data calibrations for the feed." Jan replied, "Well this is conjectural evidence, not taking the form any of scientific formula of parallax deduction."

Fili, of a dark complexion and with a long black spade beard, was puzzled by the question, because of the problem with his English. Fili was from Northern Africa. His colleague, Yomme Tuts, was from somewhere in China. He looked more Japanese and spoke better English. Yomme said, "Yes, yes, this data of ours, of Fili and myself, is an attempt to track the Ursa Star by using the proton measurement of atomic matter. It, Huuu, is a fundamentally basic theory of atom shifts in gravitational movement. We had this theory in place with the discovery of the Horblum cluster. We are still reviewing the data and the transformation to an active neutrino burst. Yes, it is still the early stages of the measurement and could be read as false data. We still agree on the movement, though; accurate readings are, however, speculative." Jan replied, "Well, the work on that will be helpful in a lot of ways if it can be done. Mr. Jeffery Philips, do you have anything to add? You too are trying to track the Ursa Star." Jeffery replied, "Yes, that is correct, Jan. The deep tracking telescope Hubble has pulled up a ton of data on the Ursa Star. As you might know, we get most of our raw data from John Captain's department. Do you agree, John?" "That's correct." Jeffery continued, "I would like to give you the latest pictures of the surrounding events connected with the star." The screen was on the side of the panel, sitting next to Jan. It came down and the pictures began to come into view. Jeffery continued, "Here is a picture of a deep space galaxy which is a Barred spiral. Now a couple of days ago, this was in the path of the Ursa Star. This galaxy is about seven billion light years away. As you see from the last photo from the Hubble telescope, there the galaxy is, being drawn by the gravitational effects. It has changed to an elliptical galaxy in a matter of days. Here is another photo of the nucleus of a different galaxy in deep space, which appears to be part of a globular cluster of galaxies. The next photo shows the giant nucleus gone and the clusters being drawn into the middle of the Ursa Star. In conclusion, it looks to have happened decades ago, despite the view we see now. Ursa is moving at a speed of hundreds of times faster than the speed of light and also growing in size and mass. It should reach our galaxy in, let's say, seven or eight years at this present rate. Although I could be wrong; it is a very unpredictable star mass."

Jan replied, "Well, that is a very interesting view of the SB and SC galaxies. Yes! The EO and, let's say, E seven galaxies in the cluster are very strange events in the wake of Ursa." John Captain said, "Excuse me, Jan. Well, I would like to add, to the data from these photos, that a radio reading in the same sector of space does show the large Magellanic Cloud around our Milky Way galaxy. Let's use the Tarantula nebula for the consideration of using all other surrounding nebulas. The data received from those points in space shows the neutrino burst that we've had has affected our planet's orbit to a point of slowing it down in its travel around the sun by about five percent. Also, it has formed a compression particle mass in these nebulas that shows that the Ursa Star is moving at a faster rate each day. It is almost foolish to estimate this star at a seven-year path to Earth. It might be seven years or seven days; it is just too much mass in too much unpredictable space!" Jeffery Philips responded, "What? It is ten billion light years out in space according to the data I have!" John answered, "That might be true, Jeffery, but it is so large that the measurements don't align with the speed of its travel!" Jeffery replied, "Speed is travel! Light is just so fast and, with elements of matter, it can only be what it is!" John replied, "I disagree. There are other factors at work here." Jan interrupted and said, "Hold it! Wait a minute; we are running out of time. Let's hear from Brad Thomas."

Brad Thomas, an astrophysicist, said, "It is clear that more research in all fields of measurement is needed to resolve these problems. Everyone on planet Earth needs answers, not discussion! I find that the data from our host, Jan, has the most assurance of being right, given the data stream of information. The diagnosis of "tired light" is the best thing we've got. The blue and red shifts in this deep space matter are just too random to have a clear dependable reading. I think the answers are there. In fact, it's her discovery, so let's work with those statistics and reports." "Thank you, Brad. Looks like we will continue to have these debates in the future. I thank you all for appearing here at YDS and we will be in touch in the future, upgrading and adding information to the tracking of the Ursa Star. I thank you." The panel stood up and Jan Lanker and all the scientists slowly walked off stage. Then Jan was seen on the top of the planet Earth, one hand up and then the other. As the camera slowly rolled back, she brought both hands together over her head in an act of prayer. Both hands together and head bowed downward, and instrumental music began in the background as the screen faded away. The narrator said, "This is the science of the world channel coming to you once every week, channel YDS, a community network. Now back to your regular network."

After the show, Jan started home to the farm, where Albert had been doing a lot of work. The main house was finished, with a nice picture window over-looking the fields. The new barn and silos had been built at a distance from the main buildings that housed the tractors. Construction was underway on other buildings further out. Jan had the limo drive her to the estate where life was quiet and peaceful. Albert had already finished building the observatory on the farm, so Jan had all the information she needed for her research on the Ursa Star. The farm was forty miles away from the city, so it would take a little less than an hour to get from the station to her new home. With a garage full of cars at the farm, Albert had hired a butler and a maid to manage the little things in Jan's life, so that she could get to her work and research. Computer access meant that all the communications equipment to have contact with anyone in the world were there at the farm. With the two huge satellite dishes as well, it was like having a personal satellite in orbit. Albert had had the farm upgraded with new plumbing and water, supplied from a new location, so that the land would bear healthy crops abundantly year after year. The crops included the simple staples of life, such as corn and wheat, and the rotating harvest of various potatoes. The market would judge the quality of the crops, but Albert had the choice of planting what he wanted, because it was not for his own profit. It was to help the church and the need for low-cost staple foods.

The limo turned off the main highway and on to a newly-paved road, where an iron gate was placed, with a security booth on either side. Out came a man from the right guard booth and, noticing the plates and the limo, opened the gate. It moved by remote control and pivoted open as the driver waved and drove over the cattle-guard without really stopping. He had about a mile to the main house, which stood like a small hotel but without advertising lights. It was not an old looking mansion; rather, it was well-designed to create a sense of the best materials that money could buy. The design motif spread to the barn and other structures on the land. Driving up to the carport in front of the main door of the house, the butler, Thomas, got out of the car and opened the door for Mrs. Lanker, He said; "Is there anything you need, Mrs. Lanker?"; "No, but thank you for asking, Thomas." Thomas then went back to the driver's seat, drove the limo around the apron of the driveway, and headed for the garage.

Jan went inside, where she was met by Lizzy, the maid, who was dusting the collection of pictures and statues. Lizzy said, "Mrs. Lanker, you're home!" Jan, holding a small briefcase, asked, "Do you know where my husband is?" "Yes, he is in the drawing room." "Thank you." Jan walked up the stairs to the hallway and entered the second door on the left. There in the room was Albert. It was a large room, well really, a large office replete with all possible office supplies. It had two office copiers and a number of computers. It was a lab of architectural drafting with flat drawers along the walls to hold large sheets of drawings. On top of these cabinets were models of buildings and samples of building products. Toward the middle of the room, there was a large drafting table and seated behind it was Albert, head down in his work in the glow of the retractable light. Albert did not notice Jan coming into the room. She slowly walked up behind him and grabbed him in a hug. Albert shifted quickly, dropping the pencils he was using. "Jan!" he said in a surprised voice. She laughed, "I could have been anybody!" Albert turned in his chair and look at Jan, "Anybody's not going to grab a crazy man." He got up, lifted Jan in the air, and carried her out of the office and down the hallway to the bedroom. He slowly put her on the bed and began to kiss her. "Albert, stop! Stop! Albert." He looked her in the eyes and said, "You know that I love you? I saw your show; you did a great job." "You saw that show?" "Sure did, madmen in space. Where in the world did you get a scientist named Yomme?" "Ha! Ha!" and then she laughed some more, "He! He! He has a good scientific mind, Ha! Ha!" Albert replied, "Yeah, a scientific mind, with a name like that? He couldn't be anything but a scientist, Ha! Ha!" "He is a good man. Not better than you, Albert, but he has a good heart." "Yeah, he did seem concerned for people in trying to explain the Dark Star." "Albert, it is called the Ursa Star. Well, I guess to you it will always be the Dark Star. I just get so confused with the input of this scientific data." "Jan, slow down. You are right to say it is the Dark Star. You should bear that in mind too. If you don't do that, the scientific academy will eat you for lunch!" "You see how much contention goes on with comparing findings? Everyone believes that they have the answer." Albert started to laugh again and said, "About *your* discovery, Ha! Ha!" Jan pushed Albert off of her and they both rolled over on their backs. "You think they will try to shut me out of the credit for the discovery?" "Brad! That guy would if he could; that's why he agreed with your findings. You should know that he is looking closely for any faults in your data." "You think so?" "Huh, know so! Look this guy writes for *The Scientific World Around Us*. In his last five editions, he has been pushing "Tired Light" ever since the moment you said it. Damn! Jan, he pulled in some strong scientists that generally refuse public appearances." "Anyhow, you are right, the Dark Star it is. I won't mention it to the public; nevertheless, I'll keep it in my mind all the time." "I think that's the best, with what we went through to get this discovery. Just don't forget about vibrations readings that will come soon, and you better believe that they will be here. Did you notice those neutrino blasts? They will taper down in the coming year and then there'll be a couple of compression forces in the atmosphere, and holy God in heaven! The sound is here!" Jan answered,

"Albert what about the compression thing you just mentioned?" "That's another thing that acts like these neutrino bursts. It might last as long. Let's see. Since the first neutrino blasts, what has it been, four years?" "I think so?" "Well, that's how long it will be in and out of the atmosphere. It will change the gravity from ten to fifty percent in waves. It all depends on which side of the planet you are on, when the waves come in." "How long do those waves last?" "I really don't know. I think it will be about hour or two for each wave." "Albert, how am I going to speak about this and what data should I have on the subject?" "Hee! Hee!" Albert laughed, "Yomme is really close to that data. He has the gravitation data on black holes; it's something in that range. Jan, I'll tell you when it is nearing time to present that data."

They both looked at the ceiling and watched the shadows overtake the curves of the room. It was true that Jan and Albert were exhausted from working on different projects. They both fell asleep on the bed as the room darkened. There would be another dream in the mind of Albert, as his rapid eye movement gave clues that Amatimas was really on his mind. His repeating dream was not going to leave him alone, because the Dark Star was moving closer every day. After a while, Lizzy realized that it was dinner time. She went to their room but, finding the door open and seeing them sleeping, closed it and took a message from the one call that came to the house. The night fell on the West coast, like drawing down a big window shade. With stars out in numbers, you could almost see the ocean that reflected off the western horizon at the farm. It was a clear night and if you were outdoors, you could see the Dark Star right around the northern star of Polaris. Going around in a slow spin, it looked like the planet Earth was no place to be with this thing overhead. If there ever was time to build a spaceship to leave the planet, it was now, because in the hope of clinging to life, you would be making your voyage in the opposite direction from where the Dark Star was coming. But, where would you go? and why? It was too big to run from and was going too fast to outrun it, based on the fact that now you could see it swallowing stars and galaxies. The mind at times in the night fears that escape from the Dark Star in a big way. You might want to hide, run, bury, lock away, or shroud yourself in some monolith under a mountain. There was nowhere to go in space to escape from this destructive matter. It would destroy the soul, because this star made it appear that everyone on this planet was already selected to feel the grappler of this Dark Star. It played havoc with groups of people all over the world. It was the only thing that made sense now; the churches were only the reminder that people had to get their minds and souls together. Membership was up so much that people demanded more church space, even in the farthest reaches of the world. Some churches were made from old abandoned buildings, and other places, such as China would change any events on Sunday at all of their huge stadiums. Even, in the Jewish areas, the Christian religion was looked at through the lonely lens of power and faith-healing. Some of the most beautiful settings in those areas were as if Christ Himself was saying the sacrifice of the mass on open ground. There was a movement to have as many amphitheater as possible built in those areas, so that people could flock to them. You should know that a hot dry sun or the wind, indeed the violent nature of a rainstorm, never discourages crowds from coming to the altar all over the world, not to mention the cold that chilled people to the bone as they prayed. The bare covering of the tabernacle was the only thing that shaded the elements when these holy masses were held in some places. Why, it is Sunday, the day the Lord's rest after He made the world. Let us give thanks. Let's give thanks to God for his creation of us and all that is around us. For the good sense to worship to Him and love Him, forever and ever, Amen. This was on the lips of those that prayed around the world

CHAPTER EIGHTEEN
Parishioners

"GOD, OH GOD! NO! NO! NO! GOD NO!!" Albert was running through the front door and out to the fields screaming, "GOD NO!" He was weeping. Jan and Albert had fallen asleep on the bed all night, fully dressed, and Albert was the first to wake up. Jan was awakened by Albert's loud voice from outside this quiet place in the flat plains of California. "NO, NO!" Jan could hear Albert shouting. She ran to the front window upstairs and saw Albert running through the fields. She called for Lizzy, at the top of her voice. "Lizzy! Lizzy!" She was downstairs and Jan was rushing down the stairs to where she was. "Lizzy! Lizzy! What is wrong with Albert?" Lizzy was confused and frightened and then she pointed to the phone that was on the kitchen wall, off the hook and swinging from side to side. Jan rushed to the phone and there was still a voice on the other end. It was Cardinal Manlin, saying, "Albert! Albert! ALLL-BERTT!! HELLO! GET A HOLD OF YOURSELF, MAN! ALBERT!" Jan picked up the receiver and said "Hello!" Cardinal Manlin replied, "Hello? Who is this?" "Who is this?" Jan asked. "Is this Jan? Where is Albert?" "He ran outside. What is wrong! What's going ON!" "Jan, you might as well know. AH, I don't know how to tell you this. But Ah, Ah, it's Fr. Anthony, AH, AH—he is dead."

Jan fell to her knees and then curled up into a fetal position on the kitchen floor. The tears began to flow down her face as she wailed out streams of grief that poured rain from her eyes. She gasped for air that was not there. She tried to make a face but her muscles could not do it. Jan was heartbroken. With the phone still close by, she could hear Cardinal Manlin exclaiming, "JAN! JAN!" She reached down for the receiver on the floor and grasped it slowly. Putting the phone next to her ear, Jan, in a change voice that was almost child-like, uttered, "hel-lo -hello." "Good, Good, Jan, JAN! Look, I'll be there tomorrow morning. ALRIGHT?" Jan looking at the floor and the pool of tears, said, "All right, yeah, OK." "Look after Albert, ALRIGHT, Jan?" She did not answer. Manlin repeated, "JAN! JAN! ALRIGHT" Jan replied, "Alright." The phone then made the sound of a click because Cardinal Manlin had hung up. With the receiver still off the hook, it began to beep. It beeped for a while until it quit, and Jan began weakly to pull herself off the floor. She used the wall and counter for support. Lizzy, who was crying in the other room, came in and helped Mrs. Lanker to her feet.

Jan finally stood up and asked Lizzy where Albert was. She replied in a low voice, "He is outside, somewhere outside." Jan, wiping her face with both hands, started toward the door of the kitchen and told Lizzy, "I'll be alright, yes, I'm alright." With tears still falling, she started toward the door and down the stairs, holding the rail with both hands. She looked through her blurry eyes, trying to focus on anything moving or standing out. She continued to walk, with the bright morning sun in her face. She looked toward the south, but she did not see Albert. She came to where the fields started away from the paved concrete around the mansion and saw footprints in the field. They were fresh and led toward the monastery. The monastery was more than a mile away; it would have taken some time if Albert had decided to walk that direction. Jan began to walk through the fields and there, about two hundred yards away, was Albert, lying face-down on the ground. He was just lying in the dirt, not caring about how he looked. At the main house, Lizzy was on the porch while Thomas had started to go out to the fields, when Lizzy said, "Thomas, let them be. It is hard for them right now."

Jan reached Albert and fell on top of him and she could hear him weeping. She was crying, too. There in the fields they lay, with the sun beating down on them. There was nothing to say or do, because they were both numb. In the distance was the half-built church. The scaffolding was on the sides of the main structure and what was to be a tall steeple was only partly finished, awaiting a gold cross to be placed on top. Yes, it was going to be a beautiful church, with imported marble from Italy and France. Albert was too much in state of shock even to think about building the church in these times of distress. In his mind, he would finish the church for the sake of Fr. Anthony. He was just so broken in will and motivation, that all he could think about were the things that Fr. Anthony had done for him that he could never repay. Fr. Anthony believed in Albert from the first moment of seeing the Dark Star. Without Fr. Anthony's strong faith, Albert would never have gotten to the Pope or even begun to build his dream of a lifetime. The Dark Star in Albert's mind had dealt a blow to them that they could not recover from. He thought of the good that he did for the church and realized that Fr. Anthony had seen the truth for what it was! And that only made Albert think about the future that they had just lost. Jan could not stand the thought of Fr. Anthony not being in her life. She cried as women cry, for she was agonized over the news. She found her strength in Albert, whom she knew would do the right thing and continue building.

They finally got up after about ninety minutes, dirty and walking slowly, holding each other. Albert brushed the dirt off of Jan and himself and looked at the house, noticing Lizzy at the window, anxiously peering out. Thomas came up to them once they had reached the concrete and said, "Is there anything I can do for you, Mr. and Mrs. Lanker?" "Yes, Thomas, if you could, but you don't have too." "What is it, Mr. Lanker?" Albert hugged Thomas around the shoulders and said, "Later tonight, Cardinal Manlin will be at the airport. Could you pick him up? I know you have other things to do at that late hour but if you could…" "No! No! Mr. Lanker, I will do it. Don't worry about me; I'm here for you and Mrs. Lanker." Albert smiled and said, "Thomas you have a life, too." "Don't worry about it, Mr. Lanker. My wife is asleep about that time." Thomas's wife lived with him above the garage. She did the gardening around the estate; well, she really just picked the flowers and arranged them, because a crew came once a week to tend to the lawns and gardens. The upper quarters above the garage were about twenty-five hundred square feet. The quarters were really a medium-sized house that overlooked the driveway and farm.

Albert and Jan were inside cleaning up when they picked up the message that Lizzy had left on the night stand in their room. It read, "Call Sister Irish," followed by a number with the area code of the Vatican. Although Albert was still wet from the shower, and Jan was still in the tub, he dialed the number. It was late night at the Vatican and Sister Irish could be reached at different location. "Hello," Albert said. "Yes? Sister Irish?" The person that had answered the phone was not Sister Irish, so she said, "Just a minute." After a few minutes, Sister Irish came to the phone. "Yes?" Albert said, "This is Albert Lanker. Is this Sister Irish?" "Yes, Yes!

Albert, I'm so sorry. It's really sad for us, too. We can hardly bear the pain. All of us, even the Pope, are in prayer now. How are you, Albert? We have you and Jan in our prayers, too." "Well, I guess we just have to bear it. It does hurt really bad. Well, thank you very much for your prayers. Jan and I really need them. It was just such a shock, a blow, and that is such a painful thing." Sister Irish replied, "Yes, he was a good priest and a good man. It is a shame. Bear up, Albert. We are still depending on you. Look, the church has Fr. Anthony's codes, so there are only two codes left for any transaction. I think there is around four or three billion dollars still left in the accounts, so if you need it, it is still there. Another thing: Fr. Anthony contacted us about some company heads at your request. I have recruited some good people from some large companies to take charge of those positions as you requested. He told us about your problem and the people we sent have a history of doing that type of job and doing it well. So Albert, don't worry about a thing on that score. Wait one moment." Sister Irish covered the phone while she was talking to someone else. When she started talking again, she said, "Albert, Yes! Cardinal Manlin is in route and should see you soon. He is on his way. Here, do you have a pen?" Albert got a pen and began to write down the flight number and airline on which Cardinal Manlin would arrive, as well as the time that the flight would be at the airport. "Yes, I have it." "Look, Albert. Remember, be strong. Fr. Anthony trusted you. Now with him gone, he will be watching over you. Remember that!" "Yes, I know, he was a good friend." "I'll tell the Pope that I have spoken to you and God bless you, Albert. Our vaults are full to overflowing; you kept your word. Fr. Anthony knew you would, so he secured the repayment of funds and more. He saw a dream come true. The Vatican sends good tidings of love to you and Jan at this time of bereavement." Albert hung up the phone right after Sister Irish had hung up.

The place was Seattle, Washington and the rain was falling like a heavy fog. It was mostly a mist of water with an occasional heavier shower at times, rather than having the water pour down the street. It was a tall church with a Romanesque's motif around the interior windows and walls. The ceiling reached up as if the ornamentation had been the craftsmen's delight. Yes! A finely-built church of solid stone that drained the water from the sky as well. He was in the back after the party of ten went out the front exit of the church, putting away his stole and priestly wear in the well-built wooden cabinets. He was the only one there after the last baptism had taken place. It was the tenth baptism on this day of misty rain and a darkened sky. There was a noise in the altar area and he went to see what it was. There, on the top of the altar, was a man dressed in a black robe, just standing on top of the holy alter with his dirty hiking boots. He went out so that he would be seen and said, "Please get down from there!" The man looked at him and said, "It is the place of our baptism into the faith!" Fr. Anthony looked at the front doors closing quickly and out in the distance was a whole group from the W.W.W., an organization that the Catholic church had not allow to join their religion because of their beliefs and sexual practices. The initials W.W.W. stood for Worthy World Worshipers, and Fr. Anthony knew at once that trouble was brewing.

He had ran back to office to call the police when some of the other members met him there. The phone lines where cut, which would explain the dead phone he got when he picked up the receiver. They grabbed Fr. Anthony by the ankles and arms and carried him a distance and placed him on the altar. Fr. Anthony howled, "STOP THIS! PLEASE STOP!" They looked at him and the person with the black robe said, "You are the famous Fr. Anthony and you are our ticket to become members of the Catholic church." "What! LET ME GO!! PLEASE! LET'S TALK ABOUT IT!" The others, dressed in jeans and plaid shirts with a red ribbon tied around their right arms, gathered round. The black-robed man went to the female members in the group of about twenty people and said, "Here is our admission to the church forever. Here is the John! The John of baptism! The one that baptized Jesus! He is the one that won't baptize us! He won't let us into the eternal life! The life we need to bring our worship to the world! HERE HE IS, BROTHERS AND SISTERS!" Fr. Anthony said, "NO! I AM FR. ANTHONY, A PRIEST!" "YES! THAT IS WHAT HE CALLS HIMSELF TODAY! ANTHONY! ANTHONY! ANTHONY! THE- SAINT- OF- PAIN-N-N-N!!!!" Just then, one of the women members pulled out a large knife and started toward Fr. Anthony, while some other members stood around and the rest held Fr. Anthony down. Up the stairs to the altar she went, as Fr. Anthony started to pray. She first cut into his groin, through his black pants, and then cut off his genitals. Fr.Anthony cried out, "GOD! NO, GOD NO, NOOO NO00! GODDDD!" The blood flooded the altar cloth, as the W.W.W. members held him down firmly.

The two holding his upper body drew back and the man with the black robe grabbed the flesh that the female member had in her dripping bloody hands. He dripped the blood over Fr. Anthony's head and said, "I TAKE AWAY THE POWER OF BAPTISM AND GIVE IT TO ME-EE!" The blood poured into the weeping eyes of Fr. Anthony and all over his face and forehead. The black-robed member then handed the flesh, drained of most of the blood, to the woman and she put in the baptismal bowl, way to the side in the cove of the church, where it leaked out the remaining blood. Fr. Anthony, lying in a daze and moaning from pain, with a faint breath coming from his mouth, spoke the words, "God no, no God, G-o-d, God!" The black-robed member motioned to one of the male members who was holding a gun and a large machete to come closer to the altar where Fr. Anthony lay. He said, "I DELIVER YOU TO HIM, I DELIVER YOU TO HIM, I DELIVER YOU TO HIM!- HEEE IS THE BAPTISM OF JOHN'S SEEED!!!" The black-robed member motioned to the male member close by to go on. This member took the large blade from his side and raised it high and came down with a swiftly slanted KNOCK! Fr. Anthony's head flew off and rolled down the stairs and then rolled onto the floor of the sanctuary and out to the nave of the church, close to the altar. There, some members picked the head up by the hair and brought it back to the altar, bloody and wet. The members flipped the cadaver over and placed the head on Fr. Anthony's buttocks, while the women members went to their knapsacks and pulled out some large needles and thick thread. They began a ritual of sewing Fr. Anthony's head to his buttocks, with his face pointed outwards. From what was left of the neck area of the head, the needles even went into some of the ears and sides of Fr. Anthony's face. After that, they all picked up Fr. Anthony's mortal remains and hung him on the tabernacle behind the altar. They scrawled their logo on the walls of the church in blood and shot a number of bullets into Fr. Anthony's dead body. They thought that the blood dripping down from Fr. Anthony's body gave a special artistic touch to the general scene. Hung under the large cross of the church, his body was placed like a doll or a flag, with his face looking out to the pews. DEPLORABLE, DREADFUL, AWFUL, just downright APPALLING! Understanding the mind of the broken WILL, the echo of OH GOD! NOOOO, NO GOD!!! still draped the walls and the statues of the church's horrifying image.

The W.W.W. were gone when the nun found the scene. The W.W.W. had left the place by the time the police looked around the grounds. The W.W.W. had escaped somewhere when the Vatican was informed of the display that was on the altar of their church. The W.W.W. had run away from the place where they had performed their worship and left their symbol, but Cardinal Manlin was informed that they were still at large. The news was carried in the Seattle papers and a few others around the country, as well as the international issue of The World Enlightenment Press. It was small news, not front page, or even an article with a picture. On television, it was only covered as a murder at the scene and nothing more. There was other news, including coverage of a plane crash in the mountains and the death of a famous rock star. So, life goes on. Still, it was big news to the Vatican and they planned to do something about it. It hurt the heart of the church to have something like this done and not to be able to find the perpetrators. That's why they sent Cardinal Manlin; he was going to find out what really happen to his longtime friend. They had been buddies for a lifetime and now Fr. Anthony, or Rick, was gone.

CHAPTER NINETEEN
Flesh And Blood

The car drove up with Thomas behind the wheel and there were two people in the back seat. Thomas parked and opened the door of the towncar limo and out came Cardinal Manlin with a small briefcase, along with a keeper that Albert did not recognize. Cardinal Manlin and his keeper were dressed in the standard black suit. They went into the house where they both hugged Albert and Jan. They mentioned that they were going to go claim Fr. Anthony's body and inform the small family that he had of his death. His family had left the details to the church because Fr. Anthony was so close to God's ministry that they felt he would always be serving Him, even in his passing. They were satisfied with the arrangements that the church had for the remains, to ship them to the Vatican and bury them there. Albert disagreed with the Vatican's idea; Albert wanted him to be buried here in the new church that was being built. He mentioned that Fr. Anthony was going to consecrate it for him and bless the altar. Cardinal Manlin, making phone calls, said to Albert after some time, "OK, looks like you have done well here with the grounds. The abbey area will do fine. I remember this place. It is as if a miracle had taken place here." Just then, the phone rang and it was handed to Cardinal Manlin. He said, "Yes, fine, that will do," and then hung up the phone.

Lizzy had set out finger sandwiches and coffee, so the meeting was ready to continue without interference in discussing the events. "Cardinal Manlin, I'll go with you to claim the body." Manlin said, "What about Jan?" "She is fine, and she just wants to rest. She does not have any meetings or shows to do this week. She needs her rest." So Albert went upstairs and told Jan that he was going with the Cardinal to Seattle to claim Fr. Anthony's body and place him in the church. She agreed and lay back in the bed as if she wanted to sleep. He kissed her and went back downstairs and out to the limo. On his way past the front door, Albert asked Lizzy to keep an eye on Jan. "To the airport, Thomas," Albert said and then said, "Stop! We will never make it in time for that flight! Thomas, let's use the chopper." Thomas drove the limo around the back of the mansion and then to the back of the garage area. He opened the door by remote and drove in where a Learjet helicopter and numerous fine cars were shined and polished. Albert got out of the car and started opening the large roll-away doors in front of the helicopter. Albert, holding the button down, kept the doors from rolling back. Cardinal Manlin and his keeper got out of the limo and started walking toward the helicopter. They knew it had to be rolled out. Thomas, checking the engine and blades, walked around the craft looking for anything out of the ordinary. All four of them pushed the helicopter straight out to the large circle outside the door, about seventy-five yards away. It moved easily because of the dolly wheels it was on. The doors closed and the dollies where taken off. Thomas was going to be the pilot and Albert the copilot. It was ironic that Albert actually had taught Thomas to fly, so he was assured that Thomas could do the job. Off and up, they took the route to the airport. Jan got out of bed and looked out the window to watch the helicopter fly by, looking at it until it disappeared, and said, "God bless you, Albert."

Heading the south and rising in altitude, the helicopter flew over the construction site of the monastery and the church. With everyone aboard the copter wearing headphones and microphones, Albert said, "There, Cardinal Manlin! There is the church!" "Ahh, yes!" Albert continued, "I based the design around the Cathedral of Altamura, built around the thirteen century. Altamura was an ancient city town in Italy close to the foot of the Apennines mountains. It was also built around farm land. I think the motif of Romanesque design is the goal here, I think it goes good with the style of all the structures in the cloister area." "Yes! That is amazing, Albert, you have done justice to the area and to the Catholic church. Looks good! I like it!" The copter flew on to the airport, where the chatter of the control tower dominated the headphones. They landed and rushed to get a flight to Seattle. Albert, Cardinal Manlin, and the keeper boarded the jet and were on their way to see Fr. Anthony.

It was general knowledge that the body had been defamed to the point of offense. It was a sight to see as the corner pulled and cut the corpse into shape. A detective was present as Dr.Ormert did his agonizing autopsy of Fr. Anthony. The doctor was dressed in a long apron made out of rubber, and blue hospital clothing under that. His hands were covered with double gloves and his hospital cap and mask made him look as if something other than surgery was happening here. Dr. Ormert was prepared for meat handling like a slaughter of the human flesh to find clues. A butcher, maybe or just a doctor with one of the sloppiest, messed-up bodies he has ever seen. They killed this man as the bag that carried the remains was toss aside. The detective took notes and at times covered his mouth. Dr Ormert was helped by two others: one was a doctor and the other just helped by keeping the place clean. Dr.Ormert pulled down the big light hanging overhead and began the long task of putting the pieces of this homicide together from a medical point of view. The first task was to pinpoint which was the first wound to the body.

The body that housed the faith of God. The body that in society should live peacefully to be a ripe old age. You know that body that loves the people and abstains from committing sin. The body that practiced the law in a living way, in a moral way, in the way of Christ. To take his pledge to serve the Most High in every way he could, he was to live his life in a different way. To sacrifice the luxurious part of this dog-eat-dog world and help whoever might call. This man of the cloth, this preacher, this minister, this deacon, this church official, this vicar did his job well. Only for the needs of the poor would the love of people be rung. Only for the wealthy and rich would his love of the public be sung. To promise to uphold the laws of the church, to pledge to keep the will of mankind in the eyes of God. To warrant a prayer to absolve the sins of the world. Not! A god, Not! A king, Not! A ruler of the throne!

Fr. Anthony, simply a strong-willed man who served the people in a educated manner. He would do his job not for the pay but for the love of the people of the world. Who was this man with the power to forgive sins and then sat "Go, sin no more"? Not Fr. Anthony, that's for SURE! I don't know any man of this power to do these THINGS? To tell someone that they are forgiven? Please! Perish the THOUGHT! PETER --Before the cock crowed three times-- He is not God!!! No, he must eat and handle his needs like every other mortal. A man, not a woman, WHY! Can't they do the same as he? A woman could pray like he does, and might even do a better job! A woman can be educated in the same manner as this man. Why NOT! Or why bother! He can't bear children or nourish them from his own body. He does not feel the phases of the moon in his life. He does not care for make-up; the nails and the hair are just a passing thought. The smell of sweet things affects each man in a different way. A man is strong and a woman is weaker, if they were the same in stature. Why! The bones are made different. Why! The ribs are in a different pattern. Why! The skin has a different texture. WHY NOT! A woman? Are there more WOMEN? Their muscles are not the same. If it really matters, there are some strongly-built women, even those that could cut the organ of a man right to the bone and never have a second thought about equal ability. Some women may be cold and some may be kind, just like a MAN! And there are men that could cut off someone's head with a blow that rings the bells of the tallest church! Yet, why not a woman in a priest's vestments to serve the Catholics? PETER!!! PETER!!! I DON'T KNOW THE MAN! No not ME! I want to live! It is the will of God to keep it simple and Kill and Eat-- YOU, you blind weak Man!!! It takes lots of really stupid questions to think that it will get you to heaven if a Man could at least be a MAN and read his Bible! And Woman could at least be a WOMAN and read the words! Born of a woman that NONE on the planet could fill the veil of MARY, that's right! The VIRGIN MARY who, in the eyes of GOD, had no desire to be compared to the shoes of a MAN!!! Peter! FEED MY SHEEP, a symbol of the church and that is IT! Who are we worshipping anyway? Surely not a mortal man and certainly not a mortal woman; they both lead to the grave! HANG HIM HIGH AND UPSIDE DOWN, YOU, YOU PETER!!! May the Holy Spirit be in your thoughts. THE SYMBOL HANGS ON THE CROSS!!!

Dr. Ormert said, "At the point of the trachea and the common carotid artery, there is a thin slice that penetrated through the subclavicle artery. This also shows signs of the internal jugular vein having been sliced thin in the same direction. The brain stem and cervical vertebrae are chipped and sliced in the position angle of less than five degrees from the jugular directional cut. Looking further in the direction of this angle, we see the sternum and clavicle injured by a blunt blow with a shave of bone loss to both. "Hmmmm. Looks like the back of the cutting weapon did this or perhaps a deflection; I can't be sure." Dr. Ormert changed the position of his instruments and continued to dig around in the upper torso. "Looks like the first rib has some fragmentation; looks like a bullet wound. Yes, here is a bullet. Looks like a forty-four special, yes! That's what it is!" Digging the bullet out of tight muscle, he placed it on the side tray. Dr. Ormert proceeded, "The trapezius, pectoralis major, and the sternohyoid all have the sharp thin slice in the same angle as the first cut; looks like a razor blade cut. Maybe not; the sternocleido mastoid is cut in the same way. Yes, by same weapon which cut the internal jugular vein through the cervical vertebrae."

"Let me see the head." The other doctor handed Dr. Ormert the head. "Yes, the sternohyiod cut is the same in the angle. The trapezius and the pectoralis major are consistent with the other analysis. Looks like a large blade did this work. Ohh - decapitation. Maybe a cleaver or that type of thing; does not look like an ax or a small knife blade, because of the lack of tear or sawing detachment in the bone area of the cervical vertebrae. On the head, Hmmm, what! Let's see that galea or the aponeurotica, OK." Dr. Ormert continued, "On the head, a blunt damage exists to the zygomatic and the facial muscles, along with the same injury to the temporalis. Looks to have the occipitalis impacted also by a blunt device and Yes!the occipital. Examining the total head area, front and back, the damage seems to be the same with the frontalis and the occipitals. The head might have fallen and done this damage because of the swelling after blood loss. Brain, eyes, nose, ears all are intact with bruised marks. Well, being rolled on a hard surface could have done it, Yes! sharp blow to the neck area and pop the head on the floor." Dr. Ormert put the head to the side with a befuddled look and then began to examine the lower portion of the body.

"Here is a bullet wound in the superior vena cave, could be the same type of bullet in the aortic arch and pulmonary artery right through the sternum and ribs." Dr. Ormert looked over the body and said, "My God, there are no genital organs." The other doctor thought it might be in the corners of the bag. He went to the bag and pulled out a small baggie with flesh inside. Dr. Ormert opened the bag of clear plastic and tried to locate the flesh from the genital area. "What do you think?" "It might fit if the drained blood was in the tissue; anyway, genital parts can be drained of blood and pressed flat." He continued, "Seems to be a knife cut, judging from the flesh rip and the jagged cut of the penis; testes and scrotum seem to be fully intact. Looking at the body, the pelvis is exposed, along with the pelvic arteries and veins and the torso arteries and veins. Let's turn the body over." Both doctors, with the help of a third man, did the task of flipping the body over. "Yes, it looks like the same weapon of cutting except for the digging of the sacrum and ilium chips and nicks. The gluteus maximus and the muscle lumbodorsal fascia and external oblique with the sartorios muscle all appear to have been done by the same knife." Dr. Ormert reached up and pulled the light into a slant position, leaving a little blood on the handle covered with plastic. He said, "It appears that the descending colon and anal canal and the rectum and anus all had the puncture wounds of a sewing device. Hmmm," Dr. Ormert said, "hand me the head; yes looks like from the temporalis and zygomatic puncture that it was placed here with thread. There is a thread in the anus and rectum area. Let's conclude this with the defiling of the body and attaching of the cut-off head to the buttocks. The death blow looks to have been in the neck area first, although the genital area looks to be cut first, with the draining of blood from the lower cavity. Internal organ temperature and quantity are as stated at the time of death: one minute past the jugular detachment. Groin area: indeterminate tissue loss because of the destructive nature. Ahhh, I give the groin area within a hour at best assessment. Finally, death caused by lack of blood and the decapitation, Ahh, thirty hours, give-or-take three hours." Dr. Ormert quickly took off his gloves and said to the detective standing in the room, "The gunshots did not matter. Who was he?" The detective replied, "A man that did so much good, and then so much bad came his way." "Oh, looks like you got a really bad murderer out there. Gives me the chills on this homicide." "Thanks, Dr.Ormert. I've got a ton or more of work to do." The detective seemed strange to the doctor because of the expensive suit and the patience with which he took down the notes that he wrote. In fact, he was not a detective at all, had the doctor asked him directly. He was with the FBI, sent by the President. Or perhaps, he was with the CIA, and sent by the Vatican. Or the mob? Or the Russian police? Or someone from China? Or France, England, Africa, Australia, Canada, Japan, Mexico, Israel, or even a Palestinian government official? Who knows! There are a lot of countries on this planet. Dr. Ormert did not get a name; he only knew that the coroner's office had no problem with his credentials and had allowed him in. The body was sewn together for the second time, pieced together with skill. It was the best they could do with what was left of this man named Rick.

CHAPTER TWENTY
Retribution

They arrived and went straight to the coroner's office, Albert, Cardinal Manlin, and his keeper. There, they found Rick in a cabinet drawer, a long drawer with the cold of ice smoke clinging to him. Albert looked at Fr. Anthony and said, "He was a faithful man to have his life snuffed out this way. Murder," he said to Cardinal Manlin, who was holding back the tears. Albert was in grief, yet it was covered up with anger. "He was murdered, wasn't he?" Cardinal Manlin, from the shadows, said, "Yes, they killed him." The keeper stepped up and took a look and said, "It was brutal; looks like a ritual sacrifice." "Do you know who could have done something like this?" Cardinal Manlin looked at his keeper and said, "W.W.W. did this work, and for the first time in the United States, too." "W.W.W.?" said Albert. "The Worthy World Worshipers. They are a sect of anti-baptism people. They were not allowed in any church, so they are going about their business of making it rough for society." "So this was not a random act, was it?" "No, premeditated." The coroner's helper looked at the group and said, "You recognize the body?" Albert spoke first, "Yes, we all do. It is him." Cardinal Manlin said, "Give me a moment." He pulled out a rosary that Fr. Anthony had owned when he was at the Vatican and laid it on him. He began to pray and the keeper did the same. Albert stood silently with his head bowed and at the end added an "Amen." The attendant started to close the drawer, when Manlin said, "We need to take the body now." "The identification papers must be filled out and we need instructions where the body is to be shipped." Manlin looked at Albert and said, "We will let you do the service at the farm. Is that alright, Albert?" Albert looked at the dead body. "It would be a honor."

Albert made the arrangements and negotiated for a refrigerated truck to drive the body down to California. He called his construction workers on their cell phone to tell them to dig a hole at the base of where the altar would eventually be in the church. A proper sacramental burial would take place in about three days at the farm's church. The cardinal contacted what was left of Fr. Anthony's family, and offered a free round-trip ticket and board to see the burial of their loved one. They got word, and some of them agreed in a sad and grieving fashion. Still at the coroner's office in Seattle, they waited on the rented cold-storage truck and the ordered casket because Fr. Anthony would not be embalmed. He was already ice cold and would be in an expensive airtight box. There was no reason to cut the body any more. This had been suggested by the corner. They watched the body being loaded into a slumber chamber and locked and driven away. All three of them would be staying in a local hotel, in individual rooms on the top floor, with a flight back home planned for the morning. Albert called Jan and told her that he would be home tomorrow and to stay home and rest. With all three of them still at the hotel, it was about five o'clock in the morning when a call came to Cardinal Manlin's room. He was on the phone most of the time before he fell asleep in his chair. The call, from some official, brought Manlin to his feet, ready to go. He knocked on Albert's door and then the keeper's door, saying, "Let's go! Get up, quick!" The rented car in the hotel's garage had been delivered to the lobby area as soon as they got off the elevator. It seemed that the keeper had called ahead, because he did all the driving. They hopped in the car and away they went, faster than they usually drove, when Albert asked, "Where are we going?" Cardinal Manlin pulled four sheets of paper out of his briefcase and said, "Read this, Albert." It was the autopsy report on Fr. Anthony along with the description of the crime scene. Albert started reading it, with his mind's eye looking at the details. His face changed expression after looking at the page where Fr. Anthony was put on the tabernacle. A explosion of air came out of Albert's mouth after flipping the page. The next page showed a number of photos, and caught Albert's full attention. He said, "My God! Who are these people?"

Their car was speeding up the highway going north toward the mountains outside of Seattle. The small cell phone that Cardinal Manlin had in his briefcase began to buzz. Manlin answered it. "Hold on! Five minutes; we want to be sure!" Albert looked back at Manlin. "Where are we going?" "We are almost there." The keeper turned off the highway and headed up a smaller road that had been paved in black asphalt. He stepped on the gas like he was in a race car. Another federal agent's car was blocking the middle of the road. Suddenly, behind the car that they were in, a police car came flying up from behind, as if they had gone past him. The keeper stopped when the police car swerved in front of the car. The keeper quickly pulled out his wallet and showed something to the officer out the window, as if to say get out of the way. The federal agent's car was about three hundred yards away from where they were stopped. Then the police car moved to the side and the officer put his hands in the air, as if to say I'm sorry and then he turned around. The keeper stepped on the gas and flew past the federal car with a wave out the window. The car went around the last bend in the road, where a number of federal cars were parked to the side of the road as if they were hiding from sight. The keeper pulled behind them and asked Albert to stay in the car. "Come on, I am with you!" Cardinal Manlin bent down and ran up to a man holding a walkie-talkie that had been handed to him. The keeper, watching Albert, did not want him to get too close to the Cardinal. Both of them got close enough to see what everyone was looking at.

The house was a large one, with a deck looking into the canyon. They all looked and it would be hard to see the road above them from the house because it was banked into the mountain. An odd-looking bus was out in front of the house, which had another small road to get to the location. It was as if you could only get there by going down the mountain and starting up the other side again. Albert wondered how they were going to contact these people from this location. There was another house about a mile down the mountain on that side, and beyond that two more on the same side at the same distance from the one at which this team of agents with Albert was located. Cardinal Manlin was handed some binoculars by one of the gun clutching agents and he looked through them at once. In view was a group of about twenty to thirty people in the house that was under surveillance. With the deck going all the way around the structure that overhung the slope, it was important for everyone on the opposite side of the mountain to stay down and out of sight. Large sliding doors of glass went around the deck, so that anyone inside could see the whole canyon. Manlin said to the person on the radio he was holding, "Pull back!" At the bottom of the slope, it was a long way down and you could see two flashes of light as the men signaled that they were moving further down the canyon and away from the house. Manlin looked through the field glasses once more and said, "Look at this MOTHER F***Ker! HE IS WEARING FR. ANTHONY'S STOLE AROUND HIS NECK! SON OF A B****CH!!" Albert looked at Manlin and saw he was about to explode with rage, and was about to do something to the head priest, who was leaning on the deck and drinking out of the consecrated chalice stolen from Fr. Anthony.

There in the house, cult members from all over the U.S. were having a gathering in the mountains outside of Seattle. Their minds were focused on the ritual they had done just days ago and were rejoicing over the success of the kill. The time was approaching noon and the sun had a haze like a veil over the heavens. It looked like a good day to have the bowels of evil set straight. Cardinal Manlin went to the radio in his hand and said, "Ten seconds." Everyone on the road got their rifles ready to do some shooting. Leaning on the rail in the black robe, the head member on the deck was joined by two other members; they continued to relax as they all talked. It was the quiet of the canyon between the road and the house of crime that made Cardinal Manlin stand up and yell, "Judas!, JUDAS! JUDAS!!!" They looked up and some of the cult members ran out after they had grabbed their guns and began to take aim at Cardinal Manlin. And just then it went off. The first boom came from inside the house and threw some members out onto the deck. It was not that loud but it was enough to do damage to the inside of the house and made the people and the man with the black robe look back quickly. Manlin said, "Everyone get DOWN!" The noise was such a loud boom that everyone on the road began to pray that mountain wouldn't slide and the large trees behind them begin to fall. However, the trees shook as if it was at least a magnitude five or six earthquake. The house on the other side, which everyone laying on the road was watching, began to fall. The land under the house was blown away so much that the fall out would come the way of everyone on the other side. "LOOK OUT!" The keeper said. It was big, like tons of explosives had gone off. The people standing on the deck flew straight up in the air about one hundred feet. The whole mountainside around the house began to fall, together with the road that led to the house. Yes, it was tumultuous, taking with it the bus and the trees all around the area. All of it began to fall down the slope into the canyon. It looked like someone had taken a bite out of the mountain. The exposed land looked almost virgin, with no plants or trees in the big cut. It tumbled and flipped as the house moved down the canyon wall, with dirt and rocks moving behind the broken wood and roofing material of the shattered house. When it was halfway down, there was another huge explosion. This time it was a fire ball combined of numerous other smaller fire ball explosions. Again the keeper said, "GET DOWN!" Everyone knew he was not saying that for his health but for his life! There must have been about ten or maybe twenty, but the fire balls were like the pit of Hell! The heat was so hot that no one could look down the canyon. It kept getting hotter, so it was no surprise that everyone began to run to their cars. The keeper jumped in the driver's seat and Manlin and Albert got in the back seat; no time to get to the other side of the car. The keeper started to back down the mountain with all the other cars on the mountain. It was a fire storm coming out of the canyon, with fire balls shooting up in the air about a half a mile. After finding room on the road, the keeper turned around like all the others coming down the mountain. They were moving fast. Albert, who had been leaning in the back seat with Manlin, finally straightened up to check the direction they were traveling. At the base of the mountain, about a mile from the main highway, the car pulled over and stopped. A military helicopter was about to land about one hundred yards away in a clear flat patch of dirt. The other cars drove by and waved to Manlin and the keeper. Albert got out of the car, still shaking, and looked at the mountain; he could see a huge fire and miles of smoke going into the air. Just then, two jet fighters flew overhead and launched two missiles. It was something to see the rockets flying the distance and hitting the side of the mountain and canyon where the W.W.W. was located. The jets made a second pass and launched two more missiles and then another set of jets did the same. Balls of flames could be seen, even at a distance. "The boys need some target practice; might as well be this part of the mountain." Albert said to the keeper, "What about the other two houses up there?" "We moved those people out this morning. They'll get compensated and can rebuild on the other side of the mountain. No, we made sure they were empty before we began." Looking at the mountain, Manlin said, "That is that!" And then told the keeper. "Good job, Datton!" Albert, looking at Manlin, was thinking that it was the first time he had heard him mention the name of the keeper. Datton said, "Let's go," and then gave Albert the keys to the car. The military helicopter was on the ground, waiting to take off. Datton started toward it as he motioned to Manlin to tell Albert something. Cardinal Manlin came closer to Albert because of the noise of the chopper and said, "Here take this. It was Fr. Anthony's." It was his wallet with a badge inside and some money that Manlin took out, saying "Hmmm, two hundred and forty dollars and a couple of one dollar bills."

Manlin put that in his pocket. He looked some more and there was a race track ticket, ten to win on the number five. Manlin looked at it and said, "This might be good," so he put that in his pocket also. Manlin opened his wallet and showed Albert his badge. It was gold and red with the symbol of the Crusaders. Albert was shocked and wanted to speak, but Datton said in a loud voice, because of the helicopter noise, "Let's go! got some Black Hawk Squadrons coming in!" Albert looked at the mountain and two jets had just pulled up over the mountain after dropping a large number of napalm bombs. Manlin shook Albert's hand as he gave Fr. Anthony's wallet to him, "Drive down; Fr. Anthony's body is waiting in Eureka, California, for you to drive it to the farm. He liked you and Jan a lot. You had guts, Albert, to come to him with the idea. You proved it and that made him happier than you'll ever know." Manlin turned and ran to the helicopter, which took off quickly and flew away from the mountain, going north. The dust that blew in Albert's eyes was almost like a blessing of nature. Albert looked in Fr. Anthony's wallet and saw the same badge as Manlin's, the symbol of the Crusades. He closed it and looked at the mountain as it burned like a volcano. Just then, a large rocket came from out of nowhere and hit the mountain with a huge boom. It probably was loud enough to be heard in Seattle. There were no jets in sight, Albert thought, and so he ran around the car and got in the driver's seat and sped away to get to the highway.

Now that Albert had gotten back off the mountain, he had to fill the car with gas just off the highway. Like a thunder cloud, the smoke filled the sky. Being far enough away from the city, you still could hear the sound of a distant explosion. "Fill it up, please," he said to the attendant. He pointed to the quality of gas he wanted. Albert turned on the radio for some music and then decided to turn to the news channel. The radio blared out "This is K-E-A-E, the all-news station. Your announcer, William Morey, with up-to-the-minute every minute news! The latest: With all the phone calls coming in from all over the city about the fire and explosions in the northern mountains above Seattle, I would like to explain this to everyone. We have word from the Banner Military Base. Commander John McCain states, 'This planned bomb and targeting exercise is a war-game live-ammo operational activity in the mountains above the city. It is completely safe! In addition, a controlled burn is being undertaken by the National Department of Forestry in the same area.'" William Morey said, "Please! Please! People, stop calling in. Here's an example of the type of calls that have been coming in to the station. A caller from East Seattle wanted to know about the volcano. Another caller in the mid-city area wanted to find out about meteoric impact. We had one caller wanting to know how long we have left to live because the Ursa Star had hit the planet." William Morey continued, "Ladies and gentleman, please, this is a controlled occurrence done by our proud Armed Forces. In other news, the stock market is up seventy-nine percent with an average DOW Industrial at nine thousand and fifty-four, point twenty-four. Gold, up one dollar, four cents, oil up ten cents, and the dollar is steady at ninety-seven. The powerhouse company Ultra has increased their stock strong hold with the buy-out of the plastics manufacturer Fury. Fury, the main developer of insulation for cars, appliances, and boat products will keep its name and come under the wing of the Ultra management group. Now, looking into sports, Jim Boom-Boom Walker scored another victory over Danny Homer in a knock-out in the third round. Jim Boom-Boom increased his record to thirty seven and zero. He....." Albert turned off the radio and rolled down the window to pay the attendant. He then drove to the highway and headed to California. He eventually reached Eureka and on the side of the road the small truck containing Fr. Anthony's body was parked. He pulled in behind it and a man came out of the cabin and handed him the keys. Albert did the same with the rental car he was driving. It would be about midnight by the time that Albert got to the farm and put the truck next to the church ready for burial. Security gave him a ride to the main house and there, asleep in the bed, was Jan. He kissed her and jumped into bed, thought for a minute, and fell asleep holding Fr. Anthony's wallet.

CHAPTER TWENTY-ONE
The Visit

I t was late at night in the middle of the country in a town outside of
Kansas City. The factory there was where the hearing devices were being
made. They were typical modern hearing-aids with the symbol of a small
cross on the middle of them. A small device with a small reminder of what
the Vatican would have done if not for Albert's suggestion beforehand. A
simple hearing-aid for everyone to keep the ill effects of the Ursa Star from
reaching the mind. The batteries have been installed and will last at least
five years, plenty of time with the expected two years of sound vibration
that would take place. This plant was a big one and they were sure to be
ahead of the deadline for producing five hundred million of them. The
other plants would do the same, making five to seven hundred million by
the year's end. With about five billion people in the world, the production
of all the devices would be an apportioned to the world's population.

The Kansas site would have new orders to be the main producer of
the hearing device. That would make jobs and businesses grow in the
area for now. This plant was expected to double its production and down
the line to build at least one billion of the hearing devices. With the
gravitational shifts going on slowly, and in some cases, definitely felt, there
was a demand that the hearing-aid devices be expedited for shipment much
more quickly. The stratosphere was now going through contractions with
the forces of the compression of space. It would alter some of the weight of
the inhabitants on the earth's surface and everything under the surface of
the planet. This brought about changes in aircraft, with the use of less fuel
in flight. Ground transportation was also affected by the changes of heavy

loads such as trains hauling material. Things that did change actually only lasted a month and then returned to normal. Not that much took place in the world, except that ten to twenty percent of the total weight of matter was somehow lost to the sky. The real effect was the opposite that did the most damage to the world. The gravity change made some buildings collapse without notice, only and blame was put on the gravitational shift. Most of the incidents that could be reported were reported and, outside the media, were just a brief mention of what took place in those remote areas. What did get mentioned were natural occurrences such as earthquakes, rain storms, tornadoes, or typhoons, but not the strange gravitational shift. In some cases, prediction of the next event became a full time job for some people with the right connections. Most were wrong or out of answers, and only tried to predict the next episode of the power of the Ursa Star.

Albert had the only explanation for the sound that would come to the planet in a form of agitating waves. It was dangerous to mankind, because it would affect the balance and nerves of the human head. The only way to stop this damage was to have the sound mixed with a low small whine that would keep the brain focused on the task of attentive cognition. Also this sound would affect all living creatures on this planet. Jan had lots to do in her observatory that Albert had built. It was situated in the rear of the house, complete with a ninety-inch mirror-aided telescope. The instruments in the observatory building gave the lab a flawless connection to the world. With links to radio, space and other telescopes, it was a state-of-the-art workroom. So Albert again began to travel, this time to Kansas too oversee the details of the production of the hearing devices made for public distribution.

Albert said, "Jan, you going to be all right here?" "I'll be fine. The Ursa Star is getting close and I am getting ready to present the explanation of the sound in the background radiation: the subatomic particle AXIONS and WIMPS explanations. It's pretty boring stuff, so you might enjoy this trip, Albert. I have a guest speaker on a mission to try to explain the state of hydrogen particles with the Big Bang in mind." "The Big Bang? What is that they see in the sky in the north? Yap! Big or Bang really slays me! Jan, you sure do know how to pick your speakers." "Wait! On second thought, I'll go with you to Kansas. That's how much I would like to hear this guy speak. He is a cosmologist that knows a lot about stars, so it might help to explain a little star theory. I don't have to be present." Albert replied, "A little about zilch to do with this Dark Star. It is moving faster than theory can explain in the particle analysis. I can't see the reason to start looking at those discoveries of active particles in a common star. The Dark Star is not a common star; it is an irregular star or something like that. Damn it! I know this! The Dark Star is headed right here, and soon. The public should get a hint of this, so that they could be warned to use the ear devices to ease their pain, and really, their lives." Jan replied, "They know it is coming this way. They can see the sky and it has grown, so there should be no problem in getting that message to them." "No! Jan, I am suggesting that you get a sociologist or someone in the field of psychiatry in your programs. You have a bunch of no-name people in the field—well, I might as well say it—astrology!" "What is wrong, Albert? You can't fool me. It is Fr. Anthony, isn't it?" Albert looked at Jan and said, "Nothing is wrong." Jan came up to Albert and hugged him. "I know you, crazy person. You can't dupe your wife, you cretin." Jan held Albert tighter and tighter. "That is it? I know, don't I?" "What is a cretin?" "You are, you big clown. OK, Albert, I'll go with you to Kansas. I can read you like a book." "You don't have to; I'll be alright." Albert looked at the wall as Jan had him in a bear hug. "Jan, I can't breathe." Jan laughed, "Now that's clear. The Dark Star does not have to get any closer for you. I've got all the answers right here. I just have to squeeze the information right out of this big cretin. I'll go with you and that is that." Albert kissed Jan's head and said, "What is a cretin?"

They had Thomas drive them to the airport and told him to take care of the farm. Albert asked Thomas what a cretin was. He looked at Albert and laughed and then got serious as he saw Jan shaking her head. He then replied, "I don't know, Mr. Lanker." They boarded their private plane and went to Kansas City, the number-one production plant for the Ursa Ear, which Albert had named after the Ursa Star. That would be the name of the product, to offset the sound, the noise, the madness of the light in the sky. The remaining time was too short to not get this product out and working for the people of the planet Earth. Albert and Jan arrived at the plant just outside the city. It was big plant and looked like an aircraft factory, with huge walls and long metal structures that could house a small mountain. The parking lot alone was so big that it looked as if the workers would need trams to get to their cars. Jan and Albert were met by a limousine at the airport and then introduced to the corporation head at the plant. Mr. Dotson greeted them both and handed them each a hard-hat. They would need to travel through the plant in a small golf cart with four seats. They first went to the south end of the plant and there was bulk plastic in huge piles. The plastic was being unloaded from flat bed trucks.

The stacks were high and the exterior of the yard was full. On fork-lifts, the raw plastic was being brought into the interior of the large structure. Mr. Dotson drove the cart inside the building, where the ceiling was high and conveyer belts rolled in plastic and boxes. The framing of all the things moving inside could be seen to be a lot like an amusement park ride. This was the raw product going in to make the Ursa Ear from nothing to something. The thought of a small toy factory came to mind in this immense structure, Albert thought. The cart drove on to where workers in one area were performing quality control on the finished devices, which were small gadgets that fit over the outer ear like hanging a clothes pin on the upper lobule. This was indeed the place for the building of these devices, where two per person had to be made in order to be effective when ear-shattering sound would fill the atmosphere.

Jan and Albert rode around with Mr. Dotson until he drove the cart to the office area of the plant. They all got off the cart and walked to a hallway where a number of elevators were located. Riding up the elevator, they came to the third floor, a carpeted floor, where the three of them went into the test lab. In this room, a number of men and women were testing the devices with equipment that could measure the effects of the signals being sent out. Mr. Dotson said, "We have the latest testing apparatus to make sure that the hearing aids are at the right frequency for the data that we were given previously." Albert knew that he had given the data to them, yet it was done by another individual. You see, Albert wanted it that way so that he could do much more with his architecture and farming, like he wanted to do. The sound that was given to this plant and all the other plants making the hearing device was at the frequency thirty four times the background sound of the universe, calculated by the radiation pressure. In this case, it would be the Ursa Star's pressure that sounded off in the sky of this planet. Mr. Dotson said, "This way." Jan led first and Albert followed, looking around at the scientists testing the devices as they walked by. They were in another room where the walls had cones of acoustics all over the flat surfaces. In the middle of the room was a table with a computer monitor. Mr. Dotson closed the door behind Jan and Albert, while he turned a couple of knobs that were on the wall that made the lights dim and desensitized the sound. It was almost like a pin could be drop and you could hear it in this muffled room. "This is zero sound and with the information received from Ultra, our parent company, we will take some tests of the Ursa Ear." As Mr. Dotson went to the computer, he hit a couple of buttons to start the sound that came from the walls of the room. It started like a low rumble, something like a large waterfall. Not that loud, the sound was rather peaceful with the mixed alteration of pitch and tone. After about a minute or two, it became more metal-like in nature, as if someone were scrapping a big glass plate. It was a shriek and then a low rumble that made the sound change nature to a buzzing annoyance. Jan put her hands on her head as if she were having a major headache. Albert looked at Mr. Dotson and said, "That's a horrible sound. Does it get worse?" Albert put his hand on the side of his face and rubbed it. Mr. Dotson said, "With the right atmospheric temperature and location, this sound could get a lot worse in frequency and cycle." He then handed Jan and Albert the hearing devices and said, "Put one on the top of each ear. They are kind of nice with the soft plastic. They just fit on like a soft paper clip on top of ear lobe." Albert looked at the device and said, "These do not have a symbol on them." Mr. Dotson replied, "These are the factory test specials. I assure you both that the ones that the public will get will have the proper symbol and instruction in the package." Albert then put the devices on his ears and Jan did the same. Mr. Dotson put some of the hearing aids on his ears and said, "Notice that the small low sound of the device blocks the sound of the cycle and dampens the frequency of the sound." Albert replied, "Yes that's good. My headache is going away and I can hear everything clearly, too." Jan agreed as she looked at Mr. Dotson and Albert while watching the computer screen with the peaks and waves illustrated on the screen. Albert said, "I didn't turn anything on. Can they be on all the time and still keep running?" Mr. Dotson said, "All yes. They are on all the time. With the battery we've put in these devices, they should last for a long, long time, about three years or more. They have no gadgets to change the adjustments of the device, so that would make it tamper-free."Albert replied, "That's great! So anyone having this device would have nothing to do except to put them on their ear." "That's correct," Mr. Dotson said. "You just have a little to do with the application of these devices to make them work."Albert and Jan left the room with Mr. Dotson and went downstairs and out to the cart to take them to the limo. Albert explained to Mr. Dotson that he and Jan had to go because they were in a rush for time.Mr. Dotson wanted to show them the packaging, so he gave Albert a big box of the hearing devices, about fifty pairs, and they both got in the limo and went to the airport.

Their private jet was waiting for them. Jan and Albert were in-flight, headed home to the farm, when Albert said, "Jan, let's go to see my parents." Jan replied, "Do you want to? I would like to see Anna and

Peter, too." Albert called the pilot to re-route the jet to Los Angeles and he changed the plane's direction at Albert's request. The small Learjet landed in Los Angeles and pulled to the far terminal for private planes. Albert had called ahead for a rental car to be waiting at the airport. Albert, the richest man in the country, had no problem with being recognized, because the company Ultra was so spread out in leadership that only the top officer knew who Albert was. He was not as lucky as Jan. She was on the television most of the time with the YDS network, so that she could be spotted by some people, but it was not a problem with their dark glasses and swift movements from place to place. Albert would drive the car to Beverly Hills to his parents house, where Anna and Peter stayed, instead of the usual limo ride. At the front gate of the mansion in Beverly Hills, Albert stopped the car. There was a speaker box that Albert pushed and said, "Hello?" It answered after about a half a minute with the voice of a man. "Yes, can I help you?" "Yes, this Albert Lanker. Is Anna there?" "Yes," as the gate slowly open. Jan had called in advance to the house to tell the butler that they were in town and would stop by. After the car was driven around the long driveway up to the front door, Anna came out of the house and opened her mother's passenger door and gave her a big hug. Albert, looking at Anna, opened his door and was met by a cocker spaniel that wanted to play, jumping on him as he wagged his tail. Anna then went around to her father and said, "Hi, daddy!" as she hugged him. The butler on the porch said, "Welcome to Los Angeles." He was a tall man with a black suit and was a little on the elderly side. They walked up to the front door where Albert was hugging Anna while Jan walked ahead of them. The dog kept rubbing and biting at Albert's leg, knowing he just wanted to play. Albert went inside and said, "Is this your dog? Peter P?" Jan said, "Why did you name the dog after your brother?" "He likes Peter; it just happened like that." Albert said after trying to walk with the dog jumping and pressing against him, "Anna, can you control him or her?" "It's a him." Then she said, "P.P.!" The dog looked at Anna and then walked to the hallway and into the back of the house where the kitchen was. Just then, a fluffy cat came out, with a slow walk, and went into the living room and lay down under the baby grand piano. The butler came down from upstairs, followed by Albert's parents. His father said, "Albert and Jan, how are you! You should have given us more notice." His mother said the same. The butler motioned them with a hand gesture to be seated in the living room.

The house was beautiful with its old wall-papered walls. The antiques were everywhere, around the walls and on tables in the front rooms. The windows had silk-like curtains, hung with gold-colored rods. The fireplace was large and had strange figures in front of it, like they came from a English depository. They all sat on the Victorian-style sofa and began to talk. "So! Anna, how are you doing at your school?" "School? I'm in an internship at the hospital. I should have my license in about a year." Albert said, "I know that! So, what kind of doctor are you going to be?" "I think I would like to work with children; still, I like the field of anesthesiology and I think that's what I will be, an anesthesiologist. It's a lot of work; nothing like the easy field of architecture." "Easy?" Albert's father began to laugh and so did his mother. "What kind of work is it, where you sit down all day drawing little pictures on computers and boards? I keep telling Grandpappy that he needs to jog and get his exercise." "It is a lot of work, young lady. I keep telling you about finding the cure for arthritis." Albert laughed and said, "Walking is good. You have this big estate; you could do a couple of miles easy here." "And do the work that Anna gives us to do?" Albert looked confused and said, "Work?" Albert's father said, "Anna, got us on health food and walks us around the pool in the morning." Anna laughed, "Yeah, that's under a mile and besides we eat breakfast out there anyway." Jan said, "That's good that you look after your grandparents. Where is Peter? Well," Albert's father said, "He is pretty busy right now." "How busy can he be? He works in one of my firms." Albert's mother said, "We should have told you." Jan interrupted, "I'll tell him. Peter got married about a month or two ago." Albert looked at Jan and said, "Married? Why didn't you tell me?" Jan said, "Because you are a grandfather." "What? He has children?" "Not children; just one child, and another on the way. You were traveling at the time. He tried to tell you, but it was about the time that you were dealing with the affairs of Fr. Anthony." "Did he have a wedding?" Albert's father and mother said, "We went to Las Vegas. It was quick. He loves her dearly, so we made sure got the right girl." Albert said, "Is he still living here?" he Albert's father said, "No, he lives in a condo on Wilshire. It's a nice place overlooking the city. He has been there for some time now."

"Anna, you should have told me!" Anna called out, "P.P." And just then you could hear the dog come running into the living room. P.P. first went to Anna and then tried to jump on Albert's lap. Albert exclaimed, "What is with this dog?" Anna said, "He's just like you, daddy." "Must be the aftershave, hmm." Everyone got up to walk around the house and then to the backyard, where the pool was located."You know, Victor has been married for some time," Anna said. "Anna, my baby girl, how about you?" She replied, "I have a good friend. I am not ready for marriage, though. I want to be a well-rounded doctor before that. I've seen Peter and Victor. We all are still close, very close." Jan laughed, "You know, Anna has been getting around for me." Albert said, "See dad, my family is out of control. I don't know anything anymore."Albert's mother said, "It is a woman's thing. Do you men ever take time to look up from that drawing board and notice that the world is going on?" All four of them sat down outside. It was such a sunny day and the temperature was nice and warm. "Well anyway, I stopped by to surprise you people and it looks like I have gotten all the surprises." Just then, the butler and the maid walked toward them with some small sandwiches and cups of beverages. They all said thank you. Albert's mother had told them to prepare a little brunch for them outside when Albert was fighting off the dog who was chewing at his leg. Now Anna had the dog go to his house, way beyond the pool. Albert and Jan, after cleaning their hands with small towels, loaded their plates and began to eat and drink with everyone. They were enjoying their meal when Albert's father began looking at the sky where you could see the Dark Star, even with the bright sun out. The Dark Star was like, or just as bright as, the moon in the daytime sky. You could see the Dark Star clearly and its spin at the center. It was bigger than the moon and took some of the sky away because the color did not conform to the nice light blue of the atmosphere.

Albert's father said, "What is it going to do?" Albert watched his father looking at the Dark Star in the sky. Albert's mother said to his father, "Jan is the astronomer. You should ask her about that?" Jan said, "You will be surprised how much Albert knows about the Ursa Star." Albert's father said to Jan, "I did not mean that you did not know, Jan. Your show is a good one. We watch it all the time." "It was Albert's idea. I just go with the information I have." Albert said, "I don't know what I would do without Jan." Albert grabbed Jan's shoulder and kissed her. "Well, I am glad you asked. It is going to come closer to the planet and make this sound that everybody will hear for years." "The neutrino bursts were hard on us old people. Another thing, Albert, how did you get so much money to do all that building and even buying us this mansion?" "You know Ultra? Well, I own that company." Albert's father and mother said, "What! You mean you did all those things with the church and television." Albert looked at his mother like she already knew it and said, "Yes, it was me. No, really Jan and me. We've both been doing our share of the work." Anna, still looking at the backyard and how beautiful it was, said, "I knew that. Mom told me a long time ago. Peter and Victor knew too." Albert's father said, "Now, you see, we are the only ones that didn't know that completely!" Albert said, "Really dad, keep it a secret. I really don't tell anyone about that." Albert's father, with a smile, knowing he helped with his architecture company, said, "That means you are the richest man in the world?" "Maybe. I don't know about the world. There are some rich kings out there. Well, let's say the richest in this country and, you know, I like to stay in the background without all the media or public knowing about it. So I hear you are in a golf club and mother is in a gardening society. See how news travels, OK!" "Our lips are sealed," Albert's mother said. Albert's father looked at Albert and put his hand on his jaw, saying "Dang it, I should have put that marble in those bottom floors of the last building I designed for you, Albert. I thought it would save money to put in the tile." Albert shook his shoulders. "It was a good design with the tile. It didn't matter that much."Albert got up after everyone was pretty comfortable talking in the backyard on very expensive outdoor furniture. "Let me go get something out of the car. It is very important." They all looked at Albert as he walked into the house and P.P. made a dash for Albert. Albert saw him coming and closed the sliding door to block the fun-loving dog. Anna called, "P.P." And the dog went back to his nice-looking dog house. While Albert was away, Albert's mother mentioned, "How do you do it, Jan, being married to the richest man?" They both laughed, even Anna and Albert's father. "He is still Albert, you know, the boss!" His father laughed aloud and everyone began to laugh at that remark. "You know, it seems like just days ago that Albert wanted to design just one building and now he can't find a building he didn't design." They continued to laugh and tried to drink some of the beverage on the table. Jan regained her composure and said, "No, really, he been working really hard. Albert puts a lot into his work with me and you guys. You know he loves you all a lot." "But He is a farmer now!" Albert's father said. They all started laughing again. Anna spit part of her drink on the ground, she was laughing so much. "Yep! We all are proud of him.

We count our blessings every day for what he has done for us. Look at this place." Jan said, "Yes, it is very pretty. Who selected the roses." "Ahh, I got a little club of ladies that have monthly meetings. It's just local stuff." Jan said, "Albert's farm is a nice place too." Anna said, "Yes, it is. I told them about it. The only thing is that it is out in the basin, away from everything." Jan replied, "It is good for seeing the stars, and besides, Albert likes it there. He feels he could do more out there." Just as Jan was going to say more, P.P. began to run to the glass door. Albert said, "Anna." She got up and said, "P.P." The dog looked at her and walked back to his house slowly, watching Albert coming toward the table and chairs where everyone sat.Albert was carrying a box about as big as a shoe box and put it on the table. "So what's going on? Looks like someone has swallowed a canary." Anna replied, "We were just discussing your job as a farmer." They all laughed, even Albert. "Hey, that's no easy job plowing those fields. It's a lot of work." "What do you have there, son?" "Oh yeah. This is the device you must wear when the sound of the Ursa Star begins to come around." Albert pulled a smaller box out of the larger box. He opened the box and put two small hearing-aids on the table. Albert's mother said, "Will this help us or do we have to do something else to make these ear devices work?" Albert answered, "No, just wear them. They are really simple devices; nothing to do except put them on each ear." Anna said, "What if we don't put them on?" "Anna, don't be silly. Your pop is literally trying to ease your pain. This is no joke. The Ursa Star will do some damage soon. You will find that it will help you maintain your sanity." Jan replied, "It's true, Anna. It is very important to have this on to keep your mind focused." Albert went over to his father and put the hearing-aids on each ear. He looked at Albert's face. "I don't hear anything." "Can you hear me talking to you?" "Fine, I hear you just like before." "Good, OK, you can take them off. Your ears hurt or anything? Are the clips too tight?" "No, they feel fine. And you said we have to have these things?" "Yep, or it could be brutal. Don't worry, they will last a long time. You don't have to do anything but wear them. Also, you people have seen these first. They will be distributed all over the world. For now, it is hush-hush." Albert's mother said, "Albert, so you do know everything the Ursa Star is going to do, don't you?" "Some of the things, but after that sound comes here it is a anybody's guess," Albert said. Albert put the box on the table and said, "You have twenty-five pairs of these devices, so if you have friends who don't have a pair when the sound comes, you know you've got some spares. Anna, you know what to do with them and make sure mom and pop have them on all the time." Albert's father replied, "Come on, we're not babies!" Albert looked at Jan. "We've got to get back to the farm." Anna got up and hugged Albert and said, "Can't you stay the night? You know we miss you both." "I miss you too, Anna. Come on, you are a big girl now." "We just don't see much of each other." Jan said, "Anna, call us. You will be all right, Dr. Lanker, the first doctor in the family I might add." Albert said, "What about your boyfriends?" "You know me. I am a family person, and friends come second. I already have too many of them, really, just not like family." "OK, come with mom and pop sometime and visit us one weekend. You don't want to leave them alone, Anna." Albert's father said, "What! Do you think we are babies?" "No, pop, just trying to keep the family in one piece." Jan and Albert began to walk to the house and P.P. began running again at Albert. It was odd this time that Albert looked at P.P. and picked him up as he licked Albert's face. Albert thought it was a nice dog and said, "Oh my God! Look at the ears on this creature. I completely forgot about the animals, They will be affected by the Ursa Star, too!" Jan said, "That is right, since they should be the first to hear the star coming." "Anna," Albert pointed to the boxes on the table while everyone was standing. He put P.P. down and began to put the hearing devices on P.P.'s ears. He didn't like it and shook his head to get them off, while trying to use his paw to scrape the hearing-aids from his head. Anna said, "He'll get used to it. I'll tape it to his head if I have to." Albert was a bit concerned about what would happen to the small animals of the world with the sound coming from the star. "Don't forget the cat, too. Anna, what is the name of the cat?" "What?" "Let me guess: Tinkle?" Anna said, "No, it's Fluffy!" Albert looked at Jan, "Now I know where I get my grandchildren's names like Toby and Charlie. good grief!" They walked to living room and to the front door where the butler and the maid were standing and they said, "It has been a pleasure to meet you, Mr. and Mrs. Lanker." Albert said, "Nice to see you. Yes, the house looks marvelous. You have done a nice job, and call us Jan and Albert.

These two are Mr. and Mrs. Lanker," pointing at his mother and father. Albert also said, "You can call Anna the quack." Jan patted Albert on His back. "Albert! That's not nice." Albert laughed and hugged Anna and said, "Keep up the good work. Remember, you are my only girl. I am really proud of you. Call me anytime, Anna, promise." Anna, with little tears in her eyes, said, "OK, daddy." Albert continued, "Look, you can do anything you want. I will still be proud of you Anna, got it?" Anna agreed. "Check on Peter and get me some pictures of those children of his, and remember that Victor is your brother, too, you know! auntie." Anna had a smile on her face, "Grandpapa!" Albert said to his mother and father, as he gave them a final hug, "These are Great Grandpeople." Jan gave them a hug also, "I will be on the line. You know where to reach me; you too, Anna," in a low voice that Albert could not hear. Albert and Jan went downstairs and to the car in the driveway. Anna was holding P.P. with one device on his ear; he gave a small bark. Albert said to his parents as the butler and maid opened the door for Jan and Albert, "Remember to use those devices!" Albert's father again exclaimed, "What do you think we are, babies?" Albert moved his hand like he was drawing something on it so his father could see it. Anna looked at Albert's father and let P.P. go from her grip. P.P. was running around the car and Albert got in the car quickly to avoid the dog chewing on his leg. The butler, standing near Albert, got the dog by the collar and held him. They waved, and Jan and Albert drove away through the open gate and to the airport, where their private jet was waiting.

CHAPTER TWENTY-TWO
Bewilderment

Time had passed since that trip to see Albert's parents. Meanwhile, back at the farm, Albert and Jan were awaiting the sound from the sky to start. With the calculations that Jan had made, the Ursa Star was way overdue. Albert was patient, thinking that it would happen when it happens. There were also some more new discoveries for Jan that the company Far-Seeing would give her credit for. Jan discovered two new comets in the direction of the Orion constellation, in the southern sky, completely by chance. Albert said it was just luck because Jan was indeed just getting another reading on the telescope's spectrum. Finally, something began to happen at night. Nothing that Jan heard or that Albert could point to would explain the idea that the Dark Star was ready to do damage to the world in a big way. The two of them had gone to bed in the huge mansion on the farm, when Albert decided to watch a little television as Jan slept. She had just been so busy all day, with the third and fourth graders in a session about astronomy. It just drained the energy out of Jan. It was really a basic lecture on the YDS channel, yet it took a lot of work to keep the focus on the Ursa Star for the children to get the concept of space and its elements. Albert was about to change the channel when a special report came on the news. It would change the way the world lived and acted as the Ursa Star began to pull the mind of everyone and everything apart. It was a special report about the country of China, in the middle of the day. The news was about the animals in the surrounding forest making strange noises and attacking small villages. From wild to domesticated animals, they took to a bizarre killing spree with human beings included. It was not only the small towns of these reports but Albert was looking at reports from large cities that were now under attack from any and all animals. Knowing that this could mean the first real sign of the damaging sound of the Dark Star, Albert called his parents late in the night to tell them to lock the dog and cat in the pool house. He further explained that they would become dangerous at the morning sun. Albert then nudged Jan to make her wake up and see the news that was coming from every part of the world. He had all the channels with the satellite-linked television, so he looked at most of the countries that were on the other side of the planet. It did seem that the Ursa Star had looped the sound wave to reflect the sunny side of the planet. The daytime side would have the most affect of the sound waves from the star. Jan told Albert that this sound must act like a sonic boom, back sliding the waves to bounce back after they had passed the planet. "Strange," Jan remarked, "The wave of sound must have passed us days or weeks ago, making the star really close to us now.

Albert continued to look at the countries that had the daytime, and did not notice any other countries with a massive outbreak of animal attacks. The attacks were mostly in the area around China. Even the heavily-occupied Japan did not report anything strange with the outbreak of animals attacking humans. In the morning, Albert called Mr. Knoll at Ultra to tell him that it was time to start distributing the ear devices right away. Mr. Knoll replied that everything was ready to go and he would instruct his worldwide contacts to have the hearing devices put on the market. The devices would run about fifteen dollars for each person in United States. It was amazingly cheap, compared to the research investment and the need for the devices all over the world. Albert's company would make a small profit from only the shipping and handling of the product. Some parts of the world, such as parts of Africa and some Third World countries, would get the devices for free. In many cases, some compensation would be given to Ultra in the form of products that were then offered to the market and sold for profit. Mr. Knoll and some of the other top executives and officers would do a good job of marketing the product to places that needed them the most. The sound of the Ursa Star was at full range weeks after distribution of the hearing devices and most people had the notion that the hearing devices were not going to stop the headache that this Star caused. Every day, they went to medical professionals seeking help, anything that would help stop the sound that blared in their minds. Albert told Mr. Knoll to do more advertising to sell the product because of the rash of quackery.

The devices that Ultra marketed were the best thing for stopping the flood of sound. They were placed in airport lobbies, train stations, gas stations, grocery stores, banks, and post offices. It wasn't until the United States government stepped in with the marketing of this device, using the banks and post offices, that they became effective. They had been watching Mr. Knoll very carefully in the steps that he took in getting the product to the people at a fair price and that price was simply too much for the Government to take. The devices took a strong hold on the market competing with aspirins and other types of drugs that seemed to halt the effects of the Ursa Star's sound. There were contraptions that you could lie in for a short amount of time and find relief. There were things to put on your head to stop the sound, such as a hat that was an ear-blocking thingamajig, but there was one big problem: you could not hear a thing when you were wearing it. The products came out in the hundreds worldwide, claiming that they had the only necessary cure for the sound that rained from the sky. Some people did have a cure in their own eyes; they would do many things that made no sense. The United States government knew the only answer to do with these devices: because of the monopoly, they had to buy out the manufacturer because the military had to have the devices. The government brought Mr. Knoll to the capitol building to talk. Mr. Knoll answered everything that the government officials asked, but Ultra had such a grip on the foreign market that it made the competitive market in the United States a losing battle in the purchase of the hearing devices. It was the head of YDS, Joel Steven, Jan's brother, who put the product over the top in sales. It could have been the cheap price or the availability of the product that made the sales soar every day. So as Albert had predicted, the United States government would eventually buy out the product and with this purchase would exempt the Ultra company from ever paying taxes again.

ULTRA would become a company that was supported by the United States, with all the technology and advances in all fields that affected the public, with the help of a special committee in the government domain. Any foreign trade would be made with the seal of the United States of America on the product and a bunch of other facts that made the United States the sole bearer of the goods. Albert told of the Vatican's symbol on the hearing devices will not be compensated for this agreement. Mr. Knoll said that this deal would not affect the production of this product except that it would be sent to the United States for boxing and handling. Albert agreed and discovered that his company was doing the right thing, even if all the companies he owned led their way to him as being the sole owner. The government knew that Albert was the owner of Ultra, but they respected him and his wife for doing the best for the country by warning the people of this astronomical event. That is why they wanted the Lankers' ownership to remain a private matter, because they were actually helping the economy, financially and physically. You see, the riots and confusion did not take place because of the investment that Albert negotiated with the Pope and others that kept the public a well-advised group without altercation. People went to work and did their jobs without panicking about the Ursa Star.

The day came when the world was under the full domination of the Ursa Star's sound. Most people had the ear devices to protect them. Those that didn't have the devices had some medical treatment done to try to restore their memory of where they were. The effects of the huge star caused people to become so brainwashed that they eventually went mad.

On the street, a man was making his usual rounds, collecting things that could be recycled. His cart, a simple shopping trolley, was filled with all the bottles, cans, and paper that it could hold. This man had his hearing devices on last week, because the handout to the poor was something that Ultra wanted, knowing that they would not be able to afford them. Ultra had worked with many charities and churches to help the poor first in addition to the food and clothing that were provided to the lower class of this country. Not like a mission or rehabilitation center. Ultra allowed those that asked for a gift to have a new chance at making something of themselves by going to the Ultra camp. The camp was in a large town, or some called it a small city, in the middle of Kansas. They made products and educated people for new trades for those who asked. It was not new to the idea, except it was the only camp that provided housing at no charge to those who came. It was sure the best thing they could do with what they had, on account of the Kansas plant would later be changed to make products for housing. This was just one of the new ideas that Mr. Knoll and Albert had in mind to help people. The wages were respectable for those that enter the camp. Those who were not in the best condition due to their addiction to drugs, liquor, psychological problems would receive a lower pay, since part of their money would go to pay for support services. Sure, the regular law enforcement was present in these sectors, which looked just like neighborhoods with tree-lined streets that were maintained by the people living there. The plan worked well because of the hope of learning a trade and career, plus being employed by Ultra, the power-house enterprise that secured their future. It was only a small part of Albert's philosophy to get the organizations involved in the planning, because he knew that the poor would always be a part of everyday life, no matter what you do to prevent it. There were a total of ten of these neighborhoods around the world, so it was no surprise to see that Albert was being nominated for some humanitarian award that he felt he did not deserve because he looked at it as business.

It had been about a week that the man with the cart had been going down the street with no protection from the sound that rained on his weak mind, saying things like THUS -THAT! THUS IT! It made people gawk and stare. He put his can-filled cart in the middle of the freeway and started to shout. THUS! THUS! Strange as it might seem, the man began to fade in and out of reality. THUS! THUS IT! The cars stopped in the middle of the roadway to avoid the man from becoming vicious while waving something that looked from a distance like a large shotgun. He began to slowly dissolve into a fog, as the cars came at a standstill on the freeway. It was surreal. With the police looking at him and ready to apprehend him, he suddenly floated up to the sky in what looked just like a small cloud. In fact, it looked like a piece of broken fog or a puff of steam vapor that floated upward and out of sight. As it was heading up, just before leaving the ground, the words of the man emerged again. AMTIMAS IS REAL! --THUS! AMITMAS IS REAL! -HE TRAVELS-THUS AMTIMAS IS REAL! This was happening in main traffic and was videotaped by three or four people that were affiliated with the news. After that, the fear came to the public to dread the thought of not wearing the hearing devices. The man was clearly mad in his mind and the other things involved that took place made the public search for some type of answers.

Albert, the only one that knew what this appearance was about and to see the rush of the news about this strange occurrence, was hardly surprised. Yes, there were strange occurrences all over the world, from large swarms of bird attacks, to fish in the millions swimming so close to shore that the water for miles was white, as they thrashed around in the waves. Bug attacks and even snakes were found in office buildings in large quantities and also the constant common word of mouth about the domestic animal attacks. The attacks were made mainly on dogs and cats, and those who live close to nature where mountains were around. The deaths toll began to drop steadily after people got wise to the danger. Yet it was hard to explain the disappearances, in view of the fact that the animals would eat their victims, bones and all. Beasts of burden were not all that willing to be handled; also, they too would kick and bite at humans in the daytime. So horse races were cancelled just because of the horses acting so wild. Nighttime racing was the only thing running at all the racetracks in any country for the safety of the public.

Albert began to think about the man that had floated into space, trying to understand that why it could have happened in the daytime. Albert knew that Amatimas was a daytime dream of the future about the devastation of the planet Earth. Albert thought deeply, as best he could, to recall the dream that had revealed most of the events that were occurring. Albert sat at his desk and put both hands on his head and closed his eyes and tried hard to picture the dream. The dream of what he recalled would make it to one of his little black books. Albert started to remember the beginning of the dream that captured his mind and body.

It was at the place of Attica. It was the first unit of stone of the base of a marble structure. The dream explained that it should be at a ninety-degree angle, at the right side of the base. It controlled the celestial pattern of the zodiac for the nations. Albert stopped and wrote down some notes about this part of the dream. The celestial pattern to the nations would have to be in the range of all the zodiac signs in that type of calendar. The nations would be an enigma to him because of the time and position of the signs. Albert recalled the astrological signs: Sagittarius, Capricorn, Virgo, Leo, and so on. The months would be made with each sign of the zodiac and at this point he could not tell what that meant about the construction. Albert continued, Therefore giving, Thus, interpretation of, are the present state, "Enough!" said the robed god of his statements as he waved his golden staff and walked back to his dwelling. This instruction to the common laborer was correlated as to the calculations of the unknown numbers. The way that most calculations were done by him was to break each number into two, then that by three to show equal portion. Now with this, Albert could figure out most of this about the numbers and the meaning of the calculations. Albert wrote down the simple numbers of six divided by two, than divided by three and that equaled one. Albert, again took twelve, divided that by two and then divided it by three and got the number two. He thought about it and went on remembering more of the dream. The robed god reappeared and said, "What a spectacular display, what a fantastic view for the first of the gods of importance for the total structure. It will have the main face of the god known to the Greeks as Zeus. It will be the rim of the wharf, for the gleam and the glare of all sides of the structure's mega-penetrative walls. Again, Albert started to think about the dream's interpretation of the mega-penetrative walls. All he could think of was the deep space wall of galaxies that astronomers had talked about. Albert took this meaning to be wishful thinking and realized it might mean walls of a building.

He stood as a feather-light man, made of some fog-like image. He was not a ghost but was made of wrapped robes and a crown of dried leaves, and his name was Panitive Possideous Mandula. His age was unknown but was presented only by the stars, in which the calculations were made by the coming comets and celestial shift. That is how the duties of his work were inherently done. The speech was clear and human-like, except for the interruption of each phrase made with the word, Thus.

Thus-, Make each phase of the cut stone by the measurement of the setting sun's green phase, which can only be seen from the special area of the Mediterranean summit. Albert knew that the green phase might mean the green flash that appears sometimes at sunset. It was the light skipping off the upper atmosphere that caused that green flash, just before the sun had completed its setting. Albert had read about this some time ago and thought that northern Europe was where it could be seen. In the Mediterranean area closer to the equator, it would be strange but with the summit in that area it was possible, maybe. Thus- In which the speed of light multiplied by the distance traveled by that calculation, would yield in increments of one lunar phase. Thus- The third moon of the planet Jupiter. Thus- By material strength, it shall be measured by the gravitational compression on top of the base of the structure. Thus- The art of each framework's expression shall be the zenith of at all times of. Thus-Entre. Thus-. Albert then went to the books around his desk and could not find the one he wanted. So he left the room and found the book in the hallway, and brought the book to his desk and found what he wanted. The compression in the frame of gravity of the planet Mercury would be a little more than one third of the Earth's. With the compressed rock from this planet, it could not be as compressed as Earth and then again, the heat of the planet might just change the process of the density and the depth at which the rock is found. Albert wrote down that the rock could be a diamond type or volcano ash. He put both in his notes. He then looked up the third moon of the planet Jupiter. It would have to be either Ganymede or Europa, but Albert was not sure which one. With Jupiter's day being about four hours long, since the planet makes a complete revolution in a little less than ten hours, it could be a short time for the lunar phase. Still, Albert could not decipher what it might mean, other than a reference to the construction of some type of building. Then again, the fog-like god had told him to find answers about the construction process, but so far, he had no answers. The whole thing was as new to him as the calculation of the universe. It was as different as the planet Pluto. He was bewildered.

Thus-, The main entry shall be made of the compressed rock from the planet Mercury. It is maintained by the mass of its gravity. Thus-Giving the density of each portal entry a sound compact existence; each wall of the four square corners shall also contain substances of reliable stability. Thus-One half the base shall. Thus-Contain. Thus-

As a reference, the only way to obtain this structural substance is by direct contact with the mass, by means unknown to anyone but the fog-like god. His methods are made by his own means and by that he demonstrates his direct placement of the material.

Albert would continue to find answers and did his best to search his memories of the second dream that he had that night, so long ago in a strange land. The second dream was so different from the first, yet just as powerful. The second dream was about a silent-looking creature called a Roamart. It stood like a tree, as tall as a 50-story skyscraper, and walked like a horse. Now all that Albert could think of was a Roamart. He thought of all the zodiac creatures from Leo the lion to fishes and crabs and even the centaur of Sagittarius. But it was confusing, because there was no creature so described. Perhaps it meant a building in which people lived. Albert remembered that his knowledge of architecture had played a brief role in the dream. Albert moved into this dream again, searching for the vision. The wall of the last floor was finally put into place. It was as long as the total building, but it did not originate from the time of Frank L. Wright or Ken Venturi. Wright's cantilever in suspended horizontal fashion would not support the idea that the style of the modernistic theories existed long before the invention of steel and concrete or before the sound of music in human ears. It might as well be said that Venturi adapted an old idea with his mother's house of angles and half-circles. But who cares whether the speed of light is only relative to the framework of a fixed object. It only works from one point of view, but from an alternative view it is a man-made crayon drawing. Its adolescent existence in the framework of the other bodies presented in the universe is the most important view. Albert stopped thinking and tried to focus on the idea of drawings and symbols that would be on the buildings. But he quickly gave up on that track, because there were just too many symbols to think about. Albert remembered something about the speed of light, which is about one hundred and eighty-six thousand miles per second. The matter of light and its trajectory are faster than its own existence, but there is a point of the elements in light of where the prediction is that the speed will travel faster than the speed predicted. As it stands, the dis-appointive existence of light, as to where it's predicted target is influenced, is underestimated. By this folly, man must be more than the span of his existence. Albert remembered that he had done some calculations in the dream, now the only reasonable thing he could focus on.

Albert remembered Athens, the land of the Greeks, who found a way to develop the native architecture. As it is, the natives understand the symbols of the land. Amatimas Draconis, an unknown philosopher who was never written about or heard of before, expressed his reasoning about the geography of the land of the native people of the Greece. It stands as the morning sun and the evening star of the ancient land. The people find no direction from the sun and the sun finds no positives in the people, but the two are the same. They find how the day travels and how they should travel by day, but it's no direction. It's no direct persuasion; it simply states the reason for their existence. Real is real and fake is not real, but the two prove their existence over time. The two find no common direction but by the one complete day. But it is the way the two find the day, the complete day. Amatimas is real. To see the fact is not a fake, but the unseen fake is not the real. There is no unseen solution to the fake of what is real. There is not or could not be seen how the fake can be real but to time and that time, not by day. No! No! Not by a star, No! No! Only a product of traveling. Amatimas is real. He travels by what mankind has not conceived and he will never find his own way until he can perceive his own existence, and that does not work. No! No! It is a fake to say it is real, but Amatimas is real.

Like the architrave, the pillar stands in place, not by the road side and not by the shore, because those ideas are only for reference books. But it is real and Amatimas is real, proven by the travel of the pillar. Of the pillar, the foundation of it, is of travel and Amatimas does travel what is real. The architrave is proof of Amatimas the philosopher and the pillar is what? It is the land-Thus. Albert wrote down AMATIMAS, and looked at the newspaper and tried to figure out why this man would call for AMATIMAS?

It was not that anybody in his dream called out for AMATIMAS, except that it could have been Panitive Possideous Mandula. Yet it could have been any strange person that might have appeared with the energy of the Dark Star. Jan walked into the room, half asleep, and looked at Albert's drawing board. Albert had remembered some, but not all, of the dream. It was like pulling nails out a wet board that had been compressed in water. He looked at Jan, "Did you see this newspaper about the strange supernatural event that took place in Los Angeles somewhere around downtown?" Jan said, "The man on the news that disappeared into thin air? I heard about it on the television. I think it was some magic trick that someone planned." Albert looked at Jan again and then looked at the newspaper that Thomas brought in daily: "I guess it could have been that, but they said in the paper here that the police expected to have no explanation for the happening. The man had no identification. They did not know who he was, even with the fingerprints lifted from the shopping cart that he left behind. And in the shopping cart there was an expensive telescope made in thirteenth century, and a piece of ancient stone tablet with writings on it and a work of art that looked like a weather vane. The things they found were priceless articles." "I read this? Dirt in bags that contain the soil of strange substances. One reporter said it was like red soil from Mars and soil from the Moon or the planets. Wait! Jan look at this! Two books: one of them was the Rudophine Tables and another was about the plans of an observatory built on Hveen." Jan said, "That sounds like something that Tycho Brahe did. Let's see; fifteenth century or around that time. Now that is strange!" Albert said, "I thought so too. You know this guy was at one of the Ultra camps in Europe. How did he get to Los Angeles? His food slips that the Ultra camps used to give away were in the shopping cart as well. They were old slips from when the neighborhood projects were just getting off the ground, about the time that they started building the first housing projects, years ago."

CHAPTER TWENTY-THREE
Star Men

Tycho Brahe was a dreamer who thought he knew the world and the sky. He would build a large observatory in a small place away from everyone to find his dreams, in order to explain the universe which everyone could see and point to and make up their own ways of understanding. Why take the time to do what this Mr. Brahe did? He did not have any telescope to look closely at the stars or planets. He would do his guessing from parts of measured iron contraptions that could only give false readings and yet reinforce the idea that he was doing something worthwhile. Yes, he was wrong, and he thought he was the only one who had the answer to the motions of the heavens. What a nose to peek into the depths of space, this Mister Brahe! He was the smell of the big picture of what the cosmos had to offer. Not to say that Mr. Brahe was trying to do something in the field of looking at the sky for the answers that certainly astronomers tended to do. It was an attempt to make a statement to the world, even if his house was bigger than most. On Hveen is where he had did his work and to feel that there were answers to be found seemed reasonable. Jan had not thought to look him centuries later for the answers. His answers didn't seem relevant.

Jan knew that Mr. Brahe's work did make it into the history books. As with the work of Nicolaus Copernicus or Claudius Ptolemaeus, he had plenty of mathematical arguments. Might as well mention the rest of the bunch: Johannes Kepler and his motions and also Galileo Galilei, with time to think about the fact that a discovery might get you time in jail. But why be right, when a look at the sky could confuse you with so many conflicting ideas that would make your head spin. There are just too many things to look at in the deep night of the sky. Just too much star stuff that has been in motion for so many years before anyone here was even born. A quadrillion cube a quadrillion is still a small number when counting the stars in the universe. You can't start to count the number of what is truly infinitesimal. Where do you start? What do you look at to call the first star? From what point do you measure the light of past time twinkle? From here, we can see how their eyes glimmered as they began to chart the numbered fire balls of hydrogen gas. Or maybe just chart the elements of time, the beginning and never-ending sky of the deep, far-distant long-range sea of darkness. If the light is for the world to see, then it is just a shallow universe in all our minds. A light year might be enough to travel and then again a parsec just rounds off the numbers in the distance. How do you incorporate the kiloparsec and the megaparsec into the equation—that the light of something round goes the other way as well. It staggers the mind to realize that theories get tired, just like the light. Einstein's theories have just too much math for the stars to follow orders and return to their original spark. You might as well believe in Darwin and that creatures have evolved out of the water. It would be a stage of life to have the travel of space to the adaptation of our mortal souls to grow and change. Hard to believe, if the quadrillion cube a quadrillion stars in the sky evolved accidentally by natural adaptation. VERY, VERY HARD TO BELIEVE. I BELIEVE IN CREATION.

Tycho Brahe did see something in the sky of his folly. A supernova in full burst might have said something about the changing matter of the universe—a bright light in the sky that made its way to the eyes of a man who was taking notes. Well looking at the sky at night for a long time, it would not be uncommon to see something happening in the clear cold darkness. Still, was it the Dark Star that he saw, or a form of it? The man screaming out the name Amatimas that went to the clouds was not wrong in having the architectural plans of Tycho's home in his shopping cart. Was this man from the time of Brahe? And what were these materials he had collected? Let's not say any more. Let's just pretend that it was only a stranger among the vast crowd on the planet Earth as the Dark Star accelerated on its way here.

It was on its way, faster and faster than anybody thought it could be. The time was getting short for everyone on this planet to be judged by the elements of space, and no one could stop it. Jan said, "Albert, I have some work to do in the lab and that's all I wanted to tell you." Albert said, "I'll be right here. I'll have some more figures for you when I get finished with these notes." Jan left the room and went downstairs and outside to the observatory. Albert finished his notes on what he thought the dreams meant and what figures could be expected from the Dark Star. He looked at what the planets suggested in the figures about how it would affect Earth. In certain parts of Albert's dream, the acts of Panitive Possideous Mandula were about building a structure for the god Zeus. Albert remembered all the things about Zeus and wrote them down. Zeus had fallen from the heavens and was the god who was related to thunder. "Hmmm," Albert thought, "this sound that is coming from the Dark Star is something like that." It was the book that Albert got that really had some of the best answers to what he wanted. In it, a picture of the west pediment of the Temple of Zeus showed the answer. The battle between the centaurs and the lapiths was the answer that could explain the Zodiac sign that Albert was looking for. Sagittarius, the centaur, or archer, is a symbol on the Zodiac calendar. In the sky, the constellation Sagittarius is at about the center of our galaxy in comparison to Earth. After Albert did some more direct observation, he went on with his notes.

Now that Albert had done some more checking, he went to the planet Jupiter and found that the Zeus's name appeared in conjunction with this planet. Now Jupiter was clearly something that Albert wanted to find out about: how the planet rotated and how large it was. After checking some tables, he found his troubling answers. Amatimas was the next thing that Albert wanted to figure out. Amatimas traveled by the pillar, then he somehow used the architrave. Albert looked at some calculations and one was at a right angle to whatever the point of travel is for the direction of Amatimas. He was a philosopher of nature, so there would be some form of calculation that Amatimas would have to do to travel. Albert got his answers and then wrapped up his papers, picked up his little black book, and went to see Jan in the observatory. As Albert walked into the lab, he saw Jan busy at the computer terminal, typing in data from a long sheet of paper. Albert grabbed Jan by the shoulders as she was sitting down: "Honey, you have anything new that I should know about?" Jan replied, "Maybe. With this latest data that I have from YDS, it looks like the matter of the star is in range to get a reading on its actual speed. Another thing: it looks like the sound of the star is diminishing. The shadow of the sound is still an unpredictable echo, though." Albert said, "That looks like that would be right. The things that the Dark Star is doing right now are compatible with the nature of its origin."

It had turned morning and the two of them were still sitting at the computer monitors, eyes fixed on the data feed streaming in. Lizzy, who was awake, asked the two if they would like some breakfast. Jan replied that they would like to have a light one, with an egg or two and a couple of strips of bacon. Albert agreed, "Two cups of coffee would do fine also, Lizzy." Lizzy walked out the observatory door and across the long path to the main house. It was about two hundred yards to the house and Lizzy could see the farm clearly in all directions. The fields had just been plowed and the dirt had the appearance of being from different planet. Out in the south field and also to the west, Lizzy could see the large tractor that Albert sometimes drove. She could tell by the smoke that shot into the air like a canon whenever the gas was applied. She turned away from the south as she got closer to the house and looked at the northern sky. Below, the north fields, heading a little to the east, did not look like the other fields. The small plants still remained on the surface, like they did after the harvest. Some of the plants had begun to grow again and were higher than the others. In the distance, as far as she could see, there was a group of trucks with open backs, and the workers were filling them up with plant material. Lizzy looked up at the sky and there, taking some of the horizon with it, was the Dark Star. Spinning like a huge drain in someone's bath tub, taking in parts of space that could only be huge stars and distant galaxies. It looked so big that the natural sky seemed different. The planet looked like a piece of flat land out in space, the next thing to be in the path of this huge distorted eye.

Lizzy reached the back door and went into the house in obvious fear as she took a second look at the sky and then the gleaners in the field. Albert, with Jan in the observatory going over his notes in the little black book, began to watch the data still coming in from the computer and said, "You see the numbers on this? They are not what they were the day before. They are showing a dramatic increase in the speed and size of the Dark Star." "Yes, I do see the increase and the size of the matter's outer edges." "Jan?" "What do you want to tell me, honey?" Albert turned to Jan, after taking a final glance at the computer screen. "Do you think this Dark Star is going to reach us this year?" "That's something that I have been trying to figure out, Albert. I do not think it will be this year, Albert. It is growing in size, so the size might be larger, but the distance is still light years away. It is hard to tell, but I know it will be soon. I have made a parallax assessment of some of the galaxies in the distance. They show the speed. It makes tracking the Dark Star like taking pictures of a speeding jet plane.

It is moving so fast that it is hard to depend on some of the calculations that have a back history." "Jan, I know when the Dark Star will be here." Jan replied, "You do? When? Tell me." Just then, Lizzy walked in with a lunch basket and thermos bottle with a handle on the side. "Breakfast is served." Jan got up and helped Lizzy with the bottle. "Just like some men, making us women do all the work." Albert turned around, "Lizzy I am sorry. I was planning to meet you at the house and bring the breakfast here. Can you ever forgive me?" Lizzy said, "No, I cannot; you have to do the dishes." Albert laughed, knowing that when Lizzy put things in their favorite basket, she also included plastic plates and eating utensils. "Now that sounds just about right. He should help us women with these things." Lizzy replied, as she placed some of the covered plates on the table next to the computers, "Mr. Lanker, did you see the Ursa Star this morning?" Lizzy, in a jogging suit and ready for her morning run, was putting the creamer and sugar bowl on the table as she finished the set-up. "Pretty big. isn't it? Don't let it frighten you. We are all here together." With a concerned look on her face, Lizzy closed her eyes and replied, "Yeah, you are right. I'm going out to jogging for a mile or two." She went to the door and shouted, "We're all going to die!" She looked up at the Dark Star and started running in the opposite direction, with her hands waving over her head. Jan and Albert were looking through the glass door of the observatory and saw Lizzy running to the south. Jan looked at Albert and did not say a word, like she was just about to laugh out loud. Drinking a cup of coffee, Albert held the cup up to his mouth longer than normal, as Jan could see the smile on his face was wider than the cup.

They finished their breakfast and went back to their notes and sat again in front of the computer screen. Albert, looking at his black book, said to Jan, "Do you know the position of the Sagittarius constellation?" "I think I can find it. You do know that it is in the direction of the center of this galaxy." "Well, when this constellation comes into view, it would be in the direct line of the Dark Star's center." "Now looking at the figures that I have here, the time, month, and day can be set up at the point of the Dark Star's entry into our solar system." Jan said, "The Dark Star is so large that this constellation, Sagittarius, is too small to have any effect on the matter." "Well, it will give the point of speed with the parallax measurements by using this constellation as a very important piece of the puzzle—the pillar of Amatimas, remember, the name that was called out by the person in the street that disappeared." "I can't relate to things like that, Albert. You know that I only concentrate on figures and times and dates." "Anyway,

Amatimas is real. He travels by the parts of the abstruse materials of the temple of Zeus. You take the structure with six pillars in the front of it and the other parts that I won't go into right now. But from some of my notes, the angle of most of the figures goes to the ninety degree angle from the point of origin. You see, the architrave in the structure is part of the key. By using the pillar, you would be able to get some more figures supporting this calculation."

Jan looked at the computer and said, "Albert, look at this. The computer is saying that it has finished the calculations." Albert took a closer look at the screen and could see the figures that were downloaded from Far-Seeing, the astronomy company. Jan continued, "It is only months away from here. The size, wait, light years, wait, parsec, that is vast distances: It is huge!" Albert said, "Look at this month; I came up with, September to make contact. It is June now and the months left that the Dark Star has to reach us would put it here next year. But the sign of Sagittarius falls in September." Jan looked at Albert and then looked back at the computer screen, as if she knew that Albert was right on the button with these calculations. The date looked like it would be around September 23rd, right before the holidays. Jan replied to Albert, "The sign of Sagittarius falls in the month of November, that is right, but the sign of Libra falls in September. Albert, I don't understand these calculations, even if you and the computer are on the same page." "Sagittarius is the constellation in September and is still visible from the city of Athens. Yes! Libra is the sign that falls, for some strange reason, in September as far as astrology goes. Because they are in the sky, a number of signs in the Zodiac are still visible in the month of November, just as Sagittarius is still visible in September." Jan replied, "I don't know where you got those calculations. There is no confusion here between the computer's data and yours about the time of contact."

Albert looked at his book once more. "Take each number and break it into two parts and then into three to show the equal portions. This is what we have to remember, Jan, with everything from now on. The calculations for what side of the Earth will be hit first will show the side that will have the most and direct blast from Dark Star." Jan looked at Albert and then wrote down some notes on her pad and got up from the table. Walking to the other side of the room, as Albert followed her with his eyes and a small head turned, he could hear Jan say, "Lizzy was right. We all are going to die." Albert, hearing it, got up and went to the side of the room where Jan was getting a large globe. As she had it in her hand, Albert said to her, "Jan, put down the globe." Jan put the globe on the floor and Albert hugged her and said, "Jan, it does not have to be that way. We've got a good chance of making it with a little luck and the grace of God to help us. What am I saying is that God will have to be in our corner for this star to do its thing to Earth. I am not going to fool you anymore with the dream and numbers because from now on we are in this for the ride." "Albert, how are we going to make it? You saw what I saw, didn't you?" "Yes! I did. The full stream of charged particles that the Dark Star is carrying with it. Now that is not going to leave any matter in its path untouched." Still holding Jan around her waist, Albert lowered his hands and grabbed each side of Jan's butt cheeks and jiggled them. Jan called out, "Albert, stop that!" Albert dropped his hands, "Pick up the globe." He walked back to the table where they were working and said, "The back side is what will do us in if any." "From behind? I don't get it." Jan, taking the globe to the table and setting it down, looked around the room of the lab for a model of the solar system. She saw one on a stand by the large telescope against the wall. Albert, sitting down at the table, took his hand and spun the globe and stopped it with his finger. Albert did this over and over until Jan reached the table and sat the model of the solar system on the table. Albert looked at the model and pointed to the larger planets and said, "This is our only hope: Jupiter and Saturn." "What could these planets do?" "I am not sure, except if they are in the path of the direction of the matter stream, we might have a chance."

Albert moved over to Jan in his chair, "Let me see your writing pad." Jan flipped the pages that she had been writing some notes on and slid it to Albert. Albert took a large marker out of a cup of writing utensils in front of the computer screen and said, "Nature has a lot of things that are always the same. Things might not go in the same direction, but they are always identical." Albert took the marker and drew a circle and went around it over and over, like a child making a picture of a tornado. "Now, in a system like a tornado, the top is the slowest part. The bottom of is the fastest, or, let's say, the winds are more condensed. The damage is done at the base. Do you agree, Jan?" Jan, having one of her hands on her jaw and her elbow on the top of the table as she leaned on it, said, "Umhum." With her hand against her face, she moved her mouth a little. Albert, looking at her as he knew he had her undivided attention, continued flipping the paper and drew another circle. "In this a hurricane, the damage of this system is done on the edges, you agree?" Jan replied in the same manner. "In an earthquake, the center is always the strongest, and in a volcano, the rounded center is the most powerful, depending on the shape of the mountain. What I am trying to explain is that the circular form of many things in nature is the key to the substance that forms the material. It is vital. The elements that are affected by gravity are affected by their matter alone. Strong forces take place when gravity is just the main factor in making the elements work the way they do. The other things that happen to any controlled or out of control forms of nature, there is so much a variable that guessing is the only way to predict the outcome. I am guessing that we can endure this event with a little luck." Jan replied, "Luck and horse shoes, tell me about it. We can't move the planet or protect it from what this, this is, Yeah! This Dark Star will do! The name is right: the Dark Star. It is going to crush this planet like a concrete mixer running over a fly, and that is still giving too much credit to the fly in this case. We have no chance of getting out of the center of this, Albert!"

Albert looked at his notes. "I have had it, Albert! This is bad, really bad! There is absolutely no way around this! We are doomed!" Albert looked at Jan with both of her hands on her face as she starting to cry. "Look, Jan!" as he moved towards her and began to hug her. She put her head on Albert's shoulder and began to shed tears. Albert whispered into Jan's ear, "There is a way that we can make it." Jan, still holding Albert, said, "Stop it. Just stop, Albert." Jan, trying to regain her sense of composure, started to look at Albert. "You have been doing all you could for the people of the world, you did what you could. You have been a wonderful father and a lot of people love you dearly. This is something that you warned the world would happen. The only hope I had was that the star would disburse some of its energy before it came this far. I believed in the tired light theory so much, that I felt it would change the form of the Dark Star and make it weaker in the path that it has taken. It's growing in strength and speed and it is something that I did not want to happen because of the nature of this star. I just hope and pray, or beg for a miracle, that something will happen to the Dark Star." "Jan, look at me. All is not doom and gloom." "Yes Albert, I have had a wonderful life with everything. You have given me everything I ever wanted. What else could I ask for? Albert, you are a wonderful man, I love you, Albert, with every ounce of my being. I have always loved you and I am the luckiest girl on this planet to have you as my husband. Albert you--." Albert put his hand on Jan's mouth and said, "Will you listen. THERE IS A WAY TO GET BY THIS!!!"

CHAPTER TWENTY-FOUR
Falling Sky

The ball of doom moved like a monster in full rage, eating at will everything that it could gobble down, signaling an end to the creation of this beautiful world by such a horrible thing, made by nature. Moving faster and faster to whet its appetite on planets, stars, and the nebulas of gases in numbers that no one can count. What does the color of it matter now? It is too close to be a pretty thing. It is too close to be something to study through a telescope. It is way too close to think it is going to turn around and go the other way. Looks like it was big when it first appeared and now it is common knowledge that it is going to consume this planet, like a whale in the water feeding on a new-found meal.

Already the wall of galaxies is gone. The deep stars, or should they be considered stars or just huge quasars, they too are not around. Yes! Gone with the wind, in the breeze of the silent quiescence of uninhabited space. There in the darkness, life might have been happy and growing like we do. Yes, life in space is a strange thing to think about, maybe or maybe not. We are in space for sure now, with nowhere to go except into the mouth of the fallen angel. We should have noticed this thing a little sooner, but it was hiding in the dark, on the shelf of the universe, waiting for the right time for the dinner bell. It waited like a snake in a hole, waiting for the right time to strike out and grab its prey. It was in the walls, lying frozen, with its eyes following the motions in space, ready to close in and close the gap. In the water like a fish, keeping its position, stalking its feast as it strolled on its way. LORD HAVE MERCY. This is the death angel coming to make his claim, his piece, his cherry on the top of the cake because all the good cake has been crunched on.

The angel has blown his horn so loudly that hearing devices had to be handed to the crowd. So loud that if your ears were not protected, you would go mad. That would explain the nomads of the world away from the air drop. Not all of them got protection and, sure enough, eating each other was normal to them. Yep, surely did eat themselves into extinction in a hurry! If not for Albert's idea, what would the world be? Was it his idea, or was it someone else's? Albert got rich and all the credit for saving people in the many lands of the Earth, but for what? To see death coming in plain sight? WHAT? Everyone is going to die at one time? Or was it Amatimas's idea to make a mockery of trying to live? Like a cat plays with its kill or like a simple drowning out of breath and, waiting for the last bit of life to kick its way out of the living body. Too cold, BRRRRR, to be a human thing. Frozen in time as the world looks at the Dark Star approaching to do its natural squandering action on this planet we call Earth. Line them up, pack them in, make the herd stand together in the open spaces. Be brave and strong as this! This thing, this Ursa Star, puts the freeze on all this worthless planet. Not a penny in value, nowhere to be saved, and you can particularly believe that the words "you are next" are on the menu-CHECK PLEASE! The other side of the universe has not been touched, yet! The sound devices have been tossed aside for about eight months but I still have mine. Check me out! The dinner was great; I'll have the dessert later. I apologize for eating and running, but standing up to be sacrificed is not my idea of being strong. CHECK, PLEASE! I AM FULL!!!

Albert looked again at the church over in the south, and as he headed that way a sunbeam was shining down from the clouds that were clearing the sky. Albert noticed this beauty and began to think of how he designed that church and how radiant and heavenly it looked. It was an excellent job, he thought. Completely a picturesque view of holy structure, barely visible from the top floor of the house, Albert was just amazed at the beautiful view. He stared and pondered. Albert hit the gas on the tractor and started to plow another row and thought of how far he had come to see the sky being taken away every day. Driving faster and lifting the plow's arms on the tractor, he headed to the barn. He still wanted to go over the data in observatory, knowing that Jan had gone to the station. Albert had done enough for today because he had been daydreaming over half of time, wondering about the Ursa Star. He put the tractor next to the other mechanical equipment used to move dirt, put the key under gas pedal, and stepped off the apparatus. Albert, seeing one of the workers in the barn working on some other equipment, said to him, "I think this one needs gas and a lube." "I got you, Mr. Lanker, will do." Albert headed to the main house, where Lizzy had his lunch ready. She was standing at the kitchen door and said, "Mr. Lanker, I tried to reach you on the radio." "You did? I thought I had it on." Lizzy replied, "It might have been my radio. I always have difficulty working it." Albert, in the kitchen, walked over next to the wine cellar door and looked at the radio. After Albert had taken a look, he said, "Look at this, Lizzy, you have to turn on the speaker switch. There are two switches to turn on." Lizzy, heading to her room, replied, "Mrs. Lanker called and she is headed home. I'll be in my room if you need anything, Mr. Lanker." Albert, sitting at the table in the kitchen, looked at the meal that Lizzy had prepared: a tuna sandwich on rye, a scoop of potato salad, a pickle, and a bran cupcake. Albert began to drink the glass of grape soda. "OK, Lizzy, thanks." Albert looked at his watch and saw that the time was 2:30 and thought about how long he had been in fields and what he had been thinking about. After drinking and eating the last of his meal, Albert got up and put the dishes in the sink. He went to Lizzy's room, with the door closed, and gave a knock. "Yes?" Hearing this, Albert said, "Lizzy, I'll be in the observatory. Tell Jan I'm there." "Alright, I'll tell her."

Albert entered the observatory and walked around, looking at telescope and touching it like it was some lucky charm. He walked over to the north wall where a large illustration of the solar system and the star charts were, and looked at them, as he needed to know the distances of each element. The sunlight shone on the marble floor, which had a huge pattern of a compass, showing the direction to the north, south, east and west. Between the directional pointers were numbers made in specially-placed stones showing the degrees to each direct true compass point. Albert looked at the floor and turned his head as if he were reading the steps to each group of compass readings. He looked at this because he designed the observatory and the light that shone on the floor was right at the point where it should have been at this time of year. He looked at the shadow creeping across the floor as he sat in the corner of the building, next to the meteorite display. He looked at his watch and thought of the time as he sat in the corner, thinking about the end of the world. The shine of the telescope had a reflection that lit the wall and highlighted the planet display. It was Jupiter that had most of the light on it. Not because it was bigger than the other planets; it might simply have been the telescope's position that made it so.

The sun was setting and Albert was still in the room and almost falling asleep, with his legs on top of the display and leaning back in the large office chair that he dragged over from the desk. Now the room was dark and Albert was asleep and snoring, with spit dripping from his mouth. Jan had been home for hours and wondered what Albert was up to, when she looked out the window and saw the lights out in the observatory. She rang the phone in the observatory and Albert, hearing this, fell to the floor, as he woke up. "Damn!" Albert said, as he got off the floor and looked at the red button flashing on the phone on the table of computers. It was the only thing that was lit in the room. He put his hands out, so that he could feel the furniture around him rather than running into it in the dark.. Feeling his shirt and noticing that it was wet, he wiped it on his leg and reached for the phone. "Hello?" "Albert, what are you doing?" "Waiting for you! Jeepers! I fell asleep." "I got here a long time; you should have called." "Wait, let me turn the lights on in here." Albert went to the wall where the light switch was and felt around and finally hit the button. A ballast noise came from the fixtures and all the lights began to light up the room. Albert went back to the phone and picked it up. "Now." Looking at his watch, he said to Jan, "Come on out here." "OK, I'll be out there in a minute or two." Albert hung the phone up and sat at the computers and then turned them on.

Jan went outside and looked up at the sky. It was a clear night. She told Lizzy to leave some dinner in the oven for them. The sky was bright because of the Dark Star, and a low rumble could be heard if you listened closely. Jan opened the door and there was Albert in the room, looking at the computer. He turned around. "Honey, how are you?" "Albert, what is on your mind? My nerves are shot. You know, the sound of the Dark Star is beginning to rumble." "I know. I was just looking at the sound right here. It's not like the neutrino sound. This is just a plain sound of stars or planets being crushed. I don't think this will affect people because this is a direct sound that is just in the stratosphere. It really sounds like the sound of air pushing and pulling the darkness apart. Like rocks of sand falling down a mountain and becoming a river of dust." Jan sat next to Albert. "This is going to get louder and louder, but it will not be bad, just disturbing if you are trying to get a good night's sleep." Jan continued, "So the sound is the last thing this doomed planet will hear, right Albert?" "I don't know. I just don't know."

Both of them got up and turned off the computers, then walked to the door and turned the lights off. Walking toward the house, they looked at the Dark Star in the northern sky. It was so big that it had taken the zenith out of the sky. Taking just about all the stars in the tail of the big dipper,even the binary star that the Middle East uses to check your eyesight. The horse rider, the double star, just Mizar and its baby B spinning around with others on the end of the Ursa system. "All gone now," Albert said to Jan. "It is so big that it looks like it has taken the sky away." Jan replied, "How long is left on the planet?" "Not long; about a couple months or less. We just have to prepare for the worst. At least we will all go together." Jan said, "There is no one in this world that I would rather be with than you." Albert hugged Jan and kissed her, as they stood between the house and the observatory. In the background, the Dark Star continued its slow spin of pops of lights as it crushed and ate its way towards the planet.

The YDS channel had gone to pictures of the Ursa Star and an update on the time remaining for the final approach of the star. The only thing that was the same was the introduction of Jan's presentation of standing on the planet Earth, with her hands in the praying position. Everything else in the program dealt with pictures of the universe, with no one talking or even being present in the studio. It was almost like the whole show was taped in advance except the live pictures of the Ursa Star. Jan would spend the rest of the remaining days at the farm with Albert. Her children would be in contact with both parents and also both families made sure they had words to say by phone. The world had the strangest reaction to what would be the end of all things that this third planet away from the sun had to offer. The planet that escaped the large rocks that flew in the darkness, just missing the mundane globe. The planet that spun in a way to have all seasons in perfect order to grow the food of its voyager, as it maneuvers through space. It is here that the flat earth theory came from. Hundreds of millions of years ago, the Pangaea continents were one. Here the creatures of large miscreants walked and ate and trod the earth like clay footprints in the valley of man. Here that the rain fell and the sun shone and the people grew. Earth, ours alone and cut off from any other living planet within reach, because where is there to go? Nature is this planet, with everything in it or on it or around it that made it what it is. Do we have a choice, tell me? No, we don't. It is home to us all, even if we take a look see at what's around this planet where you can breath and walk on the seashore as the waves count out the months, the days, the hours, the minutes. You have to believe the moment is near because the seconds are timed as well in the slap of the ocean currents on this peaceful planet.

With days left, though it only seemed like hours, the television was the only hope for people who were still around. BY GAS, BY WATER, BY DRUGS, BY ELECTRICTY, BY FIRE, BY CUT, BY FALL, BY HUNGER, BY EXPLOSION, BY LACK OF AIR OR JUST PLAIN SHOT! That would do the trick! For those whose thoughts of God had weakened in view of his pending wrath that made them guilty of the pain of their own judgments, and not God's. Being first to go to the grave is the way some thought of their sad souls. All the people of the world had stopped work and gotten together in their own groups for comfort. Some groups had living thoughts and some had death thoughts. It was just too much to think about, the problems of living that various countries were experiencing. The President of the United States that would have the last say. It was he who saw some of his military destroy themselves at sea. He could not say if their nerves were to blow the scene and do harm to everyone else. So at sea it was done, and people saw the explosion and scorned the choice. It got the attention of the world with a nuclear bomb going off as people, waiting for the end, contemplating just small apples on a tree not to touch. IT IS FORBIDDEN!

"This is the President of the United States" rang out on all the networks, a speech repeated over and over around the world. It was the President with a message of life for the world to hear. With his eyes looking right at you from all channels on the tube, it was touching. The oration by the President was simple and brief: "BE BRAVE AND HOLD ON TO THE PRICELESS LIFE THAT GOD HAS GIVEN YOU! HOLD ON, FOR GOD IS NOT A STRANGER TO YOU! BE THE FEARLESS AND STRONG PERSON OF THE WORLD AND HOLD ON FOR THE END, THE BITTER END, IF THERE IS ONE! BE THAT PERSON! WITHOUT UNWAVERING, BELIEVE, CLING TO LIFE, FOR WITHOUT IT THE HUMAN RACE IS FINISHED! BE THE ONE! BE THE ONE! BE THE ONE!!!!"

It was repeated over and over. This speech went on for hours, aired clearly until the rumble, the airlessness, began to knock the satellites out of the sky. The world was in a state of shock due to the large eye that looked down on the planet. It made the population fear the doom of death on the horizon. That silence deafening sound clearing the sky, only characterized by a taste of cold ocean water or the sight of a color of off-blue. With all the masterminds in the world looking at its coming fate, it was very strange they could not tell that the Dark Star's speed would make it come a day early.

It consumed the outer stars of the Milky Way and it entered the Earth's solar system. So fast did the Dark Star approach that it was almost like a flash in the night in the western hemisphere. Like a thief in the early morning of the phantom, moonless night. A bright flicker, a form of light, a green flash that lasted about half a minute. The wrong light, the false god, the anti everything was upon the Earth, upon us. It was here! There in the hands of Pluto, knocked like a fragment of dry lint on a dry houseplant. Now the rest of the solar system followed the pattern, except for Uranus, and Saturn became enlarged to the point that Jupiter followed suit. Those planets grew to a size that was strange among the forms of nature. Bigger and bigger in a matter of seconds, the gaseous giants dilated. They were at different positions in the solar system and that created what most called the greatest natural event the heavens had ever seen. Not supernatural, just completely natural, like the rain that falls in the meadow on a spring day. Jupiter grew larger and larger with the ammonia-filled gas that erupted to the smell of luck. It blew its way towards Earth and lifted the harmful elements of star-stuff away from the planet. It was Jupiter that made its big spinning eye a force to take a look at Earth to protect it. Jupiter would be no more, but the planet did save the world with the soft opening of the Dark Star's center, through which the Earth slipped. Jupiter was waiting for the right time to do its job and it came to the rescue to save life as we know it. Like a camel going through the eye of needle, some in history might say, and then again, maybe that would be too easy. It might just be said that Amatimas is real; he travels. Real is real and fake is not real, but the two prove their existence in time. To see the fact is not a fake, but the unseen fake is not the real. There is no unseen solution to the fake of what is real. There is not or could not be seen how the fake can be real but to time and that time, not by day. No, No, not by star, No, No, only by the product of travel. Amatimas is real; he travels by what mankind has not conceived and he will never find, till he views his own existence and that does not work. No, No, it is a fake to say it is real, but Amatimas is real!!!

You can go on and on with Amatimas by taking each letter in the name and finding the numbers of the letter or dividing the name or the numbers into mathematical problems. On and on, Amatimas could be looked at only to find even the Samarium a nuetrino absorber, kind of similar to Amatimas spelled backwards. It might be right; fake is fake and the real of the fake is not real, or is it? AMATIMAS IS REAL!

Amatimas is real; he travels and is a member of the HOLY SPIRIT. Is that an angel? Check the mind, check the heart, check the sight. I think it is time for that dessert with a glass of Holy Water because this baptism has got to stay moist! CHECK PLEASE! HOW MUCH IS THAT TAB! Not much at all; prayer is free. A little water is not bad, yet too much can do adverse things. Grains of salt are always significant and faith without works is dead, AMATIMAS is real and not a fake!

CHAPTER TWENTY-FIVE
Conclusion

The city stood strong in the haze of what has happened to the world. The shine of the cellophane-wrapped structures glimmered not from the sun but from the lights that by chance stayed on. They were waiting for this all their short lives, planted in the ground like trees in a thick forest. Reaching into the sky as if the heavens were their only equal. Stars in the darkness, they stood in a row, in a line, in the form of well-dressed women going to a great event. Not to be over-stated or under-done, glass has never been embellished with so much attractiveness as was found in this city. Any observation from any position still gives the moderately pleasurable atmosphere of the city that absolutely never sleeps, here in Las Vegas.

This city of Vegas lights, where dreams really do come true in a matter of minutes. Yes, it is true that you can become blind from the fun that can make your life a living hell, when the roll of the dice can cut your hand deep to the bone. The sleek city, as some people look at it, with the gamblers and night-life, along with legal cat houses nearby, has claimed this city the distinction of being known as Sin City. Yes, maybe there is sin in the camp of this city, like all the rest of the cities in the world. Really nothing new about what goes on when people gather. Yet, away from the Strip or the downtown area, Las Vegas is still just as slow and normal as any other American city. You don't have to tell that to Fr. Anthony's only brother, who has lived in Las Vegas most his life. Yes, the only brother of the late Fr. Anthony and his devoted ways of being his relative of a hurt heart. Sure he's gambler, and about his night life in Sin City, you'll have to ask his wife of forty years in their strong marriage. Having three children is proof that the living is easy when you are busy in your moral issues. Edward is his name, who raised his family in his typical house just east of the tall and polished buildings of the Las Vegas skyline. Just like any other city, people saw the Dark Star, and like in any other city, people did what people do.

But it is now Edward's turn, he who used to work as a doorman for one of the large hotels on the strip. One of the big tower employees, Edward worked the door until that Dark Star passed by the planet. He had seen it all, from the rich and famous to the bag ladies looking for their next meal at any cost. Edward, a simple man who does not ask for much from life, as his brother was the more famous one, what with the Pope and all. And Fr. Anthony's fame was something that put a lustrous smile on his face and later brought a heart-felt tear to his eyes with the news of his brother's tragic fate. He never went to his brother's burial. He left that to the other family members and friends to do the traveling. He did send his respects through the appropriate channels as a sign of his love for his sibling. It was just too hard, too sad; he was too despondent to attend. A quiet man that spent his life standing up and opening doors and carrying luggage with the simple response of thank you sir, thank you ma'am. What can be said? a smile for a tip, the extra money given to his wife who has never worked a day since they were married in a garden shop close to their home on the boulevard. Well, doing that is still a little work if you own it and report to your husband about how much you make, time after time. It is now that the lack of the sun created a new problem of what the Dark Star had done to the planet. Only the building lights in the deep haze could be seen in the ghost-like feel of the air and the lack of sunlight. Edward, still hearing the rumble of the Dark Star, shaking the ground in this city, knew he was still afraid. The world, in fact, was still trembling from the latest event, with the non-stop quivering of the ground. Like the old atomic blast that used to be felt in this city, it went on everywhere. That's how the world was right now, as the sky and stars could not be seen as everyone who was left on planet meditated on the next dramatic event. Edward did not care that much, only that his job was now on hold as the people, afraid of going anywhere, had neither left nor arrived in his hotel. The big flagships of hotels in the city of lights, the only city that has some type of living nature to the bad affairs that just took place. With the neon signs still sparking excitement, it gave the mind a human reality of life after death in the midst of the knockout blow of the Dark Star.

As it stood, the whole world was covered with the haze that limited one's vision to about three hundred feet. The lights, depending how bright, traveled at a greater distance in thick haze that was endorsing life. In the haze, the oxygen was just as good as always with the conventional mix of elements that were not harmful to mankind. The only thing unseen that would be discovered is that the Earth was not moving at all. It was at a standstill, like a pea on a table waiting for something or someone to set the rolling in motion. With the western hemisphere facing away from the sun, the cold was sure to come soon. The deep chill with the ice, ready to creep in any liquid form on this side of the world. Now with time passing by, from hours to days to weeks, the temperature of the planet had slowly gone down to a deep unfriendly cold. It must have been the haze that was conserving most of the heat or just the greenhouse effect doing the job of keeping the freeze manageable. As far as the science of what was going on with the planet, it was nothing but an educated guess, because the position of the Earth was not clear without looking at the sky. With all the satellites knocked out and communications at a standstill, it was even harder to travel from place to place with this cloud of haze surrounding the planet. But, it was Las Vegas where the action was. With a nice supply of food and drink and living quarters, at least the people here were more comfortable than those in the rest of the world.

In New York City, the cold had done some harmful things to the water supply, introducing a harmful bacteria into it, and not to speak of the lack of electricity, which had been out for some time. Being close to the top of the planet's pole, it was a living hell, with the darkness prowling in the windows of your personal chambers. Most of the Eastern cities had the same major problems with the cold, only to have the hospitals packed to the gills with the dead and dying. In Los Angeles, the results of the Dark Star's visit made this city less fortunate than other cities in terms of needed supplies. With the rumble under the surface of the planet continuing at constant rate, it was just enough to jolt the San Andreas Fault into significant motion. The tumultuous motion sent an earthquake of great magnitude to the area on the southwest coast of California. It happened along the fault about thirty miles away from downtown Los Angeles and it was a smackdown. Most of those living in the area thought it was simply the end, as it happened around the time that the Dark Star went by. Even the strong could not take the rumble of the Dark Star and the large shaker, because both happened about the same time. The fear, the sound, the sky, all of these at once caused an early death in many people.

Still, it was the lower coastline that the huge Pacific Ocean claimed. It was just around San Diego and a little ways up the shoreline area toward Los Angeles that was left to be in the water. Looking at the rest of the area of California, it was upsetting. Bad, really bad, for the beautiful skyscrapers that reached to the sky in the downtown area of Los Angeles. They did not fall from the shock of earthquakes, yet they were leaning so badly that it was only a matter of time before they would surrender their steel-welded beams and crash down to the street below. The street area was cleared not by choice of any special emergency, to say the least. It was just that the people who were around those pillars of iron, looking towards the sky, met their destiny from the large amounts of material falling from the sides of these mega-structures. In fact, most of the city was in ruins, with broken streets and collapsed buildings, except a good number of houses that were retro-fitted to withstand the blow with a little luck. They took the quake well and the people that left well-enough alone were living with a clear understanding that the Dark Star was not finished, as they looked at the haze in their present moment. Yes, the haze was there, too. Aside from the smell of burning smoke that smeared the darkness, the city was still running with most of its power. It looked like Los Angeles had been prepared for the worst. If something like this would happen, as bizarre as it seemed, seismology and haze were always a part of this city.

From this seat, it is a fact that the rest of the world in the darkness was indeed the better off. On the other side of the world that faced the sun, it was evident that it had been extinguished by fire. China had completely disappeared into the ashes of the burnt Earth. More than a billion people, an awful lot of souls, cooked like a frying pan on the stove, cooked too long to let the elements of the pan begin to burn. Like the pottery oven with the smell of clay or cooking haze boiling its way to make the youngest desert of the world. It was HOT! Made to BAKE! Not only was China affected, but all of the sectors in that part of the world had their share of the sun's full blaze of the fire's frying heat. The old Union of Soviet and Socialist Republics was affected also by the incinerated warmth of the sun's direct sparkle. Also included in the hot broil, the countries, of Australia and Indonesia, along with Thailand and Burma, were in the package for being roasted. Japan took it like a nation in the midst of a storm. The country endured it as long as it could, with the surrounding waters helping the haze that hung around from getting too hot. And then, in time, the heat finally got them too. Japan was baked in a kiln. The only thought that was left in the mind was what a noontime sun could do when time has stopped? This was a natural result of a stopped planet, and not having everything on the Earth flying off at once from the sudden standstill. It was the haze that compacted the atmosphere so much that it made the weight of matter stick to the surface. Yes, there was more atmosphere on the planet that might have been a part of Jupiter's atmosphere or some other dissolved planet that related to Earth's atmosphere in the common elements.

With the sun being at the zenith of the sky, it was directly over the middle of the Pacific Ocean, cooking the heated climate. It had to be an act of God that Europe had been spared, to a point; anyway, the Vatican was there in semi-darkness and that did not matter too much because the haze there was even thicker. Plenty of oxygen yet; but the inability to see was the problem with the darkened sky. There the people were alive and hoping for another miracle to bring the planet back to order. Praying to bring back the morning sunrise with its orange glow, and the evening sunset with its red haze that gave the people a sense of being alive. It would be left to the United States to find what this haze was all about and where and what was going to happen to everyone left alive on the planet. It was clear that the heat was too hot and the cold was dropping the planet into a clear-cut ice age. The President, as usual, was on the hot-seat to find answers. He once again turned to NASA, the space administration, to find the reasons that all this was happening. The questions were asked all around about how long this world would be able to support life. NASA sent up a rocket with a satellite to see what was above the haze of this strange place we used to call Earth. With the link to Far-Seeing, Albert and Jan keyed in on the probe after seeing the worst thing that they had ever experienced. They were thankful that they had survived and still had comfortable surroundings and plenty of food and power at the farm. Albert had built this farm with so much new technology that even it surprised him with the way it worked. The rocket went up about three weeks after the Dark Star had done its worst. You might as well call it the Ursa Star, because everything was changed. The satellite was deployed and the data with pictures would be downloaded to NASA and the Far-Seeing labs, where Albert and Jan would have direct access to them.

They sat in front of their computer screen in the observatory and watched the data being downloaded to the screen. The first information that came in was a picture from the cameras on the probe. It was no surprise that at a distance of one hundred and twenty miles above the Earth, the sun was bright and looked normal. An hour went by, then two and then three, and the probe had made at least three labored orbits around the planet. Albert, looking at the pictures, and Jan, looking at the down-loading data, were surprised that the planet seemed completely normal except for the haze that covered the Earth. Pictures of the Earth were as if a white cloud hung over the planet, like a large cloud of vapor that clung to the globe in a strange manner with the look of a small nebula. It was marked with red and yellow strips of clouds that had some indistinguishable comparisons to a Jovian planet. Tests of the gases above the Earth indicated some range of mixtures of hydrogen and other vapors that were being burnt off into space. The funny thing that Albert said to Jan was that he could not see the moon. It was not in any of the pictures that the probe produced at a three hundred and sixty degree photographic angle. Jan, calmly going through data, agreed with NASA's comments that the planet was in a safe range from the Sun. It had lost some of its orbit due to the shock of the event and it would be a long time before anyone would be sure what the Earth would do next. Jan looked at the data from all angles and then began to look closely at the screen.

Jan said, "This cannot be true! We are not spinning." At first, Albert thought the darkness was created by the thick layer of haze. "Yes! I thought that was it. Did you ever notice that there is no wind?" Jan replied, "No and there will be none if we stay like this." Albert was still looking at the photo coming off the probe and said suddenly, "Look, Look! Look at this, Jan! Look at this!" It was another moon or small planet right next to the Earth. And then another one next to that one. There were at least four that Albert saw that could have ranged between a five hundred thousand to three million miles from the planet. It was surely a perplexing rack of pool balls that waited for a side pocket. With the sun showing the objects in a glowing manner, it made space look like a completely new mini-solar system. Colors of blue and red and green spears made the moons and global objects a spectrum filling the limitless void of space. Waxing and diminishing in view, the sun lit up the interstellar matter with a contentment like new bulbs on a Christmas tree.

The temperature on the parts of the planet not facing the sun began to drop further to a nippy forty degrees average. The communication networks had finally done as much as they could with the resources that were left and not destroyed by the Dark Star. On all the newscasts was the President, with all the emergency agencies he could locate. They would offer food and supplies and some type of shelter in each country and state to those who needed rescue services. The whole world would be involved in this humanitarian effort, with the U.S. coordinating the help needed with the casualties of the Dark Star. Albert had representatives from his company appear to provide the technology of lights and radios and things like that, along with the equivalent products that the governmental rescue efforts offered. Albert did not worry about the capital, because he would become even richer with his company Ultra being solid in the fields of construction and technology. There was a lot of destruction in the world and it would be Ultra's job to help rebuild as much as it could handle. Information about the conditions in China and the areas around those parts was hard felt. The loss to the world, with the major part being that of the areas in and around China, came to a total of roughly two to three billion poor souls who had subjected their fate to Dark Star—a gruesome fate of nowhere to hide or run from the heat of the flaming sun. The burning sun, with its yellow inferno making the touch of matter a source of fever. A temperature that the strongest of human beings, with all their technology, could not defeat. TOO HOT, TOO WARM, TOO MUCH HEAT, was all that was said when people were asked about the other side of the planet. It was one hundred and forty degrees in the shade, with an air temperature of one hundred and twenty. The water was aboil, and fish washed up on the shorelines like waves in the heat. Trees dried up on mountains like an un-watered lawn, while the sun cracked the Earth and people sweated out the last drop of their living souls to the sky.

Albert was at the farm, with Jan doing all she could do to figure out when, or if, the sun would shine again on this part of the planet. The haze did not affect the work on the farm, because the complex had such a large indoor area. Jan, looking at some of the pictures that were on file in the computer, could see that at least the outer planets were moving in the solar system. The direction they were moving was unclear except that they were so close to the planet Earth that it was amazing and easy to observe. NASA sent up another rocket after a month to find more information about the fate of Earth. The long night of darkness was still heavy in the area of the United States, yet parts of Europe had some form of light in the sky. The sky was only lit like an obscure cloud of dim light. The temperature around both countries was stable at about forty-five degrees. It must have been the latent heat, or the heat leaving the atmosphere at the minimum, that kept the temperature from falling into freezing. That also would explain the steady temperature on the cold side of the planet Earth in the wake of the Dark Star.

It was in the second probe that Jan found the answers to what everyone was looking for and by that time the Earth was beginning to roll eastward.

The wind had begun to pick up and the sky had become more lucid. To keep the temperature in order, the moons would block some of the sun's direct light, as the planet began to whirl. The probe that was sent up showed the line of small moons or small planets revolving around the Earth. The rumble under the ground had persisted since the Dark Star's presence. It was the motion of gravity pulling on these planets' main matter that was affecting the spin of the Earth. Six objects were weaving around the planet like a victory dance of a group of gymnastic dwarfs going to the proscenium. The people of the Western hemisphere were elated by the welcome golden sunrise that pervaded the darken haze. It was not seen to be the sun, but as light in the sky that had remained dark for about three months. As it happened it was the longest day on Earth, about three days, and then was followed by three days of darkness. The days and weeks went by and the haze began to clear to some extent. Clouds began to be seen in the sky at times of the extended daylight hours that explained the light rain. The days went from two and a half days of daylight to stable thirty-hour days in a matter of months. The longer days and nights were normal for a year, until the sky was completely clear of the haze and the sun began to appear normal. Jan and Albert had been working all the time on finding answers and getting people back to their normal day-to-day routine with information about the progress of the planets' metamorphosis.

Albert would take over most of the rebuilding of Los Angeles due to the earthquake damage and Jan would do what she did best: looking to the heavens. There would be centuries of rediscovery to be done, not only by Jan, but by anyone who could pick the moons out with some knowledge of astronomy. The new moons were easy to point out, being in a line bigger than the old moon that the planet Earth used to have. The new moons numbered six or maybe five. Some explained that the sixth moon was actually a planet. Who knows? It was still too early to tell the exact orbit of all the planetary material above, below, or just around the planet. Far-Seeing would be the main source for the data that was coming in regularly for the second probe high in orbit above the Earth. Though it looked as if things were going to be normal in the sky, in truth things were not going to be. The spiral galaxy that we had with our radiant Milky Way was now a thing of the past. Our galaxy had shifted into another form, like a bared galactic group of new-found stars. Now there were more stars and in a wide range of different distances in clear view during the winter months. You could see the large double spiral neighboring galaxy and nebulas in the night sky, in plain sight of the unaided eye. Everyone knew that the solar system had just given birth to a new group of planets that numbered fifteen. Still, the third planet from the sun was Earth, even if the closer planets were not Venus and Mercury. Those planets were larger than Earth and had orbits that showed them crossing the sun in the daylight that produced a partial eclipse at certain times. The outer planets marched around like a cake walk where the music never stopped.

Albert walked to the barn and Jan yelled out of the house, "Albert, you forgot to give me a kiss." Albert, whose mind was on finding the right growing season for some of his crops, said, "I'll be right there!" The year on the Earth had lengthened by two extra months and figuring out how to grow things had become a new objective. Springuary and Webber were the two extra months. Springuary fell after April and Webber started after January. These two months had thirty five days, except in leap year, when they included a number of extra days. Four hundred and forty-five days made a complete year in the days after the Dark Star flew by. Christmas was still in December and A.D. was still attached to the numbered years in the twenty-first century. A lot of things changed and a lot of things remained the same. Tt was a human choice. With the architecture and farming at hand, Albert was a very busy man.

He turned back to the house and Jan came to meet him halfway. Albert hugged Jan and kissed her as if to say, we made it. Jan, with her mind on going to town to give another presentation at the YDS network about the solar system, asked Albert, "I'm going shopping after the taping. Can I get you anything?" "Yes, a pair of sunglasses would do! These longer days are brutal." Jan laughed as she walked away and met Thomas holding the door of the limo. In the background, the new moons of the Earth had risen in the daylight like the mirror effect in a line. Just a little bigger than the old moon, this was a sight that was breath-taking and fascinating. The planet had changed so much that the phases of the moons were still unpredictable. It would take years and years to figure out the oscillations of the orbits of this group of new terrestrial globes and their phases.

But the shine of the city had hardly changed from the events that took the world into an exceptional existence. Parking his mid-size sedan in the lot, he went to the Galaxy Star Hotel where he used to work. This hotel had laid him off for not being on his job for days on end. His gardening business had been doing poorly because of either the lack of sun or too much of it. All year, he had been gambling at so many hotels that his savings had almost been completely drained. His wife, who loved him dearly, would stick with him by asking family and friends for financial help. He was just too old to work at this hotel anymore and that would explain his truancy at his old job. He walked up the ramp to the main door of the hotel, where new faces had taken his place. Edward thought of his brother who would have helped him with his money problems like he always had, but that was long ago when the world had one moon. Now it was a different age and time, with a number of new things that had changed the world. He would have gone to Seattle to live like his brother, if not for the rain and the lack of sun that he didn't like. Edward slowly went inside the hotel: the lights, the sound, the machines rang and buzzed and flashed. With ten dollars in his pocket, Edward got a half roll of quarters from the cash cage and sat down at one of the one-armed bandits. He was so nervous from the lack of money in his pocket that he dropped two quarters on the floor. They rolled to the middle of the ornamental carpet walkway and were stopped indirectly by a man stepping on them. The man, a priest who was walking through the casino in a hurry after coming from upstairs where he had performed a private wedding, handed the two quarters to Edward sitting down, and went on his way to the front door. Edward, with a grieving tear in one of his eyes, thought again of his dead brother. He took the two quarters that had been handed to him and put them plus two others into the gambling machine with the smudge of dejected visual perception. Edward could hardly stand the feeling.

The bars, the numbers, the gold nuggets rolled around in an endless fashion and then the first line stopped and then the second and finally the third. Edward glanced at the slot machine as he reached into his hand for some more quarters, as if the escapade was on him through his water-soaked eyes. A third second went by, on the fourth second the sirens went off so loud that Edward, dazed from the lights and noise, almost fell on the floor. Through his tears, he saw the jackpot. It was big, one of the biggest one to date for this hotel. It was millions of dollars. The people in the casino area rushed to gather around Edward. The attendants and change girls got the essential information from Edward for reporting his new-found wealth. Shaking, as he reached for his wallet he dropped it there on the carpet. Edward bent down to pick up his wallet and noticed a racetrack ticket that he also picked up, that read ten to win on the five—not knowing that it was the same ticket that his brother, Fr. Anthony, had in his wallet years ago. He picked it up and stared at it like it meant something. As the people jumped up and down congratulating Edward, he was happy and mystified at the same time. He knew that he was the most fortunate man in the world at that moment because this joy would last the rest of his life.

In the background, rushing out the front door, were two elderly people with Anna and her new husband, along with P.P. jumping and biting at the leg of the groom. It was a sight as rice was being thrown and the groom exclaimed, "DOES THIS DOG HAVE A LEASH?!!!"

Yes, Ultra owned the hotel, one of their many corporate assets that they had in Las Vegas. Still, it seemed so strange that the President was in town on vacation on that day, on a stopover on his way to Lake Tahoe. Even Mr. Knoll was in town, doing some business for Albert concerning a new hotel that they wanted to build in this city. Jan had called Albert from the Galaxy Hotel earlier to say that she was still shopping and was going to be late. She and Thomas had flown to Vegas after the taping at the YDS channel to be at Anna's wedding, along with Grandpapa and Grandmama. Cardinal Manlin had his hands full in Rome. He had taken the racetrack ticket out of Fr. Anthony's wallet a long time ago and had forgotten about it after he misplaced it. With throngs of people in the courtyard at St. Peter's in Rome praying for the forgiveness of sin, Cardinal Manlin was trying to keep order. The Pope, at St. Peter's in his high parapet overlooking the square for his seasonal oration, saw the biggest crowd of people he had ever seen and loudly exclaimed to Cardinal Manlin, "THEY CAN'T ALL COME IN HERE!!!" The Pope's keepers looked at each other and scratched their heads as they gazed down as the people streaming into the courtyard. Albert, back in his drawing room after telling his helpers where he wanted the new plowing at the farm, looked again at the stairs he had designed and said, "Yes, this will work fine for this building; just fine and dandy." Albert then called his father's house in Beverly Hills. The maid answered the phone. When Albert asked for his father, the maid replied, "I'm sorry, Albert, but they have gone shopping." Albert hearing the receiver go click, quickly continued to say, "HELLO? HELLO?" Finally hanging up the phone, Albert just looked out the window with the thought of being the last to know about his family. Feeling suspicious, Albert stared at the sky from the window and saw the line of moons higher in the sky. To him, it looked like two of the moons had developed some type of atmospheres. He double-blinked his eyes and turned back to his drawing board while he rushed to open his little black book on the desk. Albert made a notation like a squiggle and then got back to drawing his latest building project.

May the love of Amatimas be with you all forever and ever-*THUS*

Dedicated to Aunt Lilo